"I don't know how to stop him this time."

It felt sinful to break the peaceful quiet that had settled around them, especially with the utterance of Cronos's name. But her mind was clear now, and all the questions were coming back, one by one, invading her space with Ryker.

"It's not something you have to do alone," Ryker said, pressing a kiss to her forehead and slipping an ambrosia-soaked strawberry into her mouth. "All the gods, old and new, are working on a solution. We'll protect Olympus."

Kyana rested her chin on her hands and swallowed the tart fruit, trying not to be distracted by the slow circles his fingers were tracing along her spine. "And the humans we've released Above to begin rebuilding? Who's going to stand guard for them?"

His circling fingers stopped and as the words tumbled out of her mouth, she wished she could yank them back. He was going to see her worries as some noble proof of growth in her and she was going to kill him for pointing it out.

"You're worried about humans? You hate humans."

She tried to move away but he tightened his arms around her, holding her to his side. "I don't *hate* humans. I just don't find much use for them. But that doesn't mean I want them all sacrificed."

Ryker's smile made Kyana growl.

"Look at you. You're all soft and mushy." He leaned in close and placed his lips against her ear. "Wonder if you taste like cotton candy now that all that bitterness is gone?"

"Bite me."

By Sable Grace

ASCENSION
BEDEVILED
CHOSEN

CHOSEN

A DARK BREED NOVEL

SABLE GRACE

AVON

An Imprint of HarperCollinsPublishers

This book is a work of fiction. The characters, incidents, and dialogue are drawn from the author's imagination and are not to be construed as real. Any resemblance to actual events or persons, living or dead, is entirely coincidental.

AVON BOOKS
An Imprint of HarperCollins*Publishers*
10 East 53rd Street
New York, New York 10022-5299

Copyright © 2012 by Heather Waters and Laura Barone
ISBN 978-0-06-207964-0
K.I.S.S. and Teal is a trademark of the Ovarian Cancer National Alliance.
www.avonromance.com

First Avon Books mass market printing: September 2012

Avon Trademark Reg. U.S. Pat. Off. and in Other Countries, Marca Registrada, Hecho en U.S.A.
HarperCollins® is a registered trademark of HarperCollins Publishers.

Printed in the U.S.A.

10 9 8 7 6 5 4 3 2 1

Acknowledgments

To the team behind Sable Grace: Our editor extraordinaire, Erika Tsang, for not cringing every time we need a little hand holding. Our fantabulous agent, Roberta Brown, who gives new meaning to the word loyalty. Our spouses, Kyle and Carmine, for bringing home the bacon while we hold down the forts. Our children—Sydney, Hunter, CJ, Laney, Andy, Kaileb, Lolley, and Hayvin . . . for sometimes understanding that Mommy is a little busy, even if it looks like she's just daydreaming.

To Jay Beeler, for all his help with the Turkish translations. Any mistakes are ours and not his.

And finally, thank you to our readers for following Kyana and Ryker on their journey and loving them as much as we do.

CHOSEN

Chapter One

St. Augustine, Florida

She watched Haven tilt her head back and let out an unladylike shout of laughter, and everything in Kyana Aslan's body warmed with contentment. This was how it was meant to be. The two of them, laughing—Haven sipping wine, Kyana sipping blood as they sat in front of the roaring fire in their shared home. Ah yes, in her dreams she still sipped fresh blood. There was no sickly sweet ambrosia here, thank you very much.

"And Ryker?" Haven's dreamy image asked, the laughter shifting to seriousness. "You're finally letting him into more places than your bed. Are you in love with him?"

Kyana wouldn't have answered that question in the wake of day, and she sure as hell wouldn't here, where *everything was perfect. Instead, she smiled and took Haven's glass. "You need more wine."*

"No. I—Kyana, I'm going to die."

She froze, mid-reach toward the wine bottle. The mood of the dream shifted, darkened. Became so heavy it was as though someone had tossed black velvet over the lovely painting she'd worked so hard to create in her head. "What?"

When she glanced back, Haven was looking directly at her, her face pale, her eyes wide. The wine was gone, the coziness and warmth now a harsh cold that brought a shudder over Kyana.

"I'm going to die, Kyana . . . Cronos is coming for me. Help me! Save me!"

But as Kyana opened her mouth to offer reassurance, the flames in the fireplace formed a claw, reached through the screen, and seized Haven's face. Her body went up in a mass of orange flames and black smoke, but it was the smell of burning flesh that snatched Kyana from her dream.

She woke with a start, her chest tight and her body coated in a slick layer of sweat. It was just a dream. Just the past weeks' events seared into her brain and her heart. She took a deep breath, peering through the dense shadows of night in her room, relaxing as she felt Ryker stir beside her.

"It's just a dream," he mumbled, his arms tightening around her.

A flicker of white light shimmered at the foot of the bed. Kyana bolted upright, her hand instinctively reaching for Ryker's arm. She blinked twice to clear her sleep-dazed vision, but it didn't help. She could still see the illuminated face staring back at her through shimmering blond hair.

Confusion settled over her as she realized whom she was looking at. Hope. Haven's long-dead twin sister—beaten to death at the age of seven by their own father.

"He's coming for her," the child sang, her blue eyes wide and glittery. "And for you. Help her."

"What the hell is that?"

Ryker's voice shattered the eerie silence that had followed Hope's warning. Kyana ignored him, her heart resuming the horrible pounding that had resided there when she'd awoken.

"Who, Hope? Who is coming for Haven?"

"Him," the child ghost said, her lips creepy pink and swollen, her eyes circled with black shadows. "She's going to die . . . you saw it. Just now."

"My dream—"

But as abruptly as she'd come, Hope vanished, leaving in her wake an icy chill that frosted Kyana's breath in the air.

"What's going on, Ky?"

Slowly, she turned to face Ryker. "You . . . you saw that, right? That wasn't part of my dream?"

"Yeah." He pulled her against his chest and pressed a quick kiss to the crown of her head. "I saw it."

"I think Haven is in trouble."

"Who was that?"

"Her twin sister." Her heartbeat was a full orchestra now, and as Kyana slipped out of the bed and shivered her way into her goddess attire, she couldn't tell if she was shaking from the drop in temperature or from stone-cold fear. "I was dreaming—Haven was eaten by fire, and then . . . I woke. There was Hope. I have to go."

She was rambling but Ryker didn't seem to have trouble following her. "She's secure Below—at the Healing Circle. There's no place safer in the world, Ky."

"And yet, I'm not reassured." So much had happened in such a short period of time that Kyana wasn't fool enough to dismiss any instincts that popped in her gut. "If she's fine, then all I've wasted is a little sleep."

Ryker climbed out of bed to stand beside her. She could read the confusion in his eyes, but he nodded. "I'll come with you."

She wasn't going to argue. She watched him dress quickly in the garb required of him as Zeus's replacement, then headed out the door. Artemis's temple was silent, the marble floors echoey, but far warmer than her own rooms. Kyana still didn't feel like much of a goddess since becoming one six weeks ago, but right now, she was determined to act like one. As Artemis's replacement, no one could stop her from doing what her instincts bade her to do. And right now, they warned her to run as quickly as she could to the portal that would take her from Olympus to the realm of magic— Below.

Ryker followed and slipped through the portal after her. Neither was winded from their sprint down the mountain, but both were silent as they jogged the cobbled roads of Below toward the Healing Circle.

While Haven was being cleansed of the evil that had possessed her, she'd been denied any visitors. Kyana hadn't fought the decree since she hadn't been ready to face Haven after everything she'd done. So it had been six weeks since she'd last seen her, and now Kyana was about to come face-to-face with the friend who, as of late, had become her biggest enemy.

As they reached the steps of the Healing

Circle, Ryker grabbed her arm, pulling her to a stop. She tried to snatch her arm free, but he held tight.

"What?"

"Something is definitely wrong." He pointed to the massive wooden doors. "Nothing would make a sentinel leave his post unattended."

Panic squeezed her chest. "I saw it, Ryker. It wasn't just a dream. There's going to be a fire. We have to get people to safety."

"Go find Haven. I'll set off the alarms."

She and Ryker separated as he ran off to ring the warning bells. Kyana sprinted through the halls, ordering everyone she saw to exit the building. She didn't stop until she reached the stairs that would take her down to the cleansing area—a place she was familiar with because when she'd joined the Order of Ancients, she'd had to be purged of the human blood she'd been feeding on for almost two hundred years.

"There's not much time." Hope's ghostly figure stood at the bottom of the stairwell, motioning Kyana forward. "Hurry."

Kyana took the stairs two at a time, following the spirit child she had no choice but to trust. She raced past rooms that looked more like prison cells than hospital rooms and skidded to a halt in front of a single door separate from the others.

"Hurry." Hope looked back toward the stairs. Her already ashen face shimmered, then began to fade. "There's not much time."

The corridor on her left was as empty as the one she stood in. Where the hell were the guards? Had they already obeyed the warning bells echoing through the halls and cleared everyone out? She immediately discarded the idea. She would have passed them.

Kyana gripped the doorknob and twisted. It didn't budge. Taking half a step back, she slammed her shoulder into the door hard enough to make the wood vibrate, but it held its ground. Stepping back, she kicked the door with all her strength. Nothing.

"Damn it," she yelled, pounding her fist against the magic-fortified wood. "Haven!"

A hand on her shoulder caused Kyana to spin around, instantly alert. "We have to get you out of here, Goddess."

Kyana glared down at the small Healer who'd come out of nowhere, shaking off the woman's touch. "Not without my friend."

"I will personally make sure my charge is brought to safety the moment the subduing potion takes effect."

"There's no time for all that. We have to get out of here, all of us, right now!"

The Healer shook her head. "I'm sorry, Goddess. She's not cleansed yet and cannot—"

"You either open this door right now or I swear to the gods I'll use your tiny little body and knobby head as a fucking battering ram."

The Healer's tiny eyes widened and her hands trembled as she pulled a small pouch from the pocket of her burlap dress and sprinkled green powder on the knob. The click of the door unlocking sounded like gunfire in the empty hallway.

"Thank you," Kyana mumbled, pushing the door open. In a second, her searching gaze took in the small room Haven had been calling home for the past six weeks. A cot, a tiny dresser and a desk, a mirror and a closet-sized bathroom, and a spellcrafting table with a small white kitten hissing in the corner. Where the hell was Haven?

She turned to question the Healer, but she'd already disappeared. Evacuated, more than likely. Kyana's stomach did a sickening somersault. Had Haven found a way to escape?

" 'Bout damned time."

Kyana spun around and found the kitten gone. In its place sat Haven, naked, and looking more than slightly irritated.

"What the—"

"I was afraid Hope wouldn't reach you in time." Haven wrapped her arms around her bare legs.

Kyana went momentarily stupid. "There was a cat . . . Why are you—never mind. We have to go. Now."

Haven pushed to her feet. "Glad to see I'm not going to have to talk you into letting me out of here. Let's go."

She snatched the blanket off the cot and wrapped it around her shoulders before making her way to the door. Kyana grabbed her by the arm. "If you try to run—"

"I won't." She shook off Kyana's hold, and together they ran back up the stairs, through the prayer rooms, and into the cool night air.

The minute they stepped outside, Kyana grabbed Haven again and pulled her toward a group of sentinels securing the perimeter around the Healing Circle. She needed to find Ryker and figure out what the hell was going on. They'd barely passed between the gates when a low rumble vibrated the ground beneath their feet. Turning, she looked at the Healing Circle. Giant fingers of fire came out of the very earth to engulf the structure.

Then a shower of blue lights rained down around the property. The building collapsed onto itself and a symphony of screams shattered the night as those who'd moved too slowly were buried alive.

Chapter Two

People ran from every direction, shouting orders, trying to put out the fires, and saving those who'd been trapped inside when the Healing Circle collapsed. The injured were moved to the streets, where soot-covered Mystics tended their wounds. In the midst of it all was Ryker. He'd only been the new God of Gods for a short time, but these people were beginning to look to him for their protection.

He wasn't letting them down.

He was so in his element that beneath the magically lit night sky, he even looked like the god everyone had counted on for millennia.

The only thing missing was his "Hera" standing at his side.

And right then, the only thing Kyana wanted was to go to him, to be his partner in all this chaos, but Haven's chattering teeth pulled her focus back to the matter at hand. She led Haven to a somewhat secluded bench, still close enough to the sentinels that she could call for assistance should she need it.

She waited until Haven settled beside her before asking the question burning in her brain since waking to find Hope standing at the foot of her bed. "How did you know what was going to happen?"

Haven pulled her blanket more tightly around her shivering, naked body. "For six weeks I've tried to purge that bastard from my blood, but I can still smell him. Still feel him."

Kyana's muscles tensed, cramping and twisting her insides. She forced herself to breathe and to find a tone that was hopefully more Artemis than Kyana. Soothing and less demanding. "Are you feeling Cronos, or just the residual effects of his possession?"

Anger flashed in the depths of Haven's eyes, and Kyana couldn't blame her. So much had gone down in the last couple of months—most of which wasn't, at the root, Haven's fault, and yet she'd been shouldered with the majority of the blame. When Haven had been on the brink of dying from a murderous, Cronos-loving son of a bitch, Kyana had turned her against her wishes. After that, Haven hadn't been just a Witch anymore. She'd become half Vampyre/Lychen like Kyana.

Now Kyana was neither of those things. She was just a goddess. But Haven was forced to carry all three breeds inside her still.

That immense power had led to Cronos's possession of her. In that state, she'd been powerful enough to bring the dead god back to life, and now he was terrorizing them all from a world away.

But he *was* a world away. He had to be. There was no way for him to get off the island they'd left him on. Only two people had the power to travel there and back—Ryker and his father, Ares—and they were the least likely people to join the dark side.

"I thought it was just . . . whatever," Haven said, drawing Kyana's attention back to her. "But it's getting stronger. Like . . . I can almost feel him breathing on me sometimes even though I know I'm alone."

Haven ground her palms into her eyes. "I saw his lackeys come into this Circle tonight in my dreams. Saw his Mages plant charms around the building that would go off like bombs. I could feel his hatred, Kyana. I knew I was his target, and I also knew it wasn't just a dream. I tried to warn the Healers but of course they wouldn't believe me. So I did the only thing I could. I dreamed of Hope. I didn't know if it would work, but I sent her to find you."

Kyana shook her head. She didn't dispute that Haven had seen or felt something but it couldn't have been Cronos. Yes, the ancient god had risen from the grave. But he couldn't get to them . . .

"He's trapped on that island, Haven. How could he get people to do his bidding?"

Haven glared at her. "He managed well enough when he was dead. Do you really think it's more of a challenge now that he's alive?"

Kyana swallowed. *Touché.*

Even though he'd been dead for millennia, Cronos had been able to possess others to do his bidding. Others who'd murdered those meant to replace the gods as their powers faded, like Haven, who'd been Artemis's first choice as the new Goddess of the Hunt and had been nearly killed because of it.

"When we left that island," Haven continued, "I felt like he was in the port with us. I've tried to convince myself that it was nothing, tried to get him out of my head, but . . . after this . . . I *know* he got off. I *know* what I've been seeing is real."

Kyana stiffened. She'd felt something strange during that port too—something she hadn't thought to mention to anyone. Hell, she'd pretty much forgotten the strange pull she'd felt until now. But at Haven's reminder, the memory was suddenly fresh again, the fear returning with a sickening twist to her gut.

She tried to steady her breathing. "What did you feel? In the port, I mean."

"*Him.* His hand on my arm. His breath on my neck." Haven turned and watched Kyana closely. "He's not trapped on that damned island. He's here. In *our* world. And every day that passes, he's getting stronger."

A hysterical sob burst from Haven and she shook her head. "I don't know where he is exactly or what he's up to, but I do know that he's back. He's really, really pissed off, and there are two people in this world he wants to make suffer while he waits for his chance to reclaim his throne. Me . . . and you."

Determined to be the voice of reason, Kyana sighed and rubbed her arm. When her hands stopped shaking, she looked at Haven.

It was odd, sitting here, having this conversation after spending so many weeks with Haven as the enemy. It was as though they'd returned to being best friends and roommates, and she had to remind herself that Haven didn't deserve her trust again. Not yet. There was still a chance she was working for Cronos. If he had managed to get his minions into the Healing Circle to blow it up, there was no reason that he couldn't have gotten them to Haven as well. Why not kill her outright? Maybe the explosion was his way of freeing Haven. Of letting her loose to work for him once again.

Kyana put her guard right back in place and sat up straight. She would play along for a few more minutes. Test the waters. See if she could tell from her heart which side Haven was playing for now.

She cleared her throat. "Let's say you're right. How do we find him? More importantly, how the hell are we going to stop him?"

"I've been asking myself that very question since I started dreaming of him."

Seeing a bit of the old Haven in the sparkle in her eyes, Kyana prompted, "And?"

"As long as I dream, we can find him. My link to him is still strong. I think that's why he's so pissed. If he knew his possession would create the link, I'm sure he figured I'd be imprisoned in Tartarus and out of his way by now. I think he's finally caught on that I can see him."

"And what exactly have you seen?"

"I've been too afraid to look at much. But if he wants me dead . . . I think I'm the one with the power. I can watch and see where he is and what he's up to." Her gaze dropped to her feet. "I can finally start to right the wrongs I've done."

"Haven, you're saying you want to remain linked to the asshat who tortured you. Who shoved his way inside you and made you do things that could still very well end with you being sent to Tartarus if your trial doesn't go well."

Even if this was a possible way to find Cronos, she didn't like it. If Haven could see him and he knew it, then he could prevent her from seeing things too. Which meant the next time his goons came after her, she wouldn't be forewarned. Maybe he could even confuse what she was seeing. Distort it so it worked *for* him rather than against him.

Or maybe it was all bullshit.

But she didn't think so. Her gut wasn't screaming at her to distrust Haven, and Kyana's gut was rarely wrong. "You do know I'm going to have to take you to Jordan Faye."

Haven blinked. "Why?"

Jordan was Lachesis's replacement, the Fate who could find the truths within a soul. If Haven was lying about any of this, Lachesis would know. "You really have to ask?"

Haven's eyes narrowed and she shook her head. "Fine. Whatever. I get it. I fucked up and now I can't be trusted. Take me to her, but not yet. Please. Let me show you what I've been seeing before it's too late, then you can get whatever confirmation you need to prove I'm not lying."

"Let you show me? What do you mean?"

Haven's gaze searched Kyana's, a pleading desperation peering back at her. "You won't like it."

More than slightly uncomfortable with the way this conversation was going, Kyana folded her arms across her chest. "Try me."

"Morpheus." Haven looked away. "He can make sure you enter my dreams, and together we find Cronos and figure out what he's up to. Then we come up with a way to stop him. After I see Jordan, of course."

Kyana felt her face mold into a look of incredulity. "Not just no, but *hell* no."

Morpheus was the God of Dreams, strange and creepy as all get-out. Going to him was about as appealing as skating on broken glass in bare feet.

"Hell yes." Haven's stare was so self-assured, it looked a tiny bit insane.

"I don't trust him." *Or you.*

"No one does. But he can make sure you travel into my head when I dream."

"In order to stick me in your dreams, Morpheus's Oneiroi would have to get into our heads. Not happening. They're *demons*."

"I haven't shut my eyes once in almost ten days without him being there, Kyana. Not once. You think *demons* scare me when I've had the darkest god to ever live playing around in my head?"

Maybe not, but they scared the hell out of Kyana.

Haven pinched the bridge of her nose and squeezed her eyes shut. "Besides, you're a goddess. The Oneiroi can't taint a deity. If they could, Morpheus would be a raving lunatic by now."

Kyana raised her brow. The God of Dreams was more than a little cuckoo. "He *is* a lunatic."

"But not in the way a person gets when they're infested with Oneiroi."

"You're willing to stake my sanity on that? Never mind. You probably are. But what about yours? You're *not* a deity."

Haven drew her lips in tight. "No. Thanks to you, I'm not, am I?"

Kyana's stomach somersaulted. To say she felt guilty about that turn of events was an understatement, to say the least.

"Haven—"

"It's all right." Haven's smile didn't quite reach her eyes. "I'm not sure I have much sanity left anyway."

"Morpheus is high as a kite and wicked to boot. You want him in our heads? Really?"

"It won't be him. It will be his—"

"It will be his demons. Even better."

Haven pinned her with a stare. "Will you do it or not?"

Her shoulders fell a little and she sighed.

"You'll see Jordan the minute we're done?"

Haven nodded.

"Fine," she said, feeling the urge to vomit. "Let's go see Morpheus."

Chapter Three

Kyana used her new skills to paint a pair of jeans and a sweatshirt onto Haven before she froze to death, then dragged her through the crowd, avoiding the commotion and Ryker. She didn't want to explain what they were up to, didn't feel up to the argument she knew she'd be in for if she did.

It was easier to go now and deal with him later. If Haven was going to try anything, it certainly wouldn't be in the Underworld where Morpheus's domain was—a place she wouldn't be able to get out of if alarms were sounded.

When they rounded the corner and moved away from the chaos, she cast a sideways glance at Haven and asked the question that had been niggling her mind. "So what kind of Illusion Charm did you create to make yourself look like a cat? I didn't know you could do that."

The stench of smoke and panic hung heavy in the midmorning air. Already the rumor that Cronos was behind the attack was spreading. The way people looked at Haven with suspicion and blame as they passed made Kyana a little worried for Haven's safety. If Kyana wasn't walking beside her right now, would they stop at just glares?

"It wasn't a charm."

Kyana frowned. "I saw you in cat form. You don't *have* a cat form."

Vampyre, yes. Lychen, yes. Witch, yes. There had been no cat in that equation.

"Apparently, I do." Haven studied her chipped, unpainted nails—a far cry from the perfectly manicured French tips she'd always been so proud of. "The cleansings seemed to have killed the bitch in me. It was more prominent than the Vampyre blood you gave me, but my Witch blood seems to still rule."

Trying not to cringe at the profanity, Kyana stopped at the cavelike entrance that would take them to the River Styx. The tiny word was proof that the Haven of old who screamed, "Darn it" when stubbing her toes hadn't returned completely.

"Okay, so the Lychen is cleansed. What's with the cat?"

"I've become a fucking Grimalkin, thank you very much. Only the tenth Witch in history to have it happen to, lucky me."

The frustration on Haven's face relaxed Kyana a bit. It was a human sort of frustration rather than an animalistic rage. "Grimawhat?"

"Grimalkin. It seems I've become my own familiar."

"It is . . . permanent?"

Rolling her eyes, Haven started down the spiral steps. "Like herpes."

A snort escaped Kyana.

"Laugh all you like. But I can turn into any cat I like, and some of them are really big with really, really sharp teeth."

That feeling of contentment Kyana had felt in her dream returned as they made their way to the shores of the River Styx and onto Charon's ferryboat. They were acting like the old friends they'd once been before Hell had ripped them apart. It reminded Kyana of why she and Haven had become such fast friends. Why they'd always been there for each other. Why she'd missed her so damned much.

Haven sat in the middle of the little boat and wrapped her arms around her knees. The scrutinizing gaze she held steady on Kyana's face was uncomfortable. "You're different now."

"No shit. I'm a goddess."

Haven cracked a smile. "That's not what I mean. You're just . . . I don't know . . . easier to read."

"No I'm not."

"Yeah. You are."

Before Kyana could think of anything to say, they rounded the bend on the river and their bubble of contentment burst at the sight of Geoffrey towering in the entrance to the Underworld, two monstrous hellhounds on either side of the onyx chariot encasing him.

As Hades's replacement, he had to authorize anyone who wanted access to the Underworld, and judging by the scowl on his handsome face, he wasn't likely to give it today.

"She hasn't finished cleansing," he said.

Like Kyana's, Geoff's Vampyric heritage had faded. But his changes hadn't affected the beauty of him, thank the gods. The only instantly noticeable difference was his long dark hair, now lined with Hades's silver just above each ear—similar to Artemis's amber curls that mingled with Kyana's own black ones.

He glared at Charon. "Take them back. They do not have permission to enter today."

"Come on, Geoff. I'm not stupid. Why would I try anything this close to Tartarus?" Haven muttered, shifting uncomfortably beside Kyana. "I mean, when I'm not possessed."

As Geoff's gaze fell on Haven, his dark blue eyes softened. It was Kyana's turn to shift uncomfortably. There was a connection between Geoff and Haven that had always been there, but that had seemingly strengthened over the last couple of months since all this Cronos shit had started. Something that made Kyana feel less like part of their original trio and more like an unwanted tagalong.

"She almost died today, Geoff. Give her a break."

His eyes widened, his face turned a bit ashen. "What the hell do you mean, she almost died?"

Kyana sighed, wishing she'd kept that tidbit to herself. Now he was really going to fly off the handle. "Nothing. She's fine. The Healing Circle, however, needs a bit of repair work."

"Someone blew it up," Haven added.

A million questions were shooting out of his eyes, and Kyana cut him off, unwilling to waste the time required to answer them. "Let us pass, okay? We just want to see Morpheus. He can link me to Haven's dream."

He snapped out of whatever fog of anger or disbelief he'd been standing in. "Why the bloody hell would you want to do that? No one visits the bloke." His gaze swayed back to Kyana as he stepped off the chariot. "He's mental, and you know that. What could possibly be in her head that you'd risk romping with his demons to see?"

"She thinks Cronos is back."

His gaze narrowed. "We *know* he's back."

Kyana shook her head. "Not alive back. Here, back. As in, he got off the island."

"And you believe her?" he asked, his Irish lilt making the incredulity in his voice sound a little less condescending.

"I'm standing right here," Haven said through gritted teeth. "Can you at least pretend I exist?"

"Lass, there's no doubt you exist. I'm just never sure who I'm speaking to when I address you."

Ouch. Kyana glanced at Haven and watched the pain of those words hit her. Even more than having Kyana pissed at her, it probably devastated Haven to have Geoff acting so cold toward her.

He swung his gaze to Kyana. "What happened with the Healing Circle?"

Noting with a sigh that he wasn't going to let them get by without the details he wanted, Kyana gave in and rehashed the details of the morning.

By the time she'd finished, he looked as though he might be ill. His stare fixated on Haven, but

Kyana couldn't tell if he wanted to grab her to hold her or to throttle her.

When he pulled himself together, he leaned into Kyana and spoke quietly, but urgently. "Maybe it wasn't Cronos. Maybe *she* wanted out of the Healing Circle and made it happen."

"You think I did this?" Haven seethed. The hurt in her eyes dissolved into outrage. "I think I could hate you for that," she whispered.

Geoff's eyes were apologetic, but he didn't look ready to back down. "I'm sorry, lass, but you haven't truly been . . . *you* . . . lately." He returned his attention to Kyana. "Does Ryker know you're doing this?"

Kyana scowled. "He's not my keeper."

"Maybe he should be. You've been through hell with Cronos," Geoff said. "And you, Haven? Why go out of your way to seek him out after all he's done to *you*?"

"Don't you think I want him to leave me the hell alone? But he won't, and we might as well take advantage of it. After Morpheus links Kyana to my dreams and if she thinks there's nothing to worry about . . . then you can find me a new damned prison and I'll stay there like a good little girl and not cause you any more problems."

"And you're okay with putting her in more

danger?" He glared at Kyana. "If she really is tapping into Cronos, you don't think that's going to piss him off?"

"If she's telling the truth," Kyana said, "then it doesn't matter. He's already pissed and already burned down the damned Healing Circle to prove it."

Silence hung heavy in the air for a long moment. Finally, he let out a whistle and the self-driven chariot disappeared down the winding tunnel that led to the Underworld. With a silent command from their master, his hounds charged off as well.

"Fine," he said. "But I'm coming with you."

Kyana opened her mouth to protest but Geoff cut her off.

"Either I go with you, or neither of you go." He looked from one to the other. "The choice is yours."

Kyana studied him, trying to determine if he wanted to tag along because he thought Haven was *a* danger or was *in* danger.

"You really believe her?" he asked, finally.

She shrugged. "I'm not naïve. That's why I want to see Morpheus. Give Haven the chance to prove she's right, and then I'll take her to Jordan to make sure she's being honest about everything else."

He briefly closed his eyes and gave a slight nod. Then he took Haven's hand and escorted her back to the middle of the ferry. The softness in his touch and the tenderness in his gaze when Haven pulled away told Kyana all she needed to know. His concern that Haven might try something was nothing compared to his fear that Cronos might actually still have the ability to reach her.

To *kill* her, once and for all.

Chapter Four

To reach the upper region of the Underworld where Morpheus's realm, Erebus, lay, they had to travel along all five subterranean rivers—which meant a lot of souls reaching out, calling to them in the darkness, pleading for their journeys to be swift and painless. It was enough to make Kyana wish she'd invited Ryker along to quickly port them into the realm instead of being forced to take this slow, tortuous ferry ride.

But Erebus was one of the few places that prevented such means of travel. Security was tight, and for good reason. Cronos opening the gates of Tartarus had led to extreme measures of precaution. But even before that, the realm had been bound by magic even Olympus seemed to lack.

"We'll let Morpheus connect me to her," Geoffrey said, stepping closer to Haven. "Less emotional baggage with me."

It was painful to watch Haven ease away from him.

She doesn't trust us at all anymore. Not that Kyana could blame her. They didn't really trust Haven either.

"Less emotional baggage, my ass," Kyana muttered, longing to point out that he was still making goo-goo eyes at the woman he claimed to have more distance from. "If anyone's going to do it," she said to his back, "it will be me."

Geoffrey glared at her, then promptly turned back around to face the front of the ferry.

The poor bastard was in love with Haven. It was written all over his face. As the new God of the Underworld, however, he didn't stand much chance of finding a happily-ever-after with her. Especially if she was found guilty and sentenced to suffer in Tartarus under his watch.

She exhaled, quietly nervous about what was to come. She didn't like to dream, where she couldn't control her environment or the people inside it.

People she never wanted to see again, whether in reality or in her subconscious. When she couldn't find peaceful sleep, it was always the same people plaguing her nights. Images of her past. Images of her human life, of her abusive, murdering husband, Mehmet, and the lecherous first wife who'd rained hell upon the other women in Mehmet's harem. Images of the man who'd saved her from certain death and had turned her into the Vampyre/Lychen she'd become, who'd loved her like a daughter, raised her in this new world, and then left her, murdered as she'd watched and mourned and prayed for a death of her own.

No. Kyana didn't like to dream because she couldn't run from her past while she slept.

It totally sucked donkey balls.

She wasn't looking forward to this at all. She'd met Morpheus only once, when he'd come out of his cave to Above in an effort to rein in his little imps when they'd gone on strike in Egypt. He'd been a reefer-smoking Bob Marley look-alike whose main concern in life was making sure people had as many bad dreams as good.

She shivered as they drifted through a narrow passage where two gates, one of ivory, the other of polished horn so bright it lit the darkness, stood sentinel on either side of the water.

She could have lived two more lifetimes without ever knowing what was in this realm.

"What are those?" Haven asked.

"The gates of dreams," Geoffrey explained,

stepping closer to Haven. "False dreams pass through the ivory while prophetic dreams go through the horn." He pointed to a soft glow around the next bend. "That should be the wilted elm. Morpheus's home is not far now."

The ferry slipped around the next turn. Sure enough, she saw a wilted elm with winged phantom-shaped wisps hanging from the thick branches. The way they moved, as if pushed by an invisible wind, turning ever so slowly to stare at her with sightless eyes, caused her to take a step back.

"And those?" Haven asked again, backing away from Geoff.

"Oneiroi dreams waiting to be released to the dreamers."

The ferry docked and Kyana shivered again. She and Haven followed Geoffrey up a small rise where Kyana expected a house or, at the very least, a cave like the one the Fates worked in. She certainly wasn't prepared to see four large cabanas complete with thatched roofs. If they weren't on the far side of the River Styx with transitional souls all around them, she could have imagined herself on a beach somewhere.

"Oh look, we have guests."

A man dressed in an overly bright orange shirt

and gray ball cap, flowered board shorts, and flip-flops appeared in front of them.

He looked nothing like Bob Marley anymore, but Kyana instantly recognized the maroon in his eyes and the golf ball–sized mark on his neck to know she was staring at Morpheus.

"Who the hell are you supposed to be this time?" she asked, trying not to glare. After all, they had come to him for a favor. Better not to piss him off straightaway.

Morpheus's grin widened. "Welcome to Margaritaville." When Kyana still didn't react, he added, "Cheeseburger in Paradise?"

"Jimmy Buffet," Haven muttered, moving to stand between Kyana and Geoffrey. The minute they'd stepped onto sand, Geoffrey had placed himself between her and Morpheus. Haven wasn't a coward, however. She never had been. It was one of the things Kyana loved most about her.

"Ding, ding, ding. We have a winner." Morpheus beamed at her, flashing white Chiclets-sized teeth in her direction.

Morpheus led the way to the largest of the four cabanas, sat on one of the loungers, and poured a round of frozen drinks into three sugar-rimmed glasses. She ignored the beverage, but Haven picked hers up and moved it toward her mouth.

Geoffrey took the glass from her before she could take a sip.

There was no way they were drinking anything Morpheus offered. Anyone who could keep a frozen drink frozen this close to Tartarus couldn't be trusted. She was already sweating, her chiton clinging to her in a chafing manner that had her squirming every so often to adjust herself discreetly.

Morpheus gestured to the other bamboo loungers spread around an Igloo cooler. "Sit, sit. It's not often that I get a visit from fellow gods and goddesses. Tell me what's going on Beyond? Any luck spotting my Chosen?"

As Kyana sat, bright light lit up the small camp like the real sun, drying some of the perspiration gathering on her forehead, but doing nothing to help with the ravaging heat. "I wish."

She'd much rather be dealing with a saner, newer version of Morpheus than this crazy loon, but Morpheus's Chosen was likely dead, just like several other MIAs.

As if sensing her rising frustration, Geoff sat between Kyana and Haven and draped his arm casually around both of their shoulders. Too warm already, she shrugged him off. Her golden skin was turning pink. It was like she'd stepped into a crematorium.

"So, you've come to the great Morpheus for assistance, have you?" Morpheus sang, his face turning ruddy as the heat thickened around them. "Of course you have. Why else would you have come where no one wishes to visit?"

"You think you know why we're here?" Kyana asked.

"You'll find soon enough that our little world of gods is like a henhouse. Something happens, we're all squawking about it in a matter of minutes."

He pulled a cigar from his bright shirt pocket, on which a tiny parrot had been embroidered. "Hope you don't mind your business being bandied about. It won't be long before we all know the exact tone of your moans and groans and the squeaks of your bedsprings."

That his eyes seemed to imply he knew about her and Ryker's relationship didn't bother Kyana—they hadn't tried to keep it a secret. But that any of the gods might be privy to what they did behind closed doors nearly made her blush.

Morpheus looked at Haven. "Word is that Cronos, or at least his supporters, are running amok Below again."

He lit the cigar, took several short puffs, then let out a dozen perfect circles of smoke. The bright red tip of the cigar blazed, almost hypnotically, as he rolled it around his palm to form a little cone of the barely-there ashes.

"You think this mixed breed can show you something in her dreams."

"How the hell do you know that?" Kyana asked. She should be used to the way the gods worked by now, but it still managed to cause her head to spin a little every time something strange was presented to her.

"You spoke the words to him," Morpheus said, jutting his chin toward Geoffrey. "My name was mentioned. I was alerted."

Oh. Well. That was creepy.

"Will you help us?" Haven whispered.

"It's not often I get to watch my pets play here in my own realm." He clamped the cigar between his teeth and rubbed his hands together as though trying to strike a fire with two sticks. "Let's get started, shall we?"

He cocked his head, peering into the nothingness above the cabanas. "Hear that? My babies are home."

Three bright green parrots and one of pure white fluttered in from out of nowhere, taking roost upon the nearest cabana's roof. "They'll sing you to sleep if you find trouble."

Kyana leaned in to Geoffrey. "He's freaking loony toons."

"With the ears of a bat, Goddess." Morpheus stood, stretched out his stubby arm, which was covered in fine gray hairs. The white cockatiel lifted from her roost to land gracefully on his wrist. "This is Slumber. She'll make certain you stay tied to your friend's dreams once you find them."

Wow. He really *did* know exactly why they'd come to him. Kyana couldn't help but be a little impressed, and admittedly, a little creeped out.

"Just stay still. She's a lover, not a biter." Morpheus guffawed at his own bad joke and bent to pull a small chest from under his lounger. From it, he unraveled a scroll of blank parchment and plucked out a quill that looked crafted from one of his beloved pets.

"Are these Oneiroi?" she asked, looking the bird dead in the eye. It blinked and seemed to smile.

"Indeed. Much prettier than their normal bodies, wouldn't you say?"

Kyana agreed. The only Oneiroi she'd ever seen had looked like creatures from one of the movies Haven used to watch all the time—*Gremlins*. But Slumber was quite gorgeous. The feathers crowning her tiny head as she bobbed her neck up and down stood straight up as though praying. Flecks of silver rimmed her black eyes, and in the depths of the pupils, only if she looked hard enough, Kyana could see the small sphere of red that belied Slumber's demonic heritage.

"Here." Morpheus handed the quill and parchment to Kyana. "Write the name of your friend and feed it to my girl. Then let her"—he pointed at Haven—"do the same."

Kyana opened her mouth to question him, but Geoffrey shook his head. "Don't ask. Just do it."

Wanting to get this over with as quickly as possible, she wrote down Haven's name, then handed over the quill and parchment. While Haven wrote, Kyana rolled the parchment into a tiny ball and offered it to Slumber.

The bird gently took the parchment in her mouth, rolled it briefly on her tongue, then resumed her head bobbing before flying off to land on Haven's shoulder. The bird devoured her paper as well, then let out a loud squeal.

"That's my lovely girl," Morpheus crooned.

"What do they need to do to ensure this works?" Geoffrey asked. "I'd rather not have to repeat this process."

"They'll do nothing but get comfortable and

fall asleep. Slumber will assure their dreams find their targets." Morpheus pulled a light cover and several pillows from a trunk and set them beside Kyana before doing the same for Haven.

Kyana frowned. There was no way she could let her guard down knowing Morpheus was leering at her. The god gave her the heebie-jeebies, and even with Geoffrey standing guard, she didn't trust the pothead not to try something that would cause her to kill him before they could locate a replacement for him. He had sexual deviant written all over his squat body.

As if knowing what she was thinking, Morpheus shrugged. "I can do what you need. But you have to want it or we're wasting our time."

He stretched out on his lounger, relit his cigar, and pulled a beer from the cooler in front of his chair. "What'll it be?"

With a sigh, Kyana stood and spread the blanket in a shadow-filled corner of the cabana, then arranged the pillows before settling herself upon them. Geoffrey took Haven's hand, holding it too tightly for her to pull away, and escorted her to lie beside Kyana. Once they were both settled, Slumber fluttered inside and landed at the head of their makeshift bed.

Flicking her finger lightly over the bird's head,

Kyana said, "You better not get lost along the way or your stoned little boss there will have to find himself a new pet. Got it?"

Slumber fluffed her crown of feathers and seemed to smile as if to say, *Trust me.*

Kyana rolled her head to the side to look at Haven. "Ready?"

"As I'll ever be."

Kyana watched Haven reach out and take Geoffrey's hand. It was the first time she'd done anything so friendly since her Turning. The gesture made Kyana look away to hide her faint smile.

With a sigh, she closed her eyes and tried to focus on the sound of the water and the feel of the soft sand beneath her.

"You have to relax," Haven said. "Get out of your own way."

"I don't see you asleep yet," Kyana grumbled.

"Working on it."

Kyana rolled onto her side. Slumber shifted, her tiny little claws scrapping Kyana's thigh, but not hard enough to break the skin.

It wasn't long before the soft sounds of Haven's breath confessed she'd succeeded before Kyana. Shortly after, Kyana felt herself slowly slipping into unconsciousness.

Chapter Five

Within a moment after falling asleep, Kyana found herself deluged with the very images of her past she'd hoped to avoid. Her marriage to Mehmet. The beatings suffered at the hands of his first wife, Azime. The torturous rape that led to Kyana's own death. Then, as always, the man who'd claimed her as daughter, changed her into the Dark Breed she'd become and rescued her from a life of abuse.

She waited, her chest heavy with dread, for the images of his murder to infiltrate the other memories as they always did, but she was thankfully spared. Instead, the dream became darker, colder, and then, finally, it morphed into Cronos's face, and his eerie laugh became the sound track to the nightmare.

There was no ground below her. No sky above

her. She was surrounded by nothingness, as weightless as air. The eerie laughter ceased so that the only sound became the blood rushing through her veins. Where was Haven? Kyana wasn't supposed to be alone here! Trapped . . . on the verge of a panic attack—

Her feet smacked something firm and hard and her world became sharp, distinct pictures once again. A marshy landscape. Sounds of swampland—the croaking frogs, the sporadic splashes of gods-knew-what lurking beneath the dark water. The panic that had shrouded her dream lifted. Her breathing and heartbeat slowed as her nightmares receded and she settled into what she somehow knew were *Haven's* dreams.

Saw grass swayed in the wind, biting at her bare ankles. The gusts kicked up, causing fine sand to sting her skin and make her eyes burn as she stumbled over a cypress root. Slumber floated on the breeze above, hovering just out of reach. Each time Kyana stopped, the bird turned and circled until she once again followed.

Then she was standing at the entrance of an old cemetery where the landscape had grown over the few intact headstones. Was this what Haven was seeing right now too? She wasn't exactly sure how all of this worked, but she doubted Haven had seen the images of Azime and Mehmet and Henry. At least, she prayed not. Those were private. Too frightening for words. Too horrifying to share.

Her gaze fell to the branch rubbing against her arm, and she jumped when she saw Haven pressed against a tree trunk, watching her with frightened eyes.

"Where are we?"

Haven clutched her throat. Her lips moved, but it was as though she existed in a silent movie. Her frustration made her eyes shimmer. She finally gave up trying to make Kyana understand and gestured for her to follow down old paths to the back of the cemetery.

Kyana scanned the area. Dark Mages tended a naked man in the firelight. Cronos stood less than twenty feet away. She'd never seen him except in her dreams, yet somehow she always knew it was him. Long, waist-length ebony hair. Ivory skin. Impeccably dressed in velvet and lace as though he'd stepped straight out of the Regency era. She couldn't hear the words he spoke, but the evil smile darkening his face caused her skin to slither.

They made their way through the shadows until they stood a couple of feet behind him. Oh how she wished for a weapon, some way to kill

the bastard in her dreams—Haven's dreams?—
that would keep him dead when reality returned.
But she had no weapons, no magic that would
allow her to attempt such a thing—even if it were
possible.

She took a step forward. Then another . . . until
she was so close she could smell his scent. In this
reality, he smelled of musky sandalwood rather
than sulfur, and as much as she didn't want to,
she found it soothing . . . calming . . . alluring. She
took another step toward him.

Cronos jerked in their direction, snapping
Kyana out of what had felt like a near-trance
state. Uncertain whether he could see them, she
grabbed Haven by the arm and ducked behind
a crypt. Her heart pounding, she peeked around
the structure to find his attention had returned to
the naked man now under the blankets.

"You have the opportunity to live again,"
Cronos said. "However, for this gift to be yours,
you must pledge your life and loyalty to me. I
will be your lord and master. You will be mine to
command. Honor what I require of you, and I will
give you free rein to work your special art on the
human world with no one to stop you."

Slowly, the man reached out to grasp Cronos's
hand and was pulled to his feet. "If you refuse

my terms, the process beginning in you will end immediately. But I am merciful. Unlike your last death, this one will be quick and painless."

"What . . . what is it that you want from me?" The man huddled under the blanket. "You know who I am. What I did to be buried here."

"I do."

"I killed . . . so many." The shame in his voice was nearly palpable. "What could I possibly do for someone like you?"

"What you've always done best." Cronos smiled. "Only better. You'll have power the likes of which you've never imagined. Allow my coven to tend to you, and soon, you'll be strong enough to contain the magic that will serve me well."

"What is he doing?" she whispered to Haven.

Haven gripped her throat. Tears welled in her eyes. She slowly shook her head as though to say she didn't know any more than Kyana did. She turned back to the scene before her in time to see the man shake off his blanket and kneel before the altar erected between the rows of unmarked graves.

"I have caused enough pain and sorrow in one lifetime and spent another paying penance for what I've done. I wish no more blackness on my soul."

Kyana held her breath, not wanting to see what Cronos would do to the man who'd refused his offer but unable to look away.

"As you wish." Cronos placed his hand upon the man's head. Instantly, the man's eyes glazed over and he crumpled to the dirt. "Such a waste," Cronos muttered. Dusting off his hands, he stepped away from the body and faced his Mages. "Put him with the others."

The others? What others?

The Mages nodded and turned their attention to the twice-dead man at their feet.

"They've come, my lord."

The unexpected voice caused Kyana to jump back, whacking her head against a tree as she moved to hide again.

"At last," Cronos breathed.

Her gaze swerved to the spot in the trees that now held Cronos's attention. A figure moved through the shadows like the shades of Hades. When the figure split to outline three forms, Kyana held her breath, squinting to make any details come alive, but they simply wouldn't. They were just three faceless shadows that seemed to matter a great deal to Cronos. He waved his guests into the firelight.

Two of them stepped forward, and Kyana

stopped breathing altogether. The third figure remained in the trees, but she paid it no more attention. What held her riveted were the faces illuminated by the fiery orange lights of the campfire. For a horrifying moment, they looked just like Azime and Mehmet. But just as quickly, they looked like strangers.

Cronos knew she and Haven were there. He was screwing with their heads. He had to be. Or maybe Kyana had brought those images with her when she'd transitioned from her own dreams to Haven's.

But one thing she knew for certain. Haven had been right. This was no mere dream. There was something different, something tangible about it that made it feel more like a Seer's vision than a sleepy hallucination. Whatever this was, it was really happening. Kyana was willing to stake her life on it.

She felt a slight pull inside her belly, felt the weight of the heavy world being lifted from her mind, and slowly opened her eyes to find Haven staring down at her.

"Did *that* feel like a freaking nightmare?" she asked, her greenish-yellow eyes narrowed.

Kyana's tongue felt thick in her mouth, as though she'd just eaten the contents of a full ashtray.

"No." She tried swallowing a few times to make her throat less dry and turned her gaze to Geoffrey. "We need to find Ryker and the others."

"Why?"

"Because . . ." She struggled to her feet, swaying slightly as a wave of dizziness nearly toppled her back over. "Cronos is raising an army, and we can guess who the top five on his most wanted list is."

And there was no way in hell Kyana was going to let the bastard near any of them.

Chapter Six

The gods weren't going to like it, but Kyana was going to bring a prisoner back to her temple, and they could kiss her ass if they thought she'd give a shit about "rules" right now. Haven had a direct line to Cronos—Kyana had now seen it with her own eyes. That meant Haven was an asset they couldn't keep locked in a cell. It also meant her life was in grave danger, and the safest place was Olympus.

Ares would object the loudest, but Kyana would deal with him. Haven would stay in her temple, whether he liked it or not.

"Will you be sending for Jordan or taking me to her?" Haven asked as they approached the portal to Olympus.

"I'll send for her as soon as you're settled." Kyana glanced at Geoffrey, watched him awkwardly sneak a peek at Haven from the corner of his eye. They were a sorry pair. Geoffrey and his misplaced honor, determined not to ruin Haven's future by tying her down to the Vampyre he'd once been. Haven wanted children, something she'd never get from a Vampyric mate.

Kyana wondered if Geoffrey realized that was no longer a conflict for them. He was a god now, likely more virile than a damned rabbit. And Haven—she wasn't likely to ever have children now anyway. Unless there was something in her Witch heritage that would balance out her Vampyric blood, that dream was only one of many Kyana had killed when she'd turned Haven. Breeding Vamps were rare.

Kyana's blood ran cold. If Geoffrey could have children now . . . as a goddess, so could she. That was something that had never been an option for her, and as the possibility swirled around her head, she felt dizzy. She and Ryker were going to have to be very careful. Just because she could have children didn't mean she wanted them.

And as the goddess in charge of human fertility, she was likely to be even more fertile than Geoff was virile. Artemis hadn't had kids, but that was simply because she hadn't had sex. Everyone knew Artie was a virgin. Maybe this was why.

Maybe she'd known that if she'd had sex at all, she would have spit out a litter—maybe even have populated a small country.

"Do you really believe I'm still working for Cronos?" Haven asked. She pushed her oily hair from her face, and Kyana wondered when she'd last had a real bath. The bathing rooms at the Circle had been minimalistic. Hot water, rough soap. Nothing like the pampering Haven was used to.

Such a small detail, but one of many that had been stripped of the Haven of old—all because Kyana had had the audacity to save her life by turning her into something she should never have been.

"No," she whispered, not because she didn't want to be overheard, but because guilt was suddenly suppressing her voice. "But if you're going to stay on Olympus, you have to be cleared for everyone else's peace of mind."

Haven gave a curt nod and stepped through the portal. Kyana followed behind Geoff, her sickness intensified as the magic of the gate penetrated her bones. As they emerged from the other side, Haven let out a gasp of awe.

The first time Kyana had arrived on Olympus, she had been dumbstruck. Everything glimmered and shone here, from the cobbled walkways carved of smoothed granite to the amber and emerald mountains. Nine temples sat atop peaks of their own, from Zeus's, now Ryker's, to Kyana's new home. There was nothing drab or out of place here. It was, in fact, the most perfect place in all the three realms.

Utopia.

And all of it was in danger of being destroyed if they allowed Cronos to reach full power.

"Where the hell did you go?" Ryker appeared directly in their path as they moved toward the road to summon a chariot.

"To see Morpheus." She told him about the dream link, watched his sun-kissed face pale. "Cronos is building his army and we need to prepare ourselves."

"You're sure?"

"Yeah, I'm sure. I don't know how much time we have, but he's got a six-week head start on us. We have to call the other gods together and try to figure out how the hell we're going to stop him."

His gaze swept toward Haven and Geoff, who seemed to be in a heated argument. Haven jerked her arm out of Geoff's grasp and stepped away, nostrils flaring.

"He had me resurrect him for a reason, and it wasn't to spend his glory years rocking on some front porch somewhere!" Haven yelled. "He's coming after me—and all of you—before he carries out his idiotic plan to rule all three realms from Olympus."

"What's going on?" Kyana asked, pulling Haven aside, afraid she was going to explode all over Geoffrey.

"He," Haven said, thrusting her finger into Geoff's chest, "thinks it might have just been a nightmare, that it was me who blew up the Healing Circle! Can you freaking say *denial*?"

"I'm not denying anything, lass. I'm just trying to make you see—"

"That you're a stubborn ass? No problem. I see it clearly."

Kyana swallowed and let her gaze drift from Geoffrey's face, watched him argue with Haven without really hearing what he said. She took in Haven's face as well, then finally settled on Ryker's. All three of them were in terrible danger if Haven's dream became reality. Silas, their Witchy friend who'd become the temporary vessel for Poseidon's powers, was in danger as well. That meant every single person she cared about could lose his life because of one god's power trip.

Cronos had wanted resurrection to reclaim his old throne, and to do that, he'd have to murder his children—or, as it stood, the three men holding those children's powers now. Ryker, Silas, and Geoffrey. As the father of Zeus, Poseidon, and Hades, he'd tried to kill them all at once, which had resulted in his exile and eventually his death. Now he wanted revenge on all of them, Kyana and Haven included, as they'd been both his right hand and his biggest obstacles these last few weeks.

"I was there, Geoffrey. It wasn't a dream," Kyana said. "It was . . . different somehow. Real enough that if we could figure out where the hell we were, we'd find that man's body, as dead this time around as he was the first."

"Bollocks." Geoff rubbed the bridge of his nose, his temper infusing his cheeks with a blush of pink. "I'm not twat enough to think he's harmless, but that he might have come back and Ares and Ryker didn't notice? It was *their* ports you're claiming he violated. They should know if it felt different."

Why was he being so thickheaded?

"Every port is different, Geoff," Ryker said. "And that one belonged to Ares. If he felt anything different, he's not saying. But I agree with

Ky. We can't risk everything by sitting back and hoping none of this is actually happening."

Kyana wanted to kiss him right then and there for being on her side without question. If he had doubts, he wouldn't voice them in front of Geoffrey. He'd wait until they were alone and give her the opportunity to convince him without creating doubts in others. It was only one of the things she was so fond of about him.

She squeezed his hand in thanks.

Geoffrey cupped Haven's face, his shoulders falling a little when she pulled away. Kyana knew then why he was being so stubborn. Because if they were right, then there was a good chance something was going to happen to Haven again before he could tell her how he felt—before he could be with her the way he was dying to be. Kyana understood that fear better than he could know.

The only difference was, Kyana didn't quite know what she felt for Ryker. If she did, she certainly wouldn't wait to tell him. Not now, when their lives hung in the balance.

"Fine." Geoffrey yanked his hood back over his head. "I'll talk to Atropos, see if any of her souls are missing. Does that suit you? If they're not . . . then we'll know your theory about his raising an army isn't valid."

"And if they are?" Haven whispered.

He kissed her nose, and this time, she didn't pull away. "Then I'll develop a taste for crow, won't I?" He nodded at Kyana. "I'll tell Jordan you wish to see her while I'm there."

He stepped back through the portal to Below, his black cloak billowing behind him, making him look like a fleeing wraith.

When he was gone, Ryker hailed their chariot and directed the driver to Kyana's temple. "Haven?"

"Hmm?"

"Look at me," Ryker said.

Slowly, Haven turned her head, her eyes coated in a glassy sheen that nearly broke Kyana's heart. The longing there was so painful to see, it took all of Kyana's willpower not to take her in her arms and hold her.

"Yes?"

Ryker glanced at Kyana, his gaze apologetic. "We're going to need to know everything you learned while Cronos was possessing you. Every detail—even the ones—no, *especially* the ones you're ashamed of. "

"Fine," she said, looking neither of them in the eye. "As soon as Jordan has convinced you I'm not a liar, I'll tell you everything."

It came as no surprise to Kyana that Jordan was able to quickly clear Haven of any lies regarding the dreams, her theories, and the explosion at the Healing Circle. And she was relieved to see Ryker didn't seem very shocked either. Haven, however, looked grateful to have the whole ordeal over with as she fell into a chair in Kyana's private sitting room and prepared to tell them everything about Cronos's possession.

As she talked, her description of the black voids of memory weren't nearly as horrific as the bits she *could* remember. The desire to kill, to feed, as the Dark Breed inside her came to be. Cronos taking advantage of that need, trying to convince her to kill her abusive father who'd beaten Haven's twin sister to death at the young age of seven.

Using Poseidon's trident against him—though she didn't remember that part, she only recalled the horrible fear that came with knowing what she'd done as she'd held the bloodied weapon in her hands afterward and prayed for someone to save her from the monster Cronos was creating in her.

All of it, she'd said, were like tiny pieces of glass pricking her brain, sometimes intense images, sometimes only a dull, blurry pain that she couldn't quite pinpoint.

Poseidon, who'd finally recovered enough to return to his domain, had been so weakened by Haven's attack that he'd been forced to place his powers in a stronger vessel—Silas. His permanent Chosen still hadn't been located, and everyone was beginning to worry that Silas's job might not be so temporary—a fact that was going drive poor, nomadic Silas insane.

"His hunger for power . . ." she continued, "it infected me. Like a disease. When I killed those Mystics . . ." Her face paled as she spoke and Kyana cringed for her, knowing the scars those actions had inflicted on her once angelic friend. "I didn't want to. I remember that. But I also knew I had to get out of there. Had to find the Eyes of Power so I could bring Cronos back. I don't remember killing them, but I remember their blood."

"It wasn't you," Kyana offered, wishing she could do more than deliver meaningless words to assuage the guilt she knew Haven harbored.

"No, it wasn't," Ryker said. "But you're sure you sensed nothing of his plans once he was resurrected?"

Haven shook her head. "Only that he wanted to reclaim his throne—which meant killing those holding the powers that rightfully belonged to him." She blinked, her face growing even paler.

"Those were his thoughts, not mine. Those powers belong to you—"

"It's all right, Haven," Ryker said, his smile revealing one of the dimples Kyana adored. "We know what you mean." He stood, stretching his arms overhead before bringing them back down to rub his temples.

"Where are you going?" Kyana asked.

"To summon the gods. We need to speed up the siphoning process. If we're about to go to war, then our powers need to be protected in the event that some of us don't make it out alive."

Kyana tried not to cringe at his defeated tone. To distract herself from his words, she held out her hand to Haven, who took it without hesitation, which lightened Kyana's heart. Maybe there was still something to be salvaged between them. Gods, she hoped so.

When Ryker was gone, Kyana debated whether to question Haven about another matter that had been bugging her for a while now. In the scheme of things, it was minor. But at the time, one of Haven's lies had cut Kyana pretty deeply. She might never get another chance to ask the question.

"Haven?"

"Hmm?" Haven curled herself into a ball on the couch, her eyes droopy with weariness.

Kyana reconsidered broaching the topic, but quickly found her resolve again. "Why did you tell me you grew up in Tennessee? That your father was a youth pastor there?"

Haven suddenly looked very much awake. She sat up, her gaze falling to her bent knees, and Kyana hated herself for bringing it up. Haven was already dying under a mountain of guilt, and Kyana had just supplied another boulder to help smother her.

"Never mind. I'm sorry. It . . . it doesn't matter."

Kyana had found out the truth when Haven had gone after her father to kill him for what he'd done to her and their family in childhood. She'd been stunned that Haven would need to lie about any of it. Especially given Kyana's own background. Why hadn't Haven trusted her with the truth? That her father wasn't a pastor in Tennessee but an abusive asshole in Florida.

"You can be friends," Haven said as Kyana turned to leave her in peace, "and not know every damned secret a person has."

Kyana turned back, found Haven staring at her, a look of remorse, maybe even a little disgust, in her eyes.

"Who wants to admit to the world that their father was garbage? That they couldn't afford breakfast or lunch, and sometimes dinner? That their first touch from a man came from the man who gave them life? Who willingly admits to that, Kyana? He killed Hope, and thinking about him made me want to vomit every day of my life. So I created a man I could be proud of. A past that didn't bring me to tears every time it popped into my head. Is that so bad?"

"No," Kyana whispered. "It was your secret to keep. I'm sorry we had to find out when we were looking for you."

And truly, she was. Her own past was no better than Haven's. The only difference was, Kyana hadn't been smart enough to make up a better one to answer the nosy questions from others. One that would be retold so many times maybe she could've thought of it as real.

"Where is he, anyway?" Haven asked. "Kevin, I mean."

"Your father—"

"Kevin. Don't call him my father." The anger and hurt in Haven's voice chipped away one more defensive wall Kyana had built between them.

"*Kevin* is Below with the other refugees. Did you . . . did you want to see him?"

Haven looked at her as though she'd lost her mind. "Only if I have permission to kick his ass."

"Wow. Not kill him? Just an ass kicking? I think you're becoming tame."

Haven rolled her eyes. "Fuck you."

And there was the new Haven again. Bad-tempered and foul-mouthed. Maybe she wasn't so bad.

As she pulled Haven to her feet, Kyana smiled. "I'll call for a bath. Consider this room yours until this ordeal is over."

It would work out well. Kyana's bedchamber was connected by a single door. Haven would remain close, and she'd be able to make sure she was safe at all times. "I'll have a bed brought in too."

"Thanks." Haven's hand slid out of Kyana's hold. "Not sure I'll be able to do much sleeping, though. Besides, won't Ares insist on cuffing me to something or sealing the room in some magical prisonlike spell? Maybe you could just give me a dungeon somewhere and be done with it."

This time, Kyana rolled her eyes. "The Haven I know isn't prone to pity parties."

Half a smile cracked on Haven's face. "It's probably the last party I'm going to see for a while. Let me have it."

"Fine, but do it in the bath. You're looking funky."

As Haven saluted her with an extended middle finger, Kyana couldn't help but smile as she made her way from the room to summon a bath. The middle finger might belong to the new Haven, but the banter they'd just exchanged belonged to the old.

There was still hope, indeed.

Chapter Seven

Only minutes after Helios had finished calling forth the sun, Ryker had his council gathered in Kyana and Artemis's temple. He sat on a throne, facing Zeus's half brother Kheiron—the mighty Centaur—who had stepped out of the sky in order to make this council. Word had spread that war was coming—and since returning from the Fates' cave where he'd spoken to Atropos, even Geoffrey was no longer in denial.

"What changed your mind?" Kyana asked, leaning in so the others wouldn't be disturbed.

Geoffrey frowned. "Atropos's souls are exactly where they're supposed to be."

Surprised, Kyana's mouth fell slack. "That's not possible. Cronos is raising the dead. That means some souls have to be missing."

"Right. Hers are still intact, but some of *mine* have gone astray."

Ryker heard this last statement and stopped speaking to the council mid-sentence. "What?"

Sighing, Geoffrey stood and turned his attention to the group before them. "Several hundred of the souls locked in Tartarus have up and gone. Their bodies remain, so it's not another breakout, but they are completely lifeless now. Someone nicked them."

"Why? I don't understand . . ." This from Haven, who had spent the last several minutes receiving hate-filled stares from the gods as they arrived. At least she could face them clean. She looked a bit more like her old self since her bath, with the exception of the borrowed chiton wrapped around her too-thin frame.

"If Atropos's souls are where they're meant to be and mine are not—it is a simple thing to assume he's raising those with sins on their hands."

I wish no more blackness on my soul . . . The man in Haven's dream had said as much. Was that really Cronos's intentions? To find sinners and raise them for his army?

"It's easier to convince those who were evil in life to become evil again," she realized aloud.

Geoffrey nodded. "It's what I believe."

Ryker's head was going to explode. The entire room erupted with unintelligible dialogue, sending timpani-sounding crashes through his skull. He could feel Kyana's questioning stare burning through the side of his face—why wasn't he shutting them up so they could get on with the meeting? Simply put, because they needed a minute to come to terms with what the small group at the front of the room already recognized. That war was coming, and that some of them would very likely die when it arrived.

Finally, when the dialogue became vulgar and screeching, he stepped in.

"Enough!" Ryker's tone held no room for argument though many looked tempted. "The point of this council is to let everyone know what's going on and come up with a plan of action to assure everyone stays safe. Us as well as the humans in our care."

"And how do you intend to do that?" Kheiron stepped forward, his hooves echoing in the now silent chamber. The slight twitch that ruffled his gleaming mahogany coat suggested tension filled him as it had everyone else. "The seas are still dying. Too much damage was done while Poseidon was injured."

Kheiron was known for his wisdom and everyone seemed eager to hear what he had to say. His crystal blue eyes didn't shine with wisdom right now, however, and instead glinted with anger. Knowing he couldn't silence him, Ryker nodded for him to continue.

"There are so many of us who still haven't been replaced that it won't be long before bits of the world start disappearing altogether. The very stars are going to die out if my own Chosen isn't found soon. The constellations are willing to step from their positions and join the war. But the question isn't how do we survive, it's how many are willing to sacrifice themselves to protect Olympus?"

The chaos that ensued was deafening. It would only be a matter of time before he had a mutiny on his hands. People were going to die, and knowing he might not be able to stop it, didn't mean he wouldn't try.

"Shut the hell up!" Kyana's bellow was such a shock that all sounds immediately ceased as everyone in the chamber turned to stare at her. She wasn't paying any attention to them. Her gaze was locked on Ryker. She knew she'd overstepped her bounds, and the stiffness in her stance said she wasn't going to back down now.

Not that he would have asked her to. He loved seeing her fired up like this. Loved how passionate she was when she truly cared about something. And whether she'd admit it or not, she cared about every single soul filling the room right now.

She turned a glare to the mob. "I wish I could tell you that Kheiron's mistaken, and he's being a horse's ass—no pun intended—for striking fear with his doomsday prophecy, but lying isn't something I do well."

She held up her hand to stop the shouts before they could start up again. "We aren't going to lay down our weapons and roll over like puppies waiting to be shoved in a burlap sack. We're going to stop Cronos before he can stop us. But, we have to prepare for the possibility of him reaching *some* of us."

"What about those of us who do not have a Chosen yet?" an unseen goddess asked from the back of the hall.

Ryker had known this question would be brought up. "The Moerae are working as quickly as possible to find everyone a replacement. Their task isn't an easy one. So many have been murdered since the breakout or are still missing. But they're not going to give up searching."

"Great, but how does that help us? It was made clear from the beginning that the higher gods and goddesses came first on the list of Chosen," another faceless voice asked. "We lesser deities are just as important. When are we going to be moved to the top of the list?"

This started a whole new round of bickering. Just what he *didn't* need right now. Since he'd already requested the Moerae prioritize based on weakness, not rank, he decided to ignore the question and focus on how they were going to attempt to save everyone.

"We don't know when or even if the strike will come, but we need to guarantee everyone will continue to live on. Even those who fall."

"And how do you intend to do that?"

Ryker couldn't see who had asked the question, but it was mirrored on every face staring at him. "Once a day, each of you will join those of us who have already begun the process. You will provide a small amount of blood. In the event your Chosen isn't found in time, there will be enough of your blood to pass on your powers when your replacement is found."

"So your answer is to leave us both weak *and* exposed in the event Cronos finds a way to reclaim his throne?" Hestia asked of Zeus. "Be realistic, brothers. It is *we* who need to be priority. Cronos's children, both old and new. It is *us* he comes for. *Us* he must kill to reclaim his throne. Not the other gods. *His children*."

The old Zeus didn't stand to address his sister. "It wasn't our *sisters* he tried to kill before, and it won't be this time. It will be his sons, and even we are no more important than anyone else. Yes, he might covet your death, sister, but it is Ryker, Silas, and Geoffrey who hold the power to Cronos's reclaiming his throne. Killing those born of his blood would fulfill only a vendetta and grant him nothing in the way of power."

"You're a fool, brother," Hestia hissed.

Zeus glared but remained calm. "The new gods have already begun using this method of blood siphoning to make sure the legacy each of us has carried since the dawn of time continues. The process they've developed will take time to complete, but it will keep you from becoming weak. You will be able to protect yourselves and carry out your duties."

"Isn't that foolish?" someone asked. "Our powers will be vulnerable in your precious glass vials. What if someone should steal them? What then?"

"I have assigned my most loyal Elite Guard to the task of making sure Olympus is not breached and we all remain safe," Ares said. "That includes our siphoned powers. Only the main portal to Below will remain functional, and it has been enchanted so only those with the seal of Zeus will be allowed to travel to and fro."

This caused a slight rumble of discord. The gods and goddesses who called Olympus home had always been able to travel without being questioned. Until this matter was resolved, only a few would be allowed to use the portal at all.

When the grumblings subsided, Ares continued, "As of now, you will not be allowed entrance on Olympus unless you reside here or have the escort of someone who does, and only then if you've been summoned. You will each have a strict schedule for your individual siphoning and you will adhere to it. Do not be early. Do not be late."

Ryker felt Kyana watching him, along with everyone else in the chamber. This was the only way he could assure Zeus and Hera that their home would remain safe. If either of them took up new residence, pandemonium would likely ensue. Ryker might have Zeus's powers, but Zeus was still the god everyone looked to for comfort. It would be several centuries before Ryker could earn that kind of trust.

"Are those you've assigned to this duty prepared to die to carry out the tasks given to them?" Ryker asked Ares, voicing the question aloud only for the benefit of the others in the room. Ares wouldn't have assigned his men if the answer was not yes. He might suck as a father, but as the God of War, he was brilliant.

Still, the others needed to hear it said aloud.

"They are." Ares nodded.

"If your best is guarding Olympus, who is going to be out looking for Cronos?" someone in the back of the room asked.

"*I* will be." Kyana stepped close enough to the table to press her hands to it and look several council members in the eye. "I'm the Goddess of the Hunt. It is time I start acting as such. There is no one else."

Chapter Eight

Silence greeted Kyana's admittedly somewhat egotistical statement for a good long minute before a voice finally broke the loud hush that had filled her council room.

"There *is* someone else." The voice belonged to Haven, and all eyes in the room turned to stare at her. "There is me."

"You?" Ares demanded. "You think we'd risk sending you back to him?"

Haven shrugged, looking more put off than embarrassed by the sudden attention from everyone in the chamber. She looked at Kyana. "I don't expect to be allowed to go after Cronos on my own, and honestly, I'm not stupid enough to try. But I can certainly help. You said there is only you, but you don't have a link to Cronos. *I* do. You need me." She turned her attention to the crowd.

"I was chosen to take Artemis's place once. There had to have been good reason for that. I've been a loyal member of the Order for a long time—far longer than I was ever a threat to it."

"Ryker, she shouldn't even be here." Ares's voice boomed loud enough to make the chandelier over the grand table rock back and forth. "She's an abomination—"

"She stays," Kyana said, moving to the empty spot on Haven's bench. "If she can begin mending the wounds she caused by helping us save the friggin' world, who the hell are we to stop her?"

Ares's face turned bright red, the veins in his neck bulging. "Keep your woman in line, Ryker, lest I do it for you."

"His *woman*?" In a flash, Kyana was propelled to her feet by anger, her fist thumped against Ares's chest. "I'm a goddess now, asshat. I belong to *no one* and have as many rights as you."

"Enough." Ryker took Kyana by the shoulders and steered her away from the conflict. "Haven will be well supervised but . . ." He turned back to face Ares. "She *will* be working at our sides. Jordan's already vouched for her. She hasn't lied to us."

"Today," Ares said, every line in his face pronounced as he clenched his jaw. "She hasn't lied to us *today*. She is the reason we're facing this war."

The temperature in the room dropped ten degrees as father and son faced off, even though Geoffrey was quietly raging enough to heat the entire temple from his place on the dais. Afraid not only of what Ares might try, but also of what Haven might do if her temper was fully unleashed, Kyana made her way to Geoffrey, hoping he could put a balm on the situation.

"Take her out of here," she said. "I'll come to you when we're done."

Geoff said nothing, making his way to Haven, obviously having already contemplated getting her out of potential harm's way himself.

When he reached Haven's side, she didn't look too willing to comply, but Geoff took her hand and led her out of the room to Kyana's private chambers.

"If you wish to argue this further, we'll do so in private," Ryker told Ares. "But I won't be swayed in this matter."

"You will hear me out," Ares insisted. "As the God of War, I'll be the one figuring out how to save all our asses. The least you can do is open your mind to what I have to say."

"Fine." Ryker nodded to Silas. "Start a round of siphoning on those present. We'll be back in a moment."

"Great," Kyana muttered. "But I'm coming too."

She followed them to the massive library under the stairs and shut the door. The lock barely clicked into place before Ares whirled on Ryker, his eyes dancing with fury.

"You're bound and determined to hate me until the day you die," he said. "I've accepted that. But do *not* let it cloud your judgment in your new position. You will respect me as a god when we council, Ryker, and stop looking at me like a son pissed off by a father he never wanted!"

Maybe she shouldn't have come. Maybe they should be doing this alone. There was a very distinct glimmer of hurt in Ares's eyes and she was pretty sure he was so consumed by his dispute with Ryker that he wasn't even aware she was there. She started to back toward the door, torn between returning to the council room and remaining in case Ryker needed calming.

In case Ares said something hurtful and required killing.

"This has nothing to do with anything other than Haven's link to Cronos—which we can use," Ryker said, looking so calm it was creepy.

The topic of his parentage was a touchy one. That Ares had brought it up should have sent Ryker through the roof.

Ares stepped forward until he stood only a couple of inches from Ryker's face. "Strike me."

Huh?

"What?"

"I said, strike me. We're going to have to work together as peers now that you've taken Zeus's place. I'm no longer your commander, but you are not mine either. Strike me, take out every ounce of hatred you have in that one hit, son, because it's the only one I'll allow before striking back. Whatever you think I've done to you, whatever sort of ways you *think* I've failed you, show me. Do it now, or get the hell over yourself."

Getting the hell out of the room was looking better and better, but Kyana stayed put. Partially because she was too intrigued to move, but mostly because she was terrified Ryker might take Ares up on his offer. If fists were thrown between them, the contention between the pair would never have a chance at resolution.

"Ryker—" she started, licking her lips as she pondered the words that might pull him out of his own head.

"Don't, Ky," he said, crossing his arms over his chest. "I won't hit him. If I did, I'd likely kill him, and since he has no replacement, I know how foolish that would be." He cocked his head, still appearing far calmer than the edge in his voice would lead her to believe. "You raped my mother. Left her to bear me alone, poor and too terrified to tell me why I was so different than the other kids—"

"Ryker, I—"

"Why I was beaten by them every fucking day because of those differences. Then you took me from her so I could become your general. Would you have ever come for me had you not learned I was special? Tell me, Ares . . . how many other bastards did you sow? How many women did you leave so badly broken that the sight of the very child you forced on them sickened them?"

Kyana's heart lurched into her throat, and the need to wrap her arms around him and make this argument stop overwhelmed her. She knew Ryker's anger toward Ares's had stemmed from childhood, knew Ryker believed Ares had raped his mother and abandoned them both.

She wasn't so sure that was all fact. But the last thing Ryker needed was to feel like she was siding with Ares.

A look of utter defeat fell over Ares. He dropped his arms to the side and stepped away from Ryker. "Finally," he said. "I understand where your hatred stems from. So be it. I am a monster. But I am also a god. You will respect me as such."

Without another word, he strode from the room and shut the door quietly behind him, leaving Kyana alone with Ryker.

"You okay?" she asked.

He gave a curt nod before turning to face her. "Don't look at me like that."

"Like what?"

"Like I'm something to be pitied. Your past was filled with even less affection than mine."

Kyana's overwhelming sympathy for him crackled like a brittle twig. "You're angry at him, not me. Remember that."

He sighed and dug his thumbs into his eyes as though trying to dig out the worst sort of headache. "I know. I'm sorry. Haven will work with us. I'll make sure of it."

"Ryker, you can talk to m—"

"Let's go back. I want to make sure they're hurrying the siphoning along."

Before they could return to the council room, a trio of sentinels asked for a private word with Ryker. He gave her a brief kiss before leaving her. Rather than return to the council room, Kyana turned in the opposite direction, needing fresh air to clear her head.

Alone, her thoughts shifted back to Cronos. She plopped down on the marble steps outside so hard, her spine vibrated. She wanted answers now. The sooner they found out what Cronos was up to, the sooner they could kill him for good. She was tired of the conflict he kept stirring within her circle of friends. Tired of the fear his name instilled in her.

For the last six weeks, she'd enjoyed waking to days of learning her new tasks, tedious though some of them were. Before that, an entire month of her life had been given to fearing and hunting Cronos, and now he was back and it was starting all over again.

She heard the door behind her open, heard the soft slap of sandals on marble and instinctively knew they belonged to Artemis. The older goddess placed a hand on Kyana's shoulder before taking a seat beside her.

"Did Ryker leave?"

"The sentinels needed him for something. I'm sure he'll be back." Kyana offered a weak smile, and Artemis slipped her hand down to find hers. Artemis forced it to the chain dangling between Kyana's breasts and wrapped her fingers around the amulet hanging there.

"Focus your energies there like I taught you.

The conduit will ease some of your anxiety . . . enough to clear your mind."

Kyana squeezed the amber arrow until it punctured her skin, and even then didn't release it. In mere seconds, the knot in her stomach untied itself and whatever had been blocking her lungs lifted, allowing her to take in a gulp of air.

"Will he ever leave us alone?" she asked, her voice as tired as her body suddenly was.

"Cronos?"

Kyana nodded.

Artemis sighed and placed her finger beneath Kyana's chin, forcing Kyana to meet her gaze. "Not until he's gotten what he wants or we've rid ourselves of him again, I'm afraid. But we're not beaten yet, Kyana, so cease looking as though we are."

A bark sounded from the hedge maze in the center of the gardens, and a moment later, a blur of golden fur flew onto the marble walkway. The clattering of nails on marble, sliding and skidding, thundered in the vast area, followed by the crash of shattering porcelain as they rushed right into the vases at the foot of the stairs.

Kyana had had the sentinels take the tracking pups outside in hopes of burning off some of their ever-present energy, but apparently that hadn't worked. As much as she hated leaving them cooped in their cage while she was on Olympus, she was going to have to put them away unless she wanted to live in rubble.

With a sigh, she bent over and slipped the other chain she wore from around her neck. The golden whistle glinted against the polished stone around her as she gave it two blows and set it on the ground. The lead bitch let out a howl and led her brothers around the columns and inside the whistle.

When the whistle stopped glowing, Kyana replaced it around her neck, where it mingled with her goddess conduit. "I hate caging them up so much."

"Then train them."

Artemis's fully grown tracking hounds were now lying at her feet, a trio of well-behaved minions that put Kyana's to shame. "When should I do that? Between this Cronos crap and the things I'm supposed to be learning from you, I barely have a minute to breathe."

"True, but you'll have to dedicate yourself to both. There is still much for you to learn, Kyana. And with Cronos alive and growing stronger, it's never been more important that you focus. You said in there that it was time you started acting like a goddess. I think you've done well so far, but I do agree it's time for you to step up and learn all you can."

That didn't help her figure out what the hell to do with her wayward pups, but Kyana was too tired to argue.

Artemis, it seemed, was not at all too tired for lecturing, however. "I've let you slide on overseeing matters of fertility. I still have enough power within me to see to that task while you train in the proper ways to hunt. But eventually, even that will become too difficult for me. Learn all you can to defeat Cronos so I can finally retire, mm?"

"Well, certainly. No problemo. Easy breezy." Kyana worried at her lip, trying to figure out a way to broach the subject of her own fertility with Artemis, but Ryker's sudden appearance at the gates diverted her attention. He looked upset, all but sprinting in their direction, followed by the sentinels who'd come for him.

"What is it?" she asked when he was within hearing distance.

He stopped, barely out of breath. "War. The Castillo's under attack."

Chapter Nine

There was no denying Cronos's return any longer, but having the very headquarters of the Order of Ancients attacked after so many weeks of peace was like reopening a wound that had finally started to heal.

And there was only one question playing over and over in Ryker's mind now. What good was being a god if he couldn't stop things like this from happening?

It had never been more vital that they all learn what they were meant to know about their new positions—most especially Ryker. The others were going to look to him and Zeus for guidance and answers, and he sure as hell wasn't going to let them down.

For a moment, he thought about calling for Geoff and Silas to join them outside Artemis's temple. Perhaps their small group could come up with a plan of action without him having to alert the others to what had happened. But as quickly as the idea had come, he decided against it. They needed all hands on deck right away. Keeping any of the deities in the dark would serve no one but Cronos.

He rubbed at the knot burning his shoulder, listening to Artemis and Kyana talking over each other to question him. He had no idea what to tell them. He only knew that the Order of Ancients' headquarters in the human world had been attacked. That people had died.

He said as much.

"How many?" Artemis asked.

"Several of theirs. A few of ours. Some of the fort's structure was weakened. The uninjured are working to reinforce it again."

As he spoke, his anger slipped out of his grasp, threatening to unearth the columns supporting Kyana's temple.

"They had to have been newly born Dark Breeds," Kyana said. "Novi. No one who's been around more than a decade would be stupid enough to strike at the heart of the fort unless they had a full army at their backs. They tried when Hell first opened and were slaughtered."

"Definitely wasn't a full army," he muttered. "Ares's new general is on his way. He'll have more information."

As though on cue, a tall, dark-haired man appeared at Kyana's gates and they swung open for his entrance. At least it wasn't a stranger. The man who'd taken Ryker's place as Ares's general was someone he had served with years ago. Zach Merchant had fought by Ryker's side in more than one rogue uprising. Since Hell's reopening, he'd proven himself worthy of the promotion, desperate to keep his new, pregnant wife safe by ensuring the world Above remained intact.

"Zach." Ryker motioned him forward. "Please tell me you know more than those asses you sent in your place."

Zach gave Ryker a slight bow before nodding a greeting to the goddesses.

"Merchant." Kyana smiled. "The uniform suits you. Glad to see you accepted it."

"Ten years rusty, but yeah, Shanna seems to like it."

"The fort," Ryker interrupted. "Details?"

"Right. Sorry." Zach's face immediately re-contorted into a back-to-business expression. "Morning patrol discovered that the Huguenot Cemetery had been violated and tracers were sent out to locate the ones responsible. I posted guards at each of the nearby cemeteries. When they returned to the Castillo, it was under attack. We lost a dozen sentinels and a handful of Mystics who were tending some of the Chosen brought in last night."

Ryker's chest gave a painful squeeze. "The Chosen? They all right?"

Zach nodded. "All brought Below. They're being held at Spirits until we're given clearance to take them to their respective gods."

Ryker exhaled. Good. More of the replacements were found, safe, and soon to be ready for a power exchange. That was a plus. But none of that eased the knots in his neck and shoulders. He might trust Zach to protect the humans, along with their stronghold Above, but he hated relying on others to do a job he was used to doing himself. More than that, he hated waiting on others to provide information he'd always been able to obtain first-hand.

"Your men didn't say anything to me about the cemetery. Anything I need to worry about?"

"All the graves there have been desecrated, just like Huguenot's. The mark of Cronos was found on several of the grave markers."

Ryker tried to keep his temper in check, but

it was becoming harder by the second. "How the hell did we go from six weeks of peace to a damned nightmare in one day?"

"Told you this treaty thing was a bad idea," Kyana muttered.

"One rogue group doesn't make all Dark Breed bad," he pointed out. He still believed in the treaty he and Geoffrey had come up with. The Dark Breeds who signed it were allowed to remain free of Tartarus unless they broke the law—and since they signed the treaty with their blood, tracers would be able to immediately locate them and bring them in.

Those who didn't sign were considered enemies of the Order and brought in regardless of their actions. Once the world settled back into a routine, it would be a sound plan. But right now, nothing was going as it should, and Ryker wasn't in the mood for another round of pros and cons with Kyana.

"Were the tracers able to find anything that will tell us who is responsible for digging up the graves?" he asked Zach.

"Ares has a group of Witches working on that now," Zach replied. "But it doesn't look promising."

"We knew Cronos was raising an army, and

Geoffrey already said some of his souls were missing," Artemis said. "It's not a surprise that cemeteries are going to be ravaged. He can't raise the dead without their bones for talismans."

"I'll question the Oracles." Ryker cast his gaze up the mountain behind his temple where the Oracles resided. "Maybe they can see where Cronos will strike next—keep a watch on known offenders' graves."

He turned to Zach and held out his hand. "Appreciate you coming so quickly. Send a guard with a list of the Chosen brought in and I'll send word to the gods they'll need to meet."

Zach took the dismissal with a nod of compliance and a quick shake of Ryker's hand. "As you wish."

When Zach vanished down the path toward the gate, Ryker spun on his heel and glared at Kyana. "If you say I told you so, I swear I'll forbid your exit off Olympus and won't let you help figure this out."

She blinked. "About what?"

"The fucking treaty."

"I wouldn't dream of pointing out the obvious."

"Nonsense," Artemis said. "The treaty is still viable. Treaty or not, there will be Dark Breeds out there until the end of time just as there always has been. The more we can harness, the better off we'll be."

Even though the older goddess was essentially taking the blame off Ryker's shoulders, he didn't feel the least bit better. He led the women inside, ready, though not at all eager, to inform the rest of the Order of the events that had taken place Above.

As they strode into the council room and he took in the sight of deities sitting with Healers, their arms outstretched as the Mystics siphoned blood into tiny vials that would be transported to Ryker's temple and added to the siphoning wall, his frustration only grew.

Sitting around while others got their hands bloodied wasn't for him. He was a warrior. A fighter used to being in the thick of things, solving the problems. Instead, he was the decision maker—his job binding him to Olympus in a stationary position he was finding more and more irritating.

An hour later, Ryker had delivered the bad news and the only straggling deities left in the throne room were he, Geoffrey, Silas, and Kyana. Beside them was Haven, looking out of place and ashen-faced. No one was saying a word, but Ryker could tell precisely what each was thinking. He'd come to know them all so well in these last few weeks that their faces had become void of secrets.

Kyana's foot was tapping impatiently on the floor. She was antsy, unable to sit still. Soon, she would demand to fight, and Ryker couldn't blame her. He was nearly coming out of his own skin with the need to jump into the fray. She wanted to hunt, and judging by the twisted, puckered mouth on Geoffrey's face, he did too. They were both ex tracers, and it was in their blood.

Silas, on the other hand, was blankly nibbling at the tray of ambrosia-laced cheeses in the center of the table, his brow lined in concentration. He wasn't much of a fighter, though he was skilled enough. But as a Witch, casting spells and creating magic had brought him to this place. Not blood and glory. Likely he was contemplating what sort of charms he could manifest that would lead them to the culprits so Geoff, Ryker, and Ky could kick their asses.

Haven was a little harder to read now, but the determination in her eyes to be a part of the team reminded him of the first time he'd met her. She hadn't backed down to Kyana's insistence that she stay where it was safe then, and he knew she wasn't going to unless the orders came with chains and guards.

"Everyone stop," he grumbled, startling all four from their solemn expressions. "I know what you want me to say and it can't happen. It would be irresponsible for all of us to leave the mountain and weaken Olympus—"

Kyana raised a black brow, gracefully lifting it to nearly meet her hairline. "Irresponsible? Irresponsible would be sitting on our asses and letting this new band of Dark Breeds be born, who won't, mind you, be under the laws of *your* treaty. Which means they're untrackable. Novi. And that makes them dangerous."

"You're a goddess now, Kyana. Not a tracer," Silas said. "You might be more powerful, but your death has far more consequence than it ever did before."

The fact that Silas was taking Ryker's side made him cringe. He didn't have much use for the Witch, and that was only partly due to his once having been Kyana's lover. But if Silas was worried about them leaving their posts here for more than just their nightly patrol, maybe Ryker should rethink his own stance. He certainly didn't want to be as much of a pussy as Silas could sometimes be.

"We all know that if anyone's going to be able to do this, it will be me," Kyana said.

"And if you fail?" Artemis asked, appearing in the doorway. "Who will make certain the humans repopulate the world? Who will track and find the loosed Dark Breeds that fail to adhere to our treaty? I can only continue carrying out those duties for so long, Kyana. My powers fade more every day. It will be up to you to begin seeing to fertility and hunting more than just Cronos. If something happens to you, there *is* no one else."

Kyana leaned slightly toward Ryker. He wrapped a protective arm around her shoulder, the idea of something happening to Ky inducing the urge to vomit.

"There's enough of my blood on that siphoning wall to replace me if I fail."

Artemis strode across the room and took the empty seat on Kyana's right, her gaze so intently settled on Kyana's face that it looked as though she was peering right through her skull and into her brain.

"It is still risky. There are others we can send when we know where Cronos is going next." She tucked her finger under Kyana's chin and brushed her hair from her cheek the way a mother might do to her daughter. "I know you will go, child. But you must promise to take more care now than is your nature."

"I'll have all of them," Kyana said, sweeping her hand to indicate everyone present at the table. "And even Ares sometimes. Artemis, you saw to your duties and hunted every day of your life. Becoming the Goddess of the Hunt did not turn me into a treasure to be put in a glass box any more than it did you."

"Yes. It did," Ryker said, knowing those words would cost him later. But he'd rather fight with Ky than bury her. "At least until you've finished siphoning."

"You mean until I become replaceable."

Like that was even possible. "Whatever you want to call it."

He cocked his head at Geoff. "And you? If you leave to hunt, who's going to see to the dead? Who's going to make sure they get to where they need to go?"

Geoff leaned against the long marble table and folded his arms. He seemed to be considering the question, but Ryker could tell by the way his eyes glowed with determination that this debate wasn't going to be a quick one . . . or an easy one for Ryker to win. If Kyana was going hunting that meant Haven was going hunting. And Ryker was pretty sure Geoff wouldn't let her go anywhere without him.

"Forget it, mate," Geoff said, his gaze turning to Haven. "I'm not sitting on my arse while the people I care about are in danger."

Ryker sighed. He couldn't blame him really. He was having issues with the thought of Kyana going off without him too—especially with the threat of Cronos breathing down their necks.

A Dark Breed, she could handle, no problem. But Cronos? Ryker didn't want her coming face-to-face with that bastard without a lot of backup.

"The threat is real," he said. "Even if you take out the Novi he's raising, Cronos is out there. We can't all leave Olympus. It would be as good as handing him the mountain."

Geoff pushed to his feet. "Fine, you stay here. It's still in *our* blood to hunt. Becoming what we are hasn't changed what we've been for centuries."

"Yeah, well I've always been a fighter. Doesn't mean I can go off and risk the entire world because I miss the excitement," Ryker said, even though that was exactly what he wanted to do.

"As well you shouldn't. You're the most important of all of us," Kyana said, placing her palm to his chest. "Without the God of Gods, Above, Below, and Beyond will fall into chaos." She waved her hand to include herself, Geoff, and Silas. "Between the siphoning and the powers the old gods hold, new Chosen can be found and trained. It will take time, and it will make the Olympians as a whole weak for a while, but *we* can be replaced. Zeus had to give you everything at once to assure your strength. *You* must be protected."

"You're not going out there alone."

"You mean without you," Geoff clarified with a laugh. " 'Cause really, mate, she wouldn't be alone. She'd be with us and we've protected her back more than once."

"What's with the *we* crap?" Silas finally looked up from the plate of cheese to focus on them. "I'm not leaving this mountain except to tend the seas until this blood's been removed and I'm just a Witch again."

"We can do it without you. Any spells, potions or charms we need . . . Haven can take care of," Kyana added in a much calmer, more persuasive tone.

"We shouldn't need a Witch," Ryker said, his temples pounding. "We're gods."

"Newborn gods, Ryker," Artemis reminded them. "You've only mastered a tenth of what you can do, while we had millennia to learn all we know."

That didn't make him feel a whole lot better.

"I can help them, Ryker." Haven's eyes lit up, and she looked altogether relieved at being handed something useful to do. "And if Cronos is near, I can feel him. I can warn them, keep them safe."

It saddened Ryker to see how desperate she seemed to make up for so many things that hadn't truly been her fault in the first place. But until she finished her cleansing, it was risky to let her venture out and chance her being taken by Cronos and used against them again. He wasn't stupid enough to say so, however. Telling Kyana he didn't think Haven should accompany her would be starting a whole other kind of war he had no energy to fight.

"If Cronos is after her, then she needs to be with one of you at all times," he finally conceded. He couldn't keep any of them on the mountain. He didn't plan on sitting still the entire time himself, but he couldn't take off and leave as often as he knew they would.

"All right then." Geoff stood and rubbed his hands together. "Looks like we have ourselves a full team."

Looks like.

Kyana also stood and motioned for Haven. "Let's go to Huguenot Cemetery and see if we can trace anything back to Cronos. I want to find that son of a bitch."

Shoving aside the sheer curtain guarding the huge window that overlooked the mountain, Ryker studied the bustle of activity outside. Olympus was humming. In his gardens below, people rushed to carry out his orders while he debated whether to try to keep Kyana here with him. She needed to fight, and forcing her to stay behind was going to be a challenge.

He rested his head against the cool glass. His choices were very limited at best. These were his people now. His responsibility. His duty. He had to keep them safe. Had to make sure the craziness going on Above didn't reach the realms of Below and never came close to even touching the gates to Beyond. The human world, the world between humans and deities, and the world of the gods. All of them were in danger.

He might not have learned a lot from Ares, but he'd certainly learned about duty and what it meant to be a warrior. Now, as the new Zeus, he was going to have to learn how to accomplish those things without a sword, without bloodshed.

Maneuvering the players in this ordeal was going to be one hell of a game of chess.

And he'd always hated that damned game.

Chapter Ten

Kyana walked along the inside of the Huguenot Cemetery, inhaling deeply in hopes of catching something on the wind though she knew it
was pointless. Whoever had made the marks of
Cronos on the coquina walls had long since gone.
And so had their scents. Magic users were far
more difficult to track than humans—charms, potions, and spells cloaking them so even the most
skilled couldn't trace them.

She passed Haven, who was conducting some
sort of spell over the mark, searching for a trace of
magic that they might be able to follow. If Kyana's
nose was going to fail her, maybe Haven's witch-
ery would be a bit more successful.

Sighing, she began her third lap around the
large square, her ears picking up every door shutting, every window being boarded by the human

residents who were still too afraid to trust that the Order would protect them now that the sun had gone down. She couldn't blame them. The Order hadn't done a fantastic job protecting them when Hell had broken free. Why believe they could do better now that things had calmed again?

And if they only knew the danger that was waiting to pounce, they'd pack up and move their families as far away from the Order as humanly possible.

"Still nothing?"

Geoffrey's voice spun her around and she shook her head. "You?"

"No. Scent's too old and Hades didn't exactly leave me many tracking skills. Least Artemis could hunt."

"For all the good it's doing us now." Kyana leaned against the wall, her gaze swinging from the spot where Haven crouched, intensely focusing on the blood sickle on the wall. "I'm so sick of the threat of Cronos hovering over my head."

Geoffrey shrugged. "Kinda grateful to him just now, to be honest. He offered Haven a reason to be free of that horrid Healing Circle—gave us a reason to be near her. Gave her a way to hopefully redeem herself with the rest of the Order before her trial."

"Asshat." Kyana rolled her eyes. "There are less world-destructive ways to spend time with her. If she winds up dead, it really won't matter how her trial would have turned out, would it?"

He grumbled something under his breath and left Kyana alone to sit with Haven on the ground. While she watched Haven work, she dragged her finger over her hunting attire, changing the leather from black, to white, to red, and left it that way. The convenient method of wardrobe changing was nifty—one that Haven was going to envy the shit out of when she was more fully her shopaholic self.

Kyana smiled, wishing things could go back the way they were, then felt her face fall solemn as she realized that, without all the horrible things that had happened, she would never have gotten so close to Ryker these last couple of months. Was she truly so shallow that she could be grateful for the devastating events that had taken place because it had brought him into her life?

She was beginning to sound as illogical as Geoff.

But truthfully, she *was* grateful for Ryker. She just wished she was as useful to him as he'd been to her. His fight with Ares had really gotten to him and she had no idea how to make it better. She'd known he resented his father for leaving his mother pregnant and alone, knew he thought Ares had raped her.

Kyana wasn't so sure. Ares didn't seem to be *that* kind of god. He was way too uptight to be ruled by sexual impulse the way some of the others were. But arguing that point wouldn't help Ryker. One didn't take the side of the enemy when trying to soothe a friend.

He needed someone with actual experience in the child/parent relationship thing, and that certainly wasn't her. Her human father had sold her to the highest bidder—allowing her to become Prince Mehmet's seventeenth wife. Hardly what she'd call a doting father. And her mother was no more loving than her father had been. She'd hated being touched, hated the messiness that came with children. She'd been glad to see Kyana go at the age of fifteen. And truthfully, Kyana had been glad to leave.

Until she realized she'd traded one hell for another.

The only real parental experience Kyana had was with Henry, the man who'd Sired her, who'd saved her when Mehmet had nearly murdered her by turning her into the Dark Breed she'd become. She'd adored him, and he her, until the day a Vampyre hunter had taken him from her.

Since then, she'd pretty much just been alone. Haven and Geoffrey had become her family, and more and more, she was considering Ryker the same.

That she didn't know how to fix any of them was likely going to kill her before Cronos ever got the chance.

"Nothing." Haven stood and brushed her hands on the jeans Kyana had painted on her before they'd left, then stooped again to pack her tools. "A Witch didn't make this mark so I can't pick up any magical residue from its caster."

Grateful to finally have a break from the dark corners her thoughts had traveled to, Kyana helped her gather her belongings. "If a Witch didn't do this, what did?"

"The only other magic users I know of are Mystics and Mages, and if a Mystic is responsible for this, I'd be very surprised."

"Really?" Kyana asked, folding her arms over her leather vest, suddenly cold. "Marcus was a Mystic. So was Drake."

And both had been responsible for the deaths of a lot of Chosen. Drake had been Haven's boyfriend—a murdering, lying weasel. Marcus had been the one who'd nearly murdered Haven, forcing Kyana to turn her and start all this mess in the first place. How could Haven forget all that?

"I know," Haven said through gritted teeth. "But they were the exception, not the rule. I seriously doubt there's a sea of Mystics gone wild out there. Far more likely to be a Mage, though I really hope I'm wrong."

"Because they're strong?"

Kyana didn't know much about Mages. She'd met only one Light Mage before and he'd been a mountain-dwelling hermit who'd threatened her life for stumbling onto his territory in Scotland when she'd been desperate to feed. And if a Mage was practicing in a graveyard, it wasn't bound to be a Light Mage. No light spells required anything dead. No, if Haven was right, this would have been the work of a Dark Mage. Something Kyana had never seen before.

"Yeah, but mostly because they freak me out." Haven shuddered and let Geoff take her arm for a moment before pulling away.

Kyana watched Haven make her own path for the gate, then looked to Geoff. "She faced Cronos. You'd think a Mage wouldn't scare her."

"Mages are given their powers by Witches,"

Geoffrey said. "If a Witch doesn't have an heir, he or she usually bequeaths their powers to someone they find fitting—and when that person receives them, they become a Mage. You'd think the power would get a bit diluted as a hand-me-down, but it's actually far more concentrated and powerful than when carried by the Witch."

"So? There are a lot of things out there that are more powerful than a Witch."

"Yeah well, over time, there have been some crafty Mages who wanted more power than was bequeathed to them. They found a way to get it. Those became the Dark Mages."

"And that would be . . . ?"

"They drain the Witch while she's alive, stripping her of all her magic until it kills her."

No wonder Haven had looked terrified. She might be three breeds in one, but the Witch in her was still dominant. Being stripped of those powers probably wouldn't kill her since she still had Vampyre and Lychen beneath that layer of herself, but she'd been raised a full Witch—likely brought up on horrifying stories about what Dark Mages did to their victims.

"The good news is that the surge of power is temporary," Geoff continued. "Every few years, they have to drain a new Witch or be reduced to whatever they were before they became any sort of Mage."

"How is that good news? That means more Witches die."

He stepped over a headstone. "It also means there's a time when they're weak and very vulnerable. Not so scary."

Kyana disagreed. She'd rather come up against a fully fed, powerful Dark Breed than one desperate to survive. That sort was usually far more deadly than the former.

"Good Lord. Look at that." Haven stopped several feet ahead of them before shooting off toward the shadowed right corner of the graveyard. She looked over her shoulder at Kyana. "There are so many!"

As Kyana and Geoff headed toward Haven, her gut twisted in dread. Each and every overturned headstone in this corner of the graveyard held some semblance of the mark of Cronos. Sickles drawn in blood, dirt, and mud were everywhere.

"Haven, can you cast your visibility spell here?" Geoffrey asked, squatting to lift a finger full of dirt to his nose.

"Yeah, but it's pointless. Whoever did this wasn't traceable at the other mark . . ."

Kyana stopped listening. Her gaze had drifted

downward to an open grave, the casket splintered, revealing nothing but dust inside.

"The bones are gone," she said, lowering herself into the hole. "He's raised some from here."

"Kyana, what are you doing?" Haven jogged to the side of the hole, her eyes wide. "Get out of there!"

"I will, but . . . There's something shiny over here." Kyana disappeared into the darkness for a moment, then stood back up, holding a small silver, circular charm in her hand for the others to see.

"Kyana! No! Drop it!" Haven screamed.

But before Kyana could register the warning, something thick and prickly crept around her ankles. Two huge, spidery vines shattered the earth inside the grave to wind around her boots and up her calves.

"Kyana!" Haven threw herself onto the ground and reached for her, but before she could grab hold, Geoffrey was on his belly, his arms around Kyana's waist.

He pulled with all his god-strength. Her muscles stretched, ripped, but the ground cracked, and reaching, inching vines pulled her deeper into the damp earth.

She tried to grab for the dagger in her boot, but

the possessed roots latched on to her wrist, binding her arm to her hip as the thick limbs snaked up her body to encase her chest.

"Get me out of here!"

The ever thickening roots grew outward by the hundreds, pulling against the hands holding her. She didn't know what evil this was, but it was winning. If they didn't figure out a way to break the binds sucking her into the ever-widening hole in the grave, it would be too late.

"Hang on to me," Geoff shouted, wrapping his arms more firmly around her waist and shoulder.

She clung so tightly to him that when the ground opened again, pulling her more deeply into the hole, she dragged him halfway into the grave with her.

"What the fuck is this!" Geoff gripped the thick roots in his bare hands and ripped them away from her throat. The vines turned thick and black and slippery as though they'd been plunged in oil, and he lost his hold.

She gasped, but before she could pull in a full breath of much-needed air, the vines regrew, tightening around her throat and snaking their way into her hair and over her face.

Geoff grabbed for her again, but the roots were too thick for him to break. He climbed into the grave with her, trying to push her up as Haven pulled. Instead of hoisting her out of the ground, the vines holding her legs squeezed around her and retreated, pulling her slowly back into the earth.

"Drop the charm!" Haven's voice broke through the fog of oxygen deprivation, but it was an order Kyana didn't have the ability to follow. The vines had crept around her fist, holding the charm prisoner against her palm.

"Free her hand."

"Don't let go of me," Geoff hissed as he pulled at the vines wrapped around her throat. "Just hold on to me."

Kyana felt herself slipping into unconsciousness. Felt her hold on him loosen. He grabbed her beneath her arms and pulled.

"The roots won't stop until they bury her alive," Haven said, jumping into the hole with them.

"Get out of there," Geoff shouted. "They'll kill you."

"Got. To. Free. Her. Hand!" Haven ripped at the veins with her claws and fangs.

Warm blood slicked Kyana's wrist and pooled in her palm. Haven continued to pull at the thick vines until she freed Kyana's fingers. The bones in her hands popped and cracked, but Haven continued to fight against the vines until she had the charm in her hand and threw it out of the grave.

"Shatter it!"

When the vines slinked from her face, Kyana pulled in huge gulps of air. The burning in her chest eased and she coughed. "Get . . . me out . . . of here."

Geoff pulled himself and Kyana out of the grave, dropping her as he rolled toward the charm and shattered it with his elbow. It burst like fine crystal. With a hiss, the roots shrank and slithered back into the ground.

Geoff pulled Haven from the grave, then returned to Kyana's side.

"Holy fuck," he whispered. "You all right?"

Her heart still pounded hard enough to cause minor earthquakes, but other than the slight burn of scrapes and cuts—from both the roots and Haven's slashing—everything seemed to be working all right.

"Pissed enough to murder, but yeah, I'm all right."

She shifted, looking at her arms and hands. Tiny black lines crisscrossed her flesh, and she was pretty sure her face and throat looked ten times worse. Her body shook violently as if an iceberg had settled in her chest, freezing her from the inside out. It looked as though her veins had been injected with an inky poison.

"What the bloody hell was that?" Geoffrey asked, wrapping his arms around Haven and rocking her gently.

"Definitely Mages," Haven breathed, running her hands over her body as though to shake loose a nest of spiders. "Dark Mages. You wanted magic users, Kyana? You got them. A lot of them. And they're powerful as hell!"

Chapter Eleven

Silence hung in the cemetery like an unwanted guest until Kyana couldn't take it anymore. "What the hell were Dark Mages doing here?"

Haven rubbed her arms, her face ashen. "I don't know. Mages are solitary by nature. But to perform a spell like that"—she pointed to the open grave—"it would take at least five of them."

"What the hell kind of spell was that anyway?"

"A trap. Simple as that. They had to know the Order would send someone here to investigate. That charm wasn't exactly hidden," Haven said. "They had to know some moron would pick it up. No offense."

Kyana growled. "Offense taken."

She suddenly felt like the dumb-ass monkey sidetracked by an *ooh shiny!* All she was missing was some poo to sling.

Hoping to divert the attention away from her chimp self, she changed the topic. "So, if they're solitary, then a group of them would stand out," Kyana said. "We can track them."

Haven gave Kyana a look that said maybe she hadn't even made it to chimp status. Maybe she was just a baboon. "The only way you can take down a Mage is with magic. And you two still know jack shit about what you can do. That leaves me, and as much as it punctures my ego to admit it, I don't have enough power to take on a full group of Mages on my own."

Geoffrey flicked the conduit of Hades glimmering on his chest, its soft glow pulsing through his shirt. "I have this. Whatever I haven't learned yet, the conduit will sort out."

Kyana glanced down at her own conduit, dangling from a chain around her neck. Artemis's golden arrow wasn't nearly as powerful as Geoffrey's amulet. It wasn't one of the Eyes of Power created for Cronos's children, but it contained enough magic within its golden shell to give Kyana some semblance of comfort.

She gripped it in her fist, feeling the immediate calm that holding it brought her. Her gaze steady on Haven, she took a deep breath and voiced what she knew was going to cause an argument.

"If they feed off Witches, maybe you shouldn't come. You can stay with Artemis in my temple and just let us handle this. The last thing we need is for these assholes to gain more power."

Or for you to get hurt. Kyana wasn't sure she could take losing Haven all over again.

"Forget it, Kyana." Haven's glare was venomous. "I'm not hiding while you two run around pretending you know what you're doing. If I hadn't been here, this trap would have killed you."

"But it's your Witch heritage that will draw them to us. Right?"

"My being with you isn't going to light up the sky like the bat signal. However, I might be able to come up with a spell or two that will help us find them."

"And if they find you first?"

"Then we'll have to make sure they can't touch my power."

"How?"

Haven frowned, scratching at her wrist—a nervous tic that only came when she was truly scared or confused. "I'll think of something."

"We'll all think on it," Geoff said. "In the meantime, Kyana and I are going to be useless if we don't replenish our reservoir of ambrosia."

He was right, and while she carried a vial of

ambrosia with her, she required food in order to consume it. Undiluted ambrosia could be deadly to the gods.

"We need to get back to Beyond. It's almost sunrise, and after what just happened, Kyana, you need to heal."

She glanced down at the rips in her leather pants and the crusted, bloody wounds revealed beneath them. It would take ambrosia and sleep to heal properly, but in a few hours, there wouldn't be a mark left on her.

"Fine. I want to talk to Ares anyway. Artemis insists that he has to be kept in the loop as far as strategy since this could very well lead to war, and honestly, I'm too tired to think. Maybe his fresh perspective on this will give us a starting point."

As they crossed Castillo Drive to the fort, Haven stopped in the middle of the street and whirled around to face them, her eyes wide. "I need to see Silas."

"Why? What's wrong?" Kyana broke away from Geoffrey's side and hurried to Haven's.

"If there's even the slightest chance that we'll run into the Mages, I have to see him first. When we get back to Olympus, will you ask Ryker to summon him? I'll speak to him while you two rest."

"You need to rest too," Geoffrey said, brushing her hair away from her ear, even as she ducked to avoid his touch.

"I will. *After* I see Silas."

Kyana shrugged and ushered them all onto the grassy hills toward the fort's entrance. "I'll see what I can do."

They made their way past the sentinels and toward the portal alcove that would take them Beyond. As soon as they were away from prying ears, Kyana asked Haven, "What can Silas do for you that we can't?"

Something in the depths of Haven's yellow-green eyes sparkled and Kyana thought she saw the hint of a grin on her face. "He can lend me his powers. He has more than enough right now while he's standing in for Poseidon. He won't need his Witch blood for a while, so he can sure as hell give it to me."

Kyana blinked. "You can do that?"

Haven nodded. "It's tricky, but possible. If we succeed, then I'll have an extra layer of magic in me so it will be tougher to strip me bare if we run into the fuckers."

"What happens if we do run into Mages and they strip all of Silas's powers off of you?" she asked.

"Then when Poseidon's real Chosen is found, Silas will be left as magic-less as a human." She looked at Kyana, a light of humor in her eyes mingling with dread. "Going to be hard as hell convincing him we won't let that happen."

Damned right it would be. Silas adored his Witch lineage. Any threat to it was not going to sit well with him. But he also adored Haven, and Kyana couldn't imagine him turning down a chance to help keep her protected, even if it cost him his powers.

While Geoffrey took Haven into the grand foyer to wait for Silas to answer his summons, Kyana headed to her rooms with Ryker. He wasn't happy at all about her pending meeting with Ares. Too soon after the fresh wounds of their earlier argument, maybe? Whatever it was, he was trying to hide it . . . unsuccessfully. She watched him pace the large room, glancing occasionally out the large windows before resuming his pacing.

He was antsy, frustrated, and looking for a way to burn off the excess energy being trapped on Olympus was creating within him. Ryker was a leader, a take-charge warrior. Sitting on his ass, safe and protected, while others faced danger had to be eating away at his insides.

"Maybe we should spend this downtime doing something to work out your tension," she teased, pleased when she won a crooked smile from him.

"You called for Ares, remember? Hard to get worked up when I know we'll be interrupted by *him*."

She was trying to be patient—really she was. But he needed to get over this drama, or at least figure out how to set it aside so they could all do their jobs without so much unneeded, added conflict.

Trying to keep the exasperation from her voice, she sighed. "You're not going to be able to avoid working with him, Ryker."

He glanced over his shoulder. "I've been working with him since I was ten. I know how to put my shit aside to get the job done. Doesn't mean I have to smile while I'm doing it."

"You're going to have to resolve this at some point. That's a drawback to immortality. Eternity is a long time to hold a grudge."

Or worse, what if one of them became a casualty in what they were facing now? What if one of them was killed before any resolution could be found? No. Kyana refused to consider that. Nothing was going to happen to Ryker because *she* still had unresolved issues with *him*, and she'd be damned if she let him go before she figured them all out. But if something happened to Ares, she knew Ryker well enough to know he'd beat himself up for leaving things in such a mess. Maybe they'd never bond or have a familial relationship—but some sort of understanding could be found, couldn't it?

"I just need to find my cool before I see him again. He went too far this time."

"Because he brought up your mother—"

"Don't. I'm not going there with you either. Not right now. I'm too damned tired."

"Fine," she said, irritated that he could dismiss her so easily, yet unwilling to provoke him further. He looked as exhausted as she felt and it had been days since they'd had a real fight. She liked the peaceful existence they were creating together.

She made her way toward him and wrapped her arms around his waist, hugging his back. Sliding her fingers beneath the soft material of his tunic, she fingered his nipple and gave it a playful pinch.

"What are you doing?"

She offered a one-shouldered shrug. "Nothing wrong with a quickie."

Gods knew she could use it. She was still tender in a few places from her battle with the grave. A little ministration from Ryker couldn't hurt.

"Quickie? Not in my vocabulary."

Though his words were clipped, she knew it had nothing to do with anger now. She lowered her hands to caress his belly. "Then maybe we should expand your vocabulary."

He turned in her arms and unsnapped the pin holding her chiton over her shoulder. The gauzy material floated around her ankles, leaving her naked and slightly cold, but his heated stare fixed that problem right away.

"I always did love learning." He brushed his lips across hers, tracing the corners of her mouth with his tongue. "How much time do we have before your meeting?"

Kyana chuckled and unfastened the belt around his waist. "That's a quickie. The definition being hurry up, 'cause we don't have long."

Ryker captured her mouth as his hands trailed over her shoulders to cover her breasts. The stress of the day melted from his mind until only Ky and how delicious she tasted remained.

Pressing her back to the wall, Ryker slid his hand over her belly to her thighs. "Open for me," he whispered against her mouth.

With a sigh, Kyana complied, sliding her leg up his to rest against his hip. Reclaiming her mouth, he dipped two fingers into her heat. He matched the thrust of his fingers with that of his tongue. Her hips rocked against his hand as she moaned into his mouth and he could taste the unspoken whisper of his name in the back of her throat.

He flicked his thumb over her clit and she threw her head back. He caught her throat in his free hand, latched on to the sweet pulse there with his mouth and suckled, licked, felt her grow hot against his palm and hard against his thumb.

He was dying to be inside her, to feel that slick heat wrapped around the part of him that needed it most. But the look of pure ecstasy on her face kept him from riding inside her. He wanted her to come against his hand. To die a sweet death while he watched and waited for his time to join.

But just as a trickle of sweat beaded on her brow and that silent whisper of his name found its voice and the muscles inside began to contract against his fingers, he was jolted out of his lust by the sound of the door opening.

"Ah, mate, put away the bangers and mash."

Ryker glanced over his shoulder to see Geoffrey standing in the doorway, shielding his eyes. Kyana buried her head in the crook of his neck, her soft laughter caressing his shoulder.

"Get the hell out of here."

"With pleasure." He nodded at Kyana before

turning to leave. "Your summons has been answered. He's waiting in the dining hall."

When Geoff was gone, Kyana rocked against Ryker's palm. "How pissed would he be if we kept him waiting for a little while?"

The mention of Ares's name killed what little bit of Ryker's desire Geoff hadn't murdered. Brushing his lips across Ky's forehead, he moved out of her grasp. "Call for me after you're done with your meeting and we can take our time to finish this."

Chapter Twelve

Kyana strode through the council room, anger warming her blood. It wasn't Ares waiting for her, but one of his messengers. He sent a *messenger* to talk strategy? Did he really think that little of her?

Never mind. Of course he did.

"Forgive me, Goddess," the man said, his red cape billowing around his small frame as he swept into a low bow. "Ares bade me to tell you he has still not finished his meeting with . . . well, it is of the upmost importance that he finishes there."

Well, at least Ares had finally decided to give her some iota of respect as a goddess. A few weeks ago, he wouldn't even have bothered with a messenger. Still, she didn't believe a word of it. She had a niggling feeling Ares was avoiding Ryker as much as Ryker was avoiding Ares.

Children.

"Is that all he said?" She could be back in her room with Ryker, with him buried inside her and . . .

She squeezed her thighs together tightly to stop the sudden throbbing that had resumed between them at the thought of what Geoffrey had interrupted.

"Only that he plans to send his tracers farther north, and hopes you'll keep yours local." The messenger looked a tiny bit afraid of giving her the command on Ares's behalf. Seemed her reputation was spreading through Olympus. Good. "He says to tell you that he'll be at your side if you have any news of Cronos's whereabouts. That his port will be available to you at all times until this ordeal is over."

Ryker wasn't going to like that bit. He'd expect to be at her side for the same reason, but their porting abilities required a twenty-four-hour cooldown, so it was safest to have a backup in case they needed to get into and out of an area quickly. The two gods were just going to have to grow up and learn to deal with each other.

She rubbed her eyes, lack of ambrosia and her injuries draining what was left of her energies. She needed to eat and sleep, but the instant she closed her eyes, her mind always strayed to monsters like Mehmet and Azime and Cronos. Two of which were long dead, and the last long dead and newly revived.

She sighed, her stomach twisting into a painful knot as she replayed the dream Morpheus had given her—Azime, Mehmet, and her precious Sire, Henry. More than the fear of seeing her past husband, reliving the pain of losing Henry had been the most horrific part of her afternoon— well, that and being nearly eaten by a grave.

She had to get her mind off all that had happened so she could focus on what was to come, but she had no idea how to put it all into perspective. The world had gone fucking insane.

She meandered through the nearly empty temple halls toward her rooms and opened the door to find Geoff on his knees, peering beneath the sofa.

"What are you doing?"

Geoffrey rose to his feet and ran a hand through his hair. "Looking for my dagger."

Kyana crossed her arms and frowned. "In here?"

"I had it when Haven and I were here earlier, during the council meeting. But I didn't have it in the cemetery."

"Where is she?"

"Walking in the gardens. She's a bit antsy waiting for Silas to arrive. Think she's afraid he'll say no."

"He won't." Silas could hold his own in any confrontation. The pansy-ass attitude he'd had over the last couple of months was an act he meant to be charming, and yet others saw it as weakness. But when it came to what needed to be done or what his friends needed, he could be counted on.

This time wouldn't be different

For the next few minutes, she helped Geoff search for the dagger, but even though they looked in every nook and cranny, they came up empty.

"Maybe you lost it somewhere else," Kyana said, brushing her hair from her face.

"I didn't lose it."

Kyana gave a snort. "Okay, fine. Misplaced it then." She put her hand on his shoulder and ushered him toward the door, eager for the rest she'd been promising herself since she'd been pulled out of that damned grave.

"Maybe," he muttered. "Let me know if you find it."

She gave him a light push and closed the door after him, sinking against it, her gaze slipping through the open door to her bedchamber to

settle on the large golden tub at the foot of her
bed. Steam spiraled from the water, which was
hot all day long thanks to the magical touch of
Artie's Nymphs.

With a sigh of longing, she made her way
toward it, stripping as she walked, needing to
scrub the filth of Cronos's return from her body
as well as her mind. She just wished Ryker was
here to offer assistance. No one else seemed better
able to soothe her, when he wasn't completely in-
furiating her, and her body was suffering from a
tiny bit of depression from their rude interruption earlier.

She sank into the moan-inducing water, her
thoughts circling on Ryker. Maybe she was cruel
to keep hanging on to him when she wasn't yet
ready to make him any promises. He was in
love with her, and she'd warned him not to let
his guard down around her. She was too used
to being half Vampyre to know the meaning of
the word *monogamy*. But smart as he might be, her
warning hadn't been enough to push him away.

He'd become a part of her life, and while she'd
refused to promise him anything, she'd promised
herself to give this thing with him an honest go.
And now, as she let the steamy water slosh over
her naked body, her skin came alive with sharp

tingles as she contemplated their earlier activities and wished like hell they'd been able to finish them.

"That might be the sexiest thing I've seen in a long damned time."

As though she'd summoned him from thin air, she looked up to find Ryker standing in the doorway, leaning against the jamb and watching her with such intensity the tingles turned to fire.

"It's still hot." She wiggled her eyebrows playfully at him, straightening just enough to allow her breasts to pop free from the surface. "Feeling dirty?"

He grinned, the dimple in his cheek flashing. "Always."

He took his time removing his godly robes, placing his sandals neatly in the corner and folding the cloth before setting it on her dresser, giving her a lingering view of his backside that made her wish both that he'd hurry the hell up and that yet he'd take his time.

"When all this goes down, you won't need armor," she muttered, letting her hands fall to caress the tops of her breasts.

He turned, giving her a half view of the rest of him. He was already hard and, as always, magnificent. "No?"

She shook her head. "Bullets and blades would just bounce right off you."

"It's all that surfing."

"Keep it up."

He stepped into the tub and she scooted backward to make room. He wasn't an overly broad man, but he was tall and solid as stone. As he eased himself in, the water instantly grew hotter.

So did Kyana.

"How did your meeting with Ares go?" She trailed her toes over his chest.

"Do you really want to talk about *him* now?"

"Not even a little." Snaking his arms behind her, he gave a light yank, pulling her onto his lap.

Their slippery bodies pressed tightly together as he scooped his hands beneath her ass and lifted to maneuver her just right. Then, before she could so much as steal a kiss, he moved his fingers around her thighs and slid them into her heat.

He was wasting no time getting them back to where they'd left off, and she was thankful. Moaning, she caught his mouth with hers and plunged her tongue inside to mimic his fingers' ministrations. She'd kill anyone who interrupted them now.

She wanted no reminders of what lay outside her bedroom doors and the world beyond it. Right now, she only wanted to lose herself in Ryker. It wasn't just the sexual release she craved, and that scared the hell out of her. He had become so much a part of her life, a part of who she was becoming, that she found it hard to imagine what life would be like without him.

Not willing to consider that possibility, or what it might mean, she tightened her arms around his neck and deepened the kiss.

Ryker sensed a change in Kyana as her arms squeezed his neck and she pushed herself more tightly against him. He wanted to know what had caused her mood to shift, but her soft pleas for more while she nibbled on his lips were maddeningly distracting.

Lifting her hips, he eased her up onto him. He moved his hands to her waist, controlling her movements to make the sensation of her slick, hot pulsations around him last. Trailing hot kisses over her neck, he captured her nipple, loving the moans of pleasure she cast into the otherwise quiet chamber.

Turning his attention to the other breast, he tugged lightly on the nipple in rhythm with the rock of her hips. She buried her face in his neck. Her panted breaths heated his flesh. She nipped at his shoulder, her fingers biting into his flesh as she tried to increase the slow movements of their slippery bodies sliding against each other.

"Please," she whispered, dipping her tongue into his ear. "Now."

Easing his hands slowly up her body, he leaned her back so he could watch her face. The ring of amber around her blackish eyes faded until the entire sphere was glazed as she stared at him, her mouth parted slightly, her breasts heaving. As her muscles tightened around him, he cupped her face, stroking her lips with his thumbs.

"Come for me, Ky," he said, his entire body rigid and tense as he waited . . . waited for her to find hers so he could find his. Her tongue flicked out, her brow damp from steam and sweat as she lifted her arms to grip the sides of the tub, bucking her hips faster and faster.

She was pale. She needed ambrosia. But right now, she needed him. It was written all over her gorgeous face and it was driving him mad. She might not know it, but he was engraving himself into her life as deeply as he was engraving himself into her body right now. She wasn't just in need of sex. She was in need of *his* sex. Of his *everything*.

That thought made him come so hard, his entire body shook as she rode his pleasure toward her own and cried out his name. She fell forward, pressing her naked breasts to his chest as she buried her face in his neck.

If he died like this, would it really be death at all?

"If we could find a way," she breathed against his neck, "to insert ambrosia into *that* I'd just feed on you all damned day."

And with that, his body gave one last jolt of satisfaction as he closed his eyes and tried to remember how to breathe.

Kyana rested her head against Ryker's chest, her fingers dancing over his belly as his hand trailed over her back. After their bath, they'd moved to her bed. He'd stroked the fires again and again until her mind and body were too exhausted to dwell on her fears.

But now that the tremors had quieted, her thoughts returned to Cronos. "I don't know how to stop him this time."

It felt sinful to break the peaceful quiet that had settled around them, especially with the utterance of Cronos's name. But her mind was clear now, and all the questions were coming back, one by one, invading her space with Ryker.

"It's not something you have to do alone," Ryker said, pressing a kiss to her forehead and slipping an ambrosia-soaked strawberry into her mouth. "All the gods, old and new, are working on a solution. We'll protect Olympus."

Kyana rested her chin on her hands and swallowed the tart fruit, trying not to be distracted by the slow circles his fingers were tracing along her spine. "And the humans we've released Above to begin rebuilding? Who's going to stand guard for them? Who knows how many *untrackable* Dark Breeds are running around now. These Novi haven't signed your treaty, which means my tracers don't have a nifty GPS on them like they do the ones who have. Sentinels know what they signed up for. It's the humans we have to consider now."

His circling fingers stopped and as the words tumbled out of her mouth, she wished she could yank them back. He was going to see her worries as some noble proof of growth in her and she was going to kill him for pointing it out.

"You're worried about humans? You hate humans."

She tried to move away but he tightened his arms around her, holding her to his side. "I don't *hate* humans. I just don't find much use for them. But that doesn't mean I want them all sacrificed."

Ryker's smile made Kyana growl.

"Look at you. You're all soft and mushy." He

leaned in close and placed his lips against her ear. "Wonder if you taste like cotton candy now that all that bitterness is gone."

"Bite me."

"You don't bite cotton candy, babe, you let it melt in your mouth."

She rolled her eyes and tried again to move away. He refused to let her, and honestly, she didn't try too hard. When she met his gaze again, the smile on his face deflated her lingering frustration, expelling a whoosh of air from her lungs. "What? Why are you looking at me like that?"

He reached for her hand, dragged her onto him so they lay belly to belly, and kissed her thoroughly, making her dizzy as she struggled to remember what they were bickering about.

"The goddess in you is very sexy," he muttered against her mouth. "All soft and gooey. All heart and determination. You're out to save the world because you care this time, Ky. Not because you want the power or the glory that comes with being the one to defeat Cronos."

"So? What does that have to do with anything?"

"It has everything to do with everything." He placed another kiss to her nose, then pulled back far enough to look her in the eye. "Because it means that this time, Kyana . . . we're going to win."

Chapter Thirteen

At the sound of the light knock on her bedroom door, Kyana slipped out of Ryker's arms and padded across the room.

"Tell them to go away," he muttered, his words muffled by her pillow.

Kyana wished she could do precisely that, but they were still waiting for Silas to arrive, and if the Nymphs were bugging her at this hour, he probably finally had.

She swung the door open wide to reveal one of Artie's six-foot-tall Nymphs. "Sorry, Goddess, but you bade us to fetch you when he arrived."

Kyana nodded and closed the door again, quickly using Artie's nifty trick to dress herself in proper goddess attire.

"When who arrives?" Ryker asked, sitting up and letting her silky sheet fall into a bunch around his hips, revealing the golden, smooth planes of his oh-so-yummy chest.

"Silas." She fiddled with the gold chains around her neck. "Remember?"

"Right."

Silas had been indisposed in the Mediterranean, leaving an antsy, irritable Haven in Geoff's care since their return. Kyana was sure Geoff didn't mind watching over her, but Haven probably didn't appreciate it at all.

Ryker moved off the bed, his hair tousled from sleep and sex, his eyes still bleary from the former. He looked so incredibly hot, it was all Kyana could do not to drag him back to bed and make Silas wait until morning.

She watched him paint on the knee-length tunic he was forced to wear here and hated so much, then fasten the broad golden belt around his waist that made him look like a cross between a WWF champion and Caesar.

He glanced at her. "Your lips are puffy."

She grinned. "Because you need to shave."

Rubbing his fingers along the golden stubble on his face, he frowned. "Sorry."

"It's all right. I like it."

And she did. The stubble had burned a path over her lips and cheeks and thighs, leaving raw, red reminders of the places his mouth had visited. It made her feel delicious.

She sighed, wishing they had more time to just *be* together like this without duty always hanging like a noose around their necks. "It's almost dawn," she muttered. "We can't leave for the next cemetery patrol for another twelve hours or so. What a waste."

Haven had insisted that these resurrections would occur between sunset and sunrise on whatever days Cronos was finding his soldiers. That meant they didn't have to be at any graveyard until dark.

She shrugged off the frustration creeping onto her shoulders at the thought of standing still all day. It wasn't as though she didn't have plenty to keep her occupied. While Silas was transferring his Witch powers to Haven, Kyana could spend this afternoon letting Artemis train her.

Determined to be productive today, she followed Ryker through the temple toward the hall where visitors were taken. Already there and waiting were Silas and Artemis, and both gave Kyana and Ryker their undivided attention as they entered the room.

Kyana beckoned one of the Nymphs standing quietly in the corner and arranged for breakfast to be brought in. She wasn't the least bit interested in food, but if she was going to train with Artemis, she would need a full store of ambrosia in her system. Besides, the others looked like they could use the calming effects the food offered.

"Finally," Silas muttered. "I haven't even been to bed yet, Ryker. Why the hell did you summon me here?"

"Because I asked him to," Kyana answered. "Or rather, Haven did. She's the one who wanted to see you. Did anyone let her know you're here?"

Artemis nodded. "Of course. Geoffrey went to wake her."

Kyana and Ryker had left the bedchamber through the main door, altogether bypassing the private sitting rooms where Haven was staying. She hadn't thought to stop in and wake her along the way.

"While we wait for her . . ." Kyana sought Artie's attention. "Train me today? In every spell, every power you think I might need? What I can't master, I'll practice as I go."

While platters appeared one by one on the long table, Kyana took a seat with Ryker beside her.

"You truly think you can learn all of what Artemis needs to teach you in one afternoon?" Silas asked.

"No. I don't." Kyana reached for a wedge of goat cheese and stuffed it in her mouth. The sweetness of the ambrosia helped hide the tang of the cheese, and she swallowed, already feeling a little stronger than she had when she'd awakened. "But whatever I *can* learn is better than nothing."

"You're a skilled fighter, Kyana, but you know shit about magic," Haven said, appearing in the hall behind them with Geoffrey in tow. As Kyana looked from Geoffrey's tousled hair to Haven's disheveled clothes, she couldn't help but wonder just how close they'd gotten the last couple of days. Were they finally . . . Never mind. Kyana didn't want to know.

"Artemis can't teach you in a day," Silas added.

Kyana didn't like either of their superior Witchy, magic-know-it-all-ness one bit. "She can try. Whatever I can't wrap my head around, you two can help me with."

She could feel the doubts quietly gathering in everyone's mind and didn't need to be a Seer to guess what they were. She was the Order's hope? The same Vampyre/Lychen Half-Breed who'd turned her best friend into the monster who'd risen Cronos in the first place?

Once, not so long ago, Kyana would have thrived on the knowledge that she was the only one who could do this job. That she held so much power. However, the events of the last couple months had taught her that no matter how much power and purpose she held, there would always be someone else more important. Someone else who needed to be protected above her own life.

Right now, there were several, and one of them was watching her mindlessly chew on a strawberry.

As her gaze fell over Ryker, the tiny black strawberry seeds nearly choked her. His face was so soft, his profile so contemplative as he sipped from his cup, a thin layer of the wall guarding her heart crumbled. He was a very big reason for her determination to find Cronos and bury him for good. She found herself trying to imagine a world without Ryker in it and simply couldn't.

Whether she could save the world or not didn't matter. With these feelings stirring inside her for Ryker, even if the rest of the world was okay, she was already doomed.

"Ahem." Silas poured a glass of ambrosia-laced wine and took a sip. "Gonna tell me why I'm here now so I can go home and go to bed, please?"

"Alone?" Geoffrey asked. "Or has Sixx returned with you?"

Kyana rolled her eyes at the mention of Silas's

girlfriend. It had been pleasantly quiet without that Witch around. Granted, Kyana had begun to hate her a little less as they'd worked together to find Haven, but less hate didn't mean a BFF relationship had been born.

"I . . . made her stay put," Silas admitted.

Kyana felt her eyes grow wide. Did that mean things were actually serious between the duo? That Silas wanted to keep her safe rather than chance her getting hurt here, with what they were all facing? Wow. If she'd thought of herself as commitment-phobic, Silas was the godfather of her clan. Was he really settling down with a dreadlock-sporting, leather-clad, big-breasted Witch?

Amazing how quickly things . . . *people* . . . could change.

She gestured to Haven. "Go for it, Haven. Tell him why you wanted him here."

Kyana pushed her plate away and steepled her fingers. Knowing this conversation wasn't going to go well, but would likely be the most entertaining part of the long day ahead.

Haven cleared her throat. "Cronos has brought in some new forces and we need to level the playing field. I'm strong, but I'm going to need to borrow your powers if there's a chance I'll be running into them."

Silas looked suspicious. "What sort of new forces?"

Haven looked away. "Mages."

Silas choked, a cherry pit plopping onto his lap.

He looked around at everyone seated at the table as though expecting someone to laugh and tell him they were joking. But when his gaze settled on Artemis, his face lost all color. "What the hell is she talking about? I can't give her my powers . . . right?"

"It *is* possible," Artemis said, looking apologetic.

Haven reached across the table and slid her hand over his. "You have enough mojo running through your veins as Poseidon that you won't even miss the Witch magic, Silas. Just hear me out."

She gave him the short version of their run-in with Dark Mage residue at the cemetery. As she talked, Ryker stiffened more with each word, and Kyana cringed as he gripped her thigh, squeezing a bit tighter with each passing second.

So much for keeping the incident a secret.

She leaned over and whispered, "She's making it sound worse so he'll give up his powers," she lied. "Now stop or you'll splinter my thigh."

"We'll talk about this later," he said, his teeth gritted.

"No we won't."

Artie sent them both a silencing glare and Kyana pried Ryker's hand off her leg so she could pay attention again.

". . . you can do without your Witch skills for a little while," Haven was saying, "and it will keep me safe in case we run into these guys."

The calmness in her voice didn't ease the disbelief on Silas's face. "I'm not going to be Poseidon for much longer. Giving you my gifts will leave me with nothing once this god's blood is out of me."

Haven nibbled on her nail. "I'll give them back when we're done."

"Right, unless you're attacked and they get a good hit in before you can get the hell out of the fight. I might not want to be a god, but I sure as hell don't want to be *normal* when this is over."

There was so much disdain in the word that Kyana almost wished she could let him off the hook. For Silas, dead was better than normal. Normal was boring. Uninteresting. Not cool. And Silas thrived on being cool. At least most of the time.

But letting him off the hook wasn't an option. She had to keep Haven safe so Haven could help them bring down Cronos. She'd try her best to make sure nothing happened to his gifts, but it would be a lot easier for him to learn how to live without powers than it would be for Kyana to learn to live without her best friend.

"We're all making sacrifices," she said. "This one is yours."

He looked at her as though she'd lost her mind. "Oh really? I thought mine was carrying around Poseidon's powers while you searched for a sucker to take them off my hands permanently. Or maybe sending my girlfriend away so that I've only seen her once in five weeks and even that was interrupted by the summons you sent today. Neither of those was sacrifice enough?"

"Give her the powers, asshat, or the only sacrifice you'll be making is the permanent sort. The one we're all going to be faced with if we don't each do what needs to be done," Kyana seethed.

Did he not understand that they were all giving up things that mattered? To think she'd ever slept with the tool was making her queasy. Silas had always been a little less than eager to face conflict, but she'd never really considered him an outright coward before.

He seemed to sense where her thoughts had gone, however, because he stood with a resigned expression on his face, then hung his head. "Fine.

Take my powers. But Haven, imagine losing yours and what that would do to you and hold on to that feeling. Please, promise me you'll remain as safe as possible because when all this is over . . . if my powers are gone . . ."

He didn't need to finish. She knew what it would do to Silas to lose his Witchiness. He'd lose the part of him he loved the most, which was saying something, and would likely sink into a pit of despair that even Sixx's jiggly puffs wouldn't be able to pull him out of.

"I'll take care of them," Haven promised.

"We all will," Kyana added.

Silas nodded, digging his fingers into his eyes as though trying to pluck a headache out with a quick pinch. "Fine. How the hell do we do this?"

Chapter Fourteen

Kyana sat quietly watching Silas and Haven sit across from each other in the dining hall, their hands joined as Silas occasionally jerked violently and Haven sank deeper and deeper into unconsciousness. His powers rippled beneath his skin, making each passing second torturous to watch.

It looked like worms had infested his flesh, maneuvered by blue lighting as tiny sparks shot from his pores into the air, before being sucked into Haven's body. This process had already gone on an hour, and according to Artemis, could take several more. No quick chanting of spells for this one.

Instead, it was as tedious as a human surgical procedure and Kyana was done watching.

"Let us know when it's over," she said to Ryker, queasy and slightly dizzy at the thought of what it felt like to be Silas or Haven at that moment. To be giving away part of what you were, or to be receiving something that wasn't yours at all.

She glanced at Artemis. "Time to train."

Artemis gave a nod and followed her out, leaving Ryker and Geoff to sit with the Mystics overseeing the transfer of magic. When Artemis pulled out a bow and quiver, Kyana groaned and reconsidered going back to watch the goings-on inside. Might be less long, tedious, and nauseating.

Artemis had been trying to teach her the art of archery since becoming a goddess, and so far, she hadn't proved to be a brilliant student. She still preferred her fists and daggers to the complicated bow that required far too much precision in the middle of a spontaneous need to defend herself. But Artemis had insisted that a huntress without a bow was doomed to failure.

Kyana sighed and turned the bow over in her hand. She had asked for this training. She wanted to learn as much as possible. She'd just forgotten about the damned bow.

"These are different, Kyana," Artemis said, looking somewhat put off by the disappointed expression Kyana was certain she was wearing. "This bow was made by the Cyclopes and precision shouldn't be an issue for you anymore. Hephaestus assured me he coated the arrows with gold-plated crystals that will lead them directly to the vulnerable targets on your prey."

Kyana fondled an arrow. "Well, that explains why they're so warm . . . and heavy. When did you have time to request special weapons for me?"

Artemis smiled. "About five minutes after our first lesson proved you weren't very . . . shall we say, adept? I went straight to Hephaestus and he made my request a priority."

The God of the Volcanoes was a magnificent craftsman, and Kyana had admired his work for years, particularly in the work of Helios's chariot and the specialized swords he crafted for the sentinels. Now she had her very own weapon made personally by him. If nothing else, that knowledge made her want to learn how to use it.

Still, the crystal charms glittering on the arrows in the early morning sunlight made them even more awkward than the normal ones Artemis had first begun training her with. A lot heavier and bigger to tote.

"Not to sound unappreciative or anything, but can we lighten their weight or something? Carrying these around all the time is going to be a bitch," she muttered. "And you only gave me three arrows. What if I can't retrieve them after I've shot them?"

"When the third arrow is used, all three will reappear in the quiver." Artemis took the bow and shot the arrows at once into a large willow nearly fifty feet away in her courtyard. All three hit directly in the center of the trunk, and a second later, the arrows in the tree vanished and the quiver was full again.

"Nice, but I've seen you shoot before. You could have managed that with toothpicks."

Artemis folded her arms over her chest, a smug, knowing look on her regal face that brought Kyana's curiosity to the surface.

"You try."

"There has to be something more useful you can teach me. Something more magical. I already know how to fight. I need to know how you track." Kyana placed the arrow in the bow and pulled back. "I'm winging it without my Lychen blood."

She concentrated on the little marks in the willow where Artemis's arrows had struck before returning to the quiver and fired. Bull's-eye. "Wow."

Artemis smiled and reached out to tug the chain that hung around Kyana's neck until the arrow conduit popped free from her dress. She gripped Kyana's bow and quiver in her other hand and muttered, *"Unesco."*

The quiver and bow vanished and the conduit around Kyana's neck glowed bright amber for a quick second before returning to its normal state.

"What did you do?"

"When you don't need them, keep them in the conduit as I just did. To retrieve the bow again, simply will them into your hand and say, *Separo.* It works much like your dogs."

Kyana was going to have to start carrying around a memo pad—or maybe one of those spiffy voice recorder things now that she could get near electronics without her Lychen brain exploding. Anything would be helpful to keep a record of everything Artie had told her at this point. Kyana didn't speak Latin, or goddess for that matter. Still, she locked the words away and prayed they'd come to her when she needed them.

"As for the other things you requested to know, there are a few I can show you," Artemis said, "but I am not proud of them. They are things you must learn eventually, but I fear teaching you now . . . you'll use them in ways not meant to be."

"Still think I'll go off half-cocked every time something doesn't go my way? Haven't I proved that I'm not so impulsive these last few weeks?"

Artemis smiled. A breeze picked up, scattering leaves across her perfectly groomed garden, which were immediately swept up by invisible hands and deposited over the cliffs behind the temple.

"You've a quick mind, Kyana. And yes, I've seen a calm develop in you that is new. Whether it's due to my blood or to Ryker's presence in your life, I'm not certain, but it's a pleasant side of you to be sure."

Kyana squirmed, uncomfortable that others could see how much she'd softened when it came to Ryker. She wasn't sure what he meant to her yet, and she didn't want anyone else to make assumptions about them that would add to his assurances that they were "meant to be."

"Just teach me," she muttered, happy for a change in topic. "I won't go off half-cocked."

Artemis sat on the last step of her temple and stretched out her legs, burying her sandaled toes into the plush grass. "Watch."

She raised her hand to the sky and was immediately greeted by a dove that settled into her palm. She closed her eyes, covered the dove with her free hand, and when she revealed the bird again, she trailed one finger down the length of its body. A path of black followed her fingertip, white feathers darkening, then falling to the ground. Soon, the bird was left naked save for a purplish body that looked anything but natural. The bird spasmed and fell limp in Artemis's palm.

"You killed it?" Kyana's disbelief forced the words out more loudly than she'd desired. Artemis protected all things in nature, and yet here, in her own temple gardens, had killed a beautiful, innocent bird.

"Killing. Not killed. Watch." This time, Artemis drew her finger from tail to head. The purple was soon covered with blackened feathers again, which turned white as snow the minute Artemis's finger reached the crown of the dove's head. It stood, chirped, then soared back into the air to safety, circling overhead once before disappearing into the forest surrounding the gates of the temple.

"What the hell was that?"

"As I said, I am not proud of everything required of me as an Ancient. I hadn't wanted to teach you this until much later, given there should be no need for it with the human population cut in half these days." Artemis held out her hands and allowed her Nymphs to wash them clean while she studied Kyana. "There are but a few of us capable of what you just witnessed. Bearers of the plagues and diseases that have stripped down the human population when it became necessary to do so. The black plague, leprosy. Even rabies, though I admit that was my first such experiment and it went awry. We've yet to figure out how to cure that one."

As the Nymphs finished and moved to once again stand behind their mistress, Kyana tried to find her voice. When she managed, it came out in a squeak. "You . . . created leprosy? Whoa."

"No, Ares did. Hera is responsible for the plague, though we shared the powers and all three of us can do each disease. Blessedly, there's been no call for such duties in a very long while."

"And you're teaching me this why?"

"Because I can control the process. They are contagious because it was our way of pruning the population. We no longer use this method. In fact, we are rarely responsible for contagious outbreaks anymore, but since your knowledge of magic is lacking, this is one you can master quickly, and it will give you another weapon to add to your limited arsenal. It's possible to infect a body with the disease and kill them instantly, making certain it dies with them rather than spreading amongst those who don't deserve it."

"So everyone who died of the plague or leprosy or rabies deserved it?"

Artemis's brow furrowed. "Certainly not. It is why we do not resort to such things anymore. Too many undeserving beings caught the epidemics and died along with those we'd chosen. We'd hoped they would spread only to their circle of miscreants and criminals. We were wrong."

Nothing new there. The gods of Olympus had been wrong very often, sad to say. If humans had any idea how fallible they were, there'd be no trust at all. But the deeper this knowledge seeped into Kyana's brain, the more interesting it became. Just thinking of putting her hands on Cronos's lackeys and instantly killing them with disease was appealing in many ways.

Namely, she wouldn't have to rely solely on the bow and arrows.

This cheered her considerably. "Show me how to do that."

Artemis must have read the eagerness in Kyana because the goddess frowned and slowly shook her head. "This is not to be used lightly. If you're not careful—"

"I won't use it on a whim, promise." Kyana sat on the step beside Artemis. "But it's the most useful tool you've shown me in weeks."

Artie's frown deepened. "I've shown you how to grant the gift of life with fertility and you focus on death as the greatest tool? You're not Dark Breed anymore, Kyana. It's time you stop looking at death as your duty."

If not for the seriousness in Artie's eyes, Kyana would have laughed. She spent two hundred years as a hunter. Spent eighty of those years going after the Order's most dangerous prey. Now she'd spend the next several thousand or so as the Goddess of the Hunt. Death was a part of Kyana and always would be.

"Show me."

With a sigh that carried the weight of her decision, Artemis nodded. "Hold out your hand. The creatures here will instinctively trust you."

Kyana did as instructed and held her hand to the grass. A small brown mouse skittered out of the bushes next to the steps and climbed into her waiting palm. So much trust, especially from something so small and vulnerable, baffled her. Maybe it was just humans and those who had once been human who had the natural instinct to doubt and mistrust everything. Some called it the survival of the fittest or self-preservation. Kyana just figured it was part of her nature to expect the ill intentions of others before they could kill her.

She ran her finger over the mouse's little head. It stood on its hind legs, its nose twitching as it tested the air. For half a second, Kyana thought about releasing the creature and sending it on its way, but her need for knowledge overruled.

"What next?"

Artemis took Kyana's hand and gently covered the little mouse. "You must think of the disease you wish to inflict. It's possible to call forth any plague or disease you've ever heard of, however, I advise you stick with the three I gave you."

Kyana glance at Artemis. "Why's that? If there are so many ways to inflict pain and death, why not use whatever is most fitting?" Considering she'd had a natural immunity to disease and infection most all her life, she didn't know a lot about plagues and diseases. But, for those following Cronos, she'd make it a point to learn the most horrific in history.

A faint blush stained Artie's cheeks. "Because being creative is how rabies was born."

That Artie had a few mishaps of her own made Kyana feel slightly better about some of her own screw-ups. At least she'd never unleashed a disease on innocent creatures that killed man and beast alike. Not yet anyway.

"Do I need to concentrate on the word or the effects of the disease or . . ."

"You'll learn what works best for you. I focus on the dying. See the life being drawn out of them. It only takes a second to get the image in my head. Once it's there, I think, or say, *Sino in nex*. Then it's just a matter of trailing my hand over the parts of the body to be infected, transferring the image in my head into the victim's body."

Kyana nodded though she didn't have a single idea how to pull off what Artie suggested. Sure, she had watched more than her fair share of people die, but it was usually at the end of her dagger or fangs, not from some disease.

"Death in general, Kyana. Nothing more is needed. The key is having the disease you desire in your head before saying the words. As long as you do that, everything else will take care of itself."

Kyana closed her eyes and repeated the word *plague* over and over in her head. With it, she pictured the tiny mouse dying. Its little body being destroyed by the disease she whispered in her mind.

"*Sino in nex*," she said, opening her eyes. Slowly, she trailed her finger from the creature's little brown head, over its belly, to its tiny feet. A thin, black line trailed behind her finger. The mouse began to quiver in her palm. Its fur completely fell from its body like pine needles in autumn before it flopped onto its side. Its stomach concaved. Its breathing sped up before becoming heavy and labored, its tiny mouth lathered in white foam.

"*Refero vita*," Artemis said, taking Kyana's hand and forcing it back up the mouse's body.

In seconds, the creature was once again the picture of health, its small pink nose twitching, its tiny paws scratching at its face in a quick bath. Artemis forced Kyana's hand toward the ground. With a little tweak of its nose, the dormouse disappeared into the greenery surrounding them.

"Wow." The words *refero vita* rang over and over in her head. She didn't want to forget *that* one. "Would that have worked to bring Haven back? Before I turned her, I mean?"

A look of sorrow-filled understanding softened Artie's face. "I'm afraid not. It can only remove damage that particular god or goddess created. A spell reversal so to speak."

"Oh."

Artemis gripped Kyana's shoulder and forced her attention away from her empty hand. "This is not to be used lightly. You must understand that."

"I get it."

"Good." Artemis stood and gestured for Kyana to do the same.

Kyana thought about Cronos. Of those following him. Of those killing for him. If she had even the smallest opportunity to put her hands on them and perform the trick Artemis had just taught her, she was damned sure going to pick the most painful disease she could think of.

And there'd be no spiffy *refero vita* when she was done.

Chapter Fifteen

Feeling as though she'd received the first real moment of solitude she'd had in days, Kyana took her time patrolling Tolomato Cemetery that evening, enjoying the quiet of the near silent backstreets of St. Augustine. Ryker, determined not to be left behind after what had happened at their last cemetery patrol, was walking the military cemetery not too far away. And Geoffrey had taken Huguenot, though he'd been reluctant to leave Haven on Olympus alone. But taking Silas's powers had exhausted her and there was no way in hell she was in any sort of shape to join them tonight.

Most of Kyana's tracers had been sent to every other cemetery in the area, and hopefully, they had enough bases covered that one of them would find something that would finally give them an idea of where Cronos was hiding out. If they could catch him while he was weak, they might have a chance at stemming the brewing battle to come.

Not an optimistic person by nature, Kyana wasn't counting on it. But right now, it was the only plan they had.

She craned her neck to peer at the moon. It was nearly sunrise already, and with every minute that ticked by, the chances of finding anything amiss lessened. Soon, Ryker would come for her and they'd be forced to return Beyond and wait another full day to do this all over again. Irritation didn't begin to describe what that thought did to Kyana's already testy mood.

The faint echo of footsteps on the sidewalk outside the cemetery made her sigh. Ryker was early. That meant the military cemetery had been a dead end too. Lovely.

As she turned to face him, however, something struck the back of her skull, sending her to her knees. Before she could make sense of what had happened, something thick and black and foul-smelling was thrown over her head. She breathed in to yell as her fist struck out, catching the culprit on a bony bit of his or her body, but as the air traveled down her throat to settle into her lungs, panic burst like a balloon inside her.

Whatever she was breathing in was slowly stealing her consciousness—her ability to move. She felt her arms turn to lead, felt her eyelids close before her mind shut off and she felt the cold cemetery grass against her back.

While it had been a foul stench that had put her to sleep, it was an altogether different odor that slowly brought Kyana out of the comatose state that had overtaken her in the cemetery. One of rotting flesh and dirt.

The fog in her brain slowly lifted, but as her body was flung belly down over a hard, bony shoulder, her silent command to her legs to kick out wasn't obeyed. She felt as though she'd been dipped in concrete, her limbs heavy and stiff. Her mind raced, desperate to find the goddess inside who could stop this. Deep breaths. In and out. In and out as she tried to focus her mind and energies.

The person carrying her had an uneven gait, causing his shoulder to dig into her ribs and squeeze the air from her lungs. Even thinking became difficult. She tried to scream. Her tongue was too thick to do more than make a guttural groan. She was useless. She was vulnerable.

She was in deep shit.

A heavy amount of jostling rattled her bones, a sharp tug yanked at her hair. In the next instant, she was blinded by lamplight. When she saw the face staring down at her, she prayed for the blindfold again.

Bile rose in her throat, burning her nose and making her eyes water.

No longer the gloriously beautiful man she'd once thought him to be, her husband still had the same piercing black stare that had haunted her dreams for centuries. Though Prince Mehmet's face was gaunt and near yellow, his cheeks sunken and nose half missing, he was still as recognizable to her now as he'd been then. Still as monstrous.

"He raised you," she hissed, pleased that her tongue was back under her control. She tested her hands and feet and found them still dead to her. Cronos had done this. The small glimpse she'd seen of Mehmet in Haven's dream had been *real*. The bastard had gone out of his way to make this war even more personal, and murderous rage threatened to suffocate her.

Mehmet smiled and stepped aside so his partner could move into Kyana's view. Azime, his first wife and Kyana's past life tormentor.

This had to be a nightmare. Mehmet and Azime couldn't really be standing in front of her in this,

this . . . where the hell were they? Kyana shifted her gaze, searching for escape. Brick walls surrounded her on all sides. One window directly to the left of her chair and a door to her right. If she could just make her legs move, she could—

Azime's cold hand slapped Kyana across the cheek so hard her eyes watered and her head jerked violently to the side. She wasn't given a second to breathe before Azime grabbed a handful of her hair and forced her head back with such brutality, she thought her neck bones might snap.

"Yooooou," Azime whispered, her breath hot and as putrid as the rest of her body, "bitch!"

She slapped Kyana again, then stepped back and flung her hands in front of her. "You see what you've done? Look at me!"

This time, Kyana was ready for Azime's fist. She stiffened her back, pressing her body against the chair. Braced, the impact barely moved her head at all. She stared up at Azime, focusing all her hatred on the living corpse, wishing she could project some piece of the goddess within her out and into the creature's heart.

Once so beautiful as the Haseki Sultan, it had been hard to stare too long at Azime—her beauty nearly blinding. Now her outside was as filthy and rotted as her insides had always been. The stunning Mediterranean coloring had a greenish tint, her long, silky black hair matted and streaked with dusty gray. She looked so brittle, Kyana was surprised her hand hadn't shattered upon impact with Kyana's face.

She was the devil's handmaiden. Just as she'd been in life.

"What *are* you?" she asked, revolted by the sight of the gaping hole in Mehmet's cheek as he turned to look at his wife.

"More powerful in death than even in life," Mehmet said. He leaned down and kissed the wife who'd beaten Kyana when she'd pleased their husband, and had nearly killed Kyana when she'd angered him.

Kyana caught a glimpse of blackened tongues stretching out from blacker mouths to touch one another and her gagging resumed. This time, she couldn't control it. She vomited, the bile splashing onto Mehmet's filthy robe.

Well, there was a little satisfaction at least.

Mehmet jerked away from his wife and back-handed Kyana, sending her chair toppling over. He pulled a wand from the sleeve of his robe. *"Temizlemek!"*

With his words, the vomit disappeared and understanding dawned on Kyana. Mages. They'd been risen as Mages and Cronos had made certain they'd become Dark.

"Did you think that killing us would keep us from your life?" He tucked the wand back into his sleeve and smiled. "He is raising only those he knows aren't opposed to violence. He raised *us* because he knew we'd take great pleasure in being the ones to deliver unto him *başin*."

Your head.

Kyana flinched and tried to back away as he stepped even closer to right her chair.

"*Seni sik*," she breathed, surprised at how easily the language of her human years came back to her.

"Tsk tsk." Azime pulled a similar wand from her robe and held it in a hand that was missing its middle finger. "Such language for a wife of a prince. A pity to see all these years haven't tamed your wild ways."

Wild ways? When they'd known Kyana, she'd been docile and obedient and spineless. "Release me, and I'll let you see for yourself how much your little whipping post has grown up."

"Mm." Azime's smile revealed yellow teeth, and her black tongue flicked out to wet her dark, flaky mouth. "You killed us once. I knew it was a mistake to bring that bastard into our home. He changed you and you bit the very hands that kept you fed, you ungrateful *hayvan*."

"Ah, she is no beast my love," Mehmet said. "Merely an irrelevant pest I mean to squash."

He slid his fingers down the shoulder of Kyana's vest and pressed his nail to the seam, ripping the fabric in two.

"If I'm so irrelevant, why would Cronos bother raising you two just to come after a fucking mosquito?" The leather material slid into her lap, leaving her breasts bare and her skin icy. Kyana let her anger burrow into her marrow, warding off the fear that threatened to break her. "There's a reason Cronos wants me out of the way."

She watched him smile, watched Azime sneer. Kyana's whole body trembled, but try as she might, she couldn't lift a hand to cover herself. While nudity hadn't been an issue in years, suddenly, she was a young girl preparing to be violated by the man she'd married all over again.

"Still so supple and young. I am almost pleased Henry betrayed my trust and made you his that night, for it kept you ripe and blooming for me today."

He hunched over, dropping to his knees. Then the sickly sensation of heat on her breast, followed by sticky moisture, made Kyana scream out. He was suckling her, groping her like a sixteen-year-old virgin, his hands clumsy, his mouth too eager.

Kyana retched. Fought to pull away and cried out when she couldn't.

She looked to Azime, praying the woman would be disturbed to see her husband so blatantly fondling another woman, but the bitch looked pleased. Her fingers dropped to cup her own breasts and her hips swayed back and forth in a mockery of love play.

"You're fucking insane!" Kyana screamed.

Mehmet's teeth pulled violently on Kyana's nipple as he moved to his feet, taking the tattered remains of the vest with him, leaving her exposed and scared out of her mind. She'd have rather opened her eyes to see Cronos than these two. No Dark Breed ever created had the ability to shake the core of Kyana's foundation as Mehmet and Azime.

"If you plan on killing me, get it over with," she whispered.

"Not yet, *hanim*."

"I am *not* your wife."

"Ah, but you are and always will be. Immortality tends to bind marriage vows when till-death-do-you-part no longer matters." He pointed his wand at her again, this time speaking some word that ripped her pants directly from her body in shredded ribbons onto the floor.

A look passed from Azime to Mehmet that fed Kyana hope. The old woman was getting irritated now. Apparently, fondling Kyana wasn't as big a deal as Mehmet thinking of Kyana as his wife after all these years. Azime had loved being the Haseki Sultan, had loved being number one over Mehmet's other wives. But she'd loathed sharing his titles and gold with the other girls.

The bed, sure. The power? Never.

Kyana focused on Azime, whose black and gray hair was tumbling from her ancient, broken combs to settle about her emaciated shoulders like a death shroud.

"You don't want me in his life again, Azime. Why are you helping him?"

"You won't be in his life again, whore. You'll be dead as soon as—"

"Don't spoil the surprise. He'll be here soon enough."

Cronos? Were they really waiting on Cronos?

The knots entangling Kyana's guts gave a painful twist. If Cronos showed up here, fully in power or not, she was as good as dead. Whatever spell they'd used to bind her had made her so useless, she didn't stand a chance.

"Cronos doesn't scare me," she bluffed, snatching Mehmet's gaze with hers and pinning it in place by sheer will. "I'm surprised you let him control you. The husband I remember never obeyed anyone, and now you're nothing more than a scion for a god you never prayed to."

Mehmet simply grinned and leaned toward her, his rotting mouth brushing her ear. "I'm not obeying anyone, pet. This little reunion was my idea."

He stepped back and pulled Azime into his arms. "Death does not stop the wish for revenge. Nor does it hinder the mind from planning just how your demise will be played out."

Azime's grin pulled her decaying flesh tight and caused the cartilage in her nose to shift at a grotesque angle. She pulled out her wand and waved it before Kyana. "*Yer değiştir.*"

Before Kyana's brain could translate the words, she found herself supine on a pile of musty blankets. She struggled to stand, to roll over, to shield herself from the hate-filled stares weighing her down. Her bare ass was cold despite the sweat breaking out all over her body.

"Oh, where is the *hayvan* now?" Azime gripped Kyana's chin, tilted her head back.

Like the rest of her body, she suddenly had no

control over her eyelids and she found herself staring once again at the pair. They wore matching evil leers as they glared at her with black eyes.

Azime reached around her husband and unfastened his cloak, letting it fall to the floor. "After much debate, we agreed that you should leave this world as you were meant to over two hundred years ago. This time when you're left bleeding and broken, there will be no one to save you. This time when the demons come to claim your soul, it will be the savior of your past leading the way."

Kyana didn't need them to fill in the gaps. She would be beaten, raped, and tortured, just as she'd been the night Henry had turned her. And when they tired of the game and left her bleeding in a corner, no one would care. There was no one to save her, and for once in her new life, she was unable to save herself.

She always thought that when it was time to face her final death she'd do so on her feet fighting. Not once had she dreamed that the evil killing her would be the very two people who'd destroyed her life the first time.

A long, slow creaking caused chills to slither over her naked shin. Somehow she managed to find the will to fight Mehmet's command and squeeze her eyes tightly closed. If she would have an audience when she died, she certainly didn't want to see in their eyes that her violation had entertained them.

"Come now, Kyana, greet our guest with the respect he deserves."

It's not real. It's not real. It's not real.

Kyana struggled to wake up. This had to be a dream. That was all. It was the worst, most vivid nightmare of her life. When she woke, Ryker would be there beside her, ready to hold her tightly and offer to share the horrors with her if she'd only let him.

But she knew when she opened her eyes, it wouldn't be Ryker's arms around her, it would be Mehmet's. His rancid breath would burn her skin. His rotting member would defile her. He'd enter her and she'd die, slowly, painfully rotting away from the inside out.

As if reading her thoughts, Azime cackled. "Open your eyes."

When Kyana didn't obey, Mehmet's sharp voice pierced her ears. "Now."

Her eyes snapped open. Then an invisible hand gripped her chin and she found her head slowly turning toward the entrance through no effort of her own. Now it wasn't the potion they'd given her that held Kyana numb. It was sheer disbelief.

"Henry." His name tumbled from her lips in a whisper of uncertainty. His presence was familiar. His dark eyes, his long brown hair. But the aura around him was different, the stooped shoulders, the hollow gaze.

Slowly, that gaze fell upon her, and she found herself looking into the eyes of her Sire. Yes, it was him. But the dark glare searing her skin like a laser no longer belonged to the Vampyre Half-Breed she'd loved more than her own human kin. It wasn't kind, or soft, or looking upon her with love and care. It was hard and menacing and peering down at her like she was a feast to be enjoyed.

He wasn't on her team anymore.

Kyana couldn't control the shaking that started at her toes and ended at the roots of her hair. Tears burned hot trails down her cheek. She now knew what Azime meant by the savior of her past.

The man who had created her would now be the one who murdered her.

Chapter Sixteen

Kyana imagined there were a lot of people standing in line to send her to Hell, but not Henry. He'd seen the goodness in her, had brought her back from the edge of darkness and had given her the light she'd lived by as a Dark Breed working for the Order of Ancients. If she had to die, she did not want her death to be at the hands of the only man she'd ever considered true family.

Henry's steps on the wooden floor were heavy and hesitant. His flesh looked cracked and frail, but not falling from his bones like Mehmet and Azime's, and he was still wearing the tattered remains of the silk and leather she'd buried him in.

"This isn't real. You're not real. None of you are real!" The accusations spilled from Kyana's lips in a frantic screech. She no longer cared if they saw her panic, her fear. She only cared about waking up and forgetting this had ever popped into her morbid imagination.

"Is it not fitting that the man who'd betrayed me in one lifetime would be the one to give me back all that was taken in this one?" Mehmet circled his bony arm around Henry's shoulder.

Kyana spat at his face, which wasn't easy given the lack of moisture in her mouth.

Mehmet wiped the spittle from his cheek with the back of his hand, looking unfazed by Kyana's show of defiance. "As his Mages, we have the power to become who we were before you so savagely murdered us. All we need is the blood of our murderer. *Your* blood."

Kyana was too afraid to focus on Henry and see as much hatred staring down at her from him as was coming from her captors. If she could only move her damned hands or feet. She was supposed to go out fighting! Not laying naked and paralyzed on dirty blankets in the middle of gods-knew-where, held hostage by her own damned nightmares!

Swallowing her tears seemed to lubricate her throat enough to offer back a bit of her voice. "I should have cut off your damned heads when I had the chance."

Henry had stopped her. Hadn't allowed her to

rip them to shreds after her feeding frenzy had caused her to drain every drop of blood in their bodies. Look what that mistake was costing her now.

Damn them all!

Kyana didn't see the fist in time to brace herself. The blow to her jaw rattled her teeth and split her lip. Warm blood trickled over her cheek to pool beneath her ear and run down her neck. Now that she had better control over her panic, she'd be damned if she let them know how much pain a simple fist to the face caused her. She stared stoically up at Azime, who lowered her fist to snatch Kyana by the hair and jerk her neck backward.

"We end her life now."

"No." Mehmet pried his wife's fingers from Kyana's head and shoved her behind him. "I want the revenge I've dreamed of for over two hundred years. Then, to make it sweet justice for you, the one who gave her the power to destroy us will end her life."

"I don't care about justice, *koca*. I want her dead. Now!"

Mehmet struck her. A slab of flesh slid off the bone beneath Azime's eye and plopped onto the shabby collar of her robe. She raised a shaking hand to cover the gaping hole in her face, and

Kyana swore that if looks could kill, Mehmet would have just found his second death.

"Do not forget your place," Mehmet said, the words bringing back a flood of memories Kyana didn't want to relive. Her place. His place. A man's wife in their time was no better than chattel, no better than the dog that pissed in the corner. Step out of line and pain would follow. Or starvation. Or death. "She will die when I say."

Kyana felt the burning sensation of being watched. Slowly, she lifted her head to find Henry's gaze locked on her. The blackness of his eyes wavered from lifelessness to the bright green she remembered them to be, before fading once again to black. Since he was newly turned, and lacking a conscience, the acts he was witnessing shouldn't have any emotional effect on him. However, the tight lines around his mouth suggested he didn't want to do what his instincts demanded.

Kyana held his gaze, pleading silently with him to find the inner strength that had given him control over the beasts of his lineage so many years ago. The man who had offered her salvation before resurrecting her. Who'd taught her how to tame her own monster and live a seminormal life.

The man who had shown her the first bit of kindness she'd ever known.

Henry's eyes softened again, lightened to green.

"You don't want to do this, Henry. You're a Novus again. Whatever you do now will determine if you walk in the light or forever in the dark. You told me those very words once. Don't you remember?"

Henry hissed, his fangs grazing his lip, but he said nothing.

"Think to sway him?" Mehmet taunted. "Think you're more powerful than the very soul who raised him? I think you're in for a disappointment. I think you shall see where his loyalties now lie."

Kyana didn't look away from Henry. He was reposturing, adjusting his stance. He was going to attack her and there wasn't a damned thing she could do about it.

He lunged. Kyana turned her head and braced for impact. A scream broke her rigid posture, forcing her eyes open. Henry stood in front of her, and a bright light shot from his hand and hit Mehmet in the center of his decaying chest, pinning him to the wall.

"Go," he growled.

It took Kyana a second to realize Henry was talking to her. Hope lit her up from the inside out and her heart gave a slight tug of relief. He was coming back to her. He wasn't completely lost yet.

She tried to sit up, to stand, but still her body refused to obey her commands. "I can't."

His growl turned into a low rumble. Azime launched herself at him, her roar splitting the silence.

Henry easily sidestepped the attack without releasing Mehmet from the powerful beam of light. His mouth moved, but Kyana could hear nothing from his lips. Azime froze, her hands outstretched in claws. Before Kyana could digest the power her old Sire now wielded, he reached out with his free hand to grab Azime by the throat.

With a snarl, he tightened his fist and lifted her off the floor. When she was eye-level, he shook her like the clichéd rag doll. The nauseating sound of bone and muscle being ripped apart was the only noise that filled the room for several seconds before the thump-thump of Azime's body falling in two different directions brought silence.

The light holding Mehmet to the wall was so powerful that all he could do was gurgle his outrage. Henry closed the distance, the light centered in Mehmet's chest causing his bones to smoke.

Kyana could only watch in morbid fascination. Her Vampyre/Lychen Sire seemed to have been given some Mage juice with his reincarnation.

Big mistake, Cronos. Big mistake.

Standing chest to chest with Mehmet, Henry reached into the prince's sleeve and stole his wand. He flicked it toward Kyana so quickly, she flinched and looked away, certain she was about to experience severe pain. Instead, a tingling sensation crept down her thighs and filled her calves, inching toward her toes until she was able to move her feet.

The minute the tingling stopped and she was brave enough to test the weight of her body on her legs, she lunged for Mehmet, whose eyes were wide in terror. As she flew at him, she gripped the amulet at her throat, needing more strength to deliver the justice he deserved. Energy soared through her. Her entire body shook from power and outrage, and she directed it all at Mehmet.

Satisfied that her strength was returning, she pinned him to the wall with one hand, then smiled as she trailed her fingers over her bare breasts, down her belly, then bending slightly to reach her legs. A web of silk followed the path her finger blazed, clothing her in a chiton of pure gold.

Gold chains wove themselves into her hair, raising the tendrils off her neck and pinning them to the top of her head, tickling her scalp like tiny snakes as they found their perfect spot. Jewels appeared on her fingers and a golden band fell across her biceps, etched with an amber arrow.

This time, she wasn't going to kill Mehmet as a Dark Breed. She was going to kill him as a goddess, and by the gods, she was going to look the part.

"Scared yet, you prick?"

Mehmet gurgled something, but there was definite fear in his eyes. This would be no anger-induced death, but cold and calculated and she'd be very much in control this time to savor every blessed second of it.

The brick wall behind him vibrated and danced. A million obscenities and insults perched on her tongue, but all her focus was on her hands, and she was unwilling to expend any of her newfound energy screaming words at him that would cause him no harm. Haven said they needed magic to kill a Mage, and Kyana was damned sure going to reach into the deepest part of herself to find some to finish this fucker off.

She brought her hands toward her chest and shoved them outward, energy sparking from her hands and into his body, lifting him off his feet and backward. Mehmet flew through the solid brick and back twenty feet into the night. Kyana held her hands out before her, concentrating on the magic flowing from her fingertips. She held him suspended for several agonizing seconds until the heat of the blue sparks caused his skin to start melting from his bones.

Without a word, she dropped her hands to her sides. Mehmet's bone-splintering scream filled the night air. Kyana rushed to the gaping hole. The terror on his face just before he burst into flames would stay with her forever. With a shaky sigh, she pressed her forehead to what remained of the wall and fought to control her quivering limbs. After all these years, he'd still had the power to scare the hell out of her. But never again. His body, nothing more than ash, floated on the wind.

He was dead now, but the only way to make sure he wasn't raised again was to stop Cronos.

A hand grabbed her arm, and Kyana spun to find Henry staring solemnly at her.

"Come."

That solemn stare turned pleading, his eyes flickering from black to green. She still couldn't wrap her brain around finding her dead Sire standing before her. But as happy as she was to see him and as grateful as she was that he'd helped her get free of Mehmet and his crazy wife, she was nobody's fool. The fight against his dark side hadn't been fully won, and she wasn't willing to hand him her trust on a silver platter.

His grip tightened painfully as he tried to drag her toward the door. "Come! Now!"

He was so newly born, he was struggling to speak even one full sentence, but there was a fear in his eyes that lured her away from the wall.

She wanted desperately to throw her arms around him and believe he was her old Henry, but she couldn't. Not until she had answers. She wanted to ask him so many things. How he'd been raised. Was he in pain? Did he still love and adore her as he had in another life?

Instead, all she said was, "Tell me where I am, Henry, so I can get home."

He pierced her with his now startling green eyes. "I . . . do not . . . know." His gaze softened but didn't go black again. They settled on a warm mossy color that had once been her most favorite color in the world.

She moved her arm from his hold but he grabbed her again, this time, his eyes frantically dancing, and his fear and desperation practically oozed from his pores. "He. Comes."

"Who—Cronos," she answered herself, feeling the weakness return to her legs. Of course Cronos would come. He'd want to see her corpse when Mehmet had finished with it.

Henry nodded and resumed pulling her out

of the abandoned warehouse and down the deserted street. This time, Kyana didn't fight him. She'd rather take her chances should Henry turn black-eyed again than with Cronos if he showed up while she was unprepared to defend herself.

His quick stride and continual glances over his shoulder created a sense of urgency that cramped Kyana's stomach. The Henry she'd known hadn't been afraid of anything. He hadn't even shown fear when the Van Helsing wannabe who'd taken his Vampyric life had tortured him brutally before finally killing him.

He'd retained his Vampyric speed, and suddenly the streets were blurred as he pulled her through alleyways and down side streets toward a row of devastated buildings. He led her into the farthest one, and the minute the door closed behind them, he sank to his knees and then to his belly, pressing his cheek to the scorched floor.

"Henry?" Kyana knelt beside him and placed her hand on his back. He was cold. Far colder, even, than he'd been as a Vampyre. He shuddered beneath her hand and let out a low moan.

"Thank you," she whispered. "You saved my life. Again."

When he made no indication of response, she gently tugged his shoulder until he rolled onto his back and was forced to look up at her. What did she say to a man she'd watch die so long ago? *You okay?* seemed far too inadequate. Her mind numb, Kyana sighed. There was nothing she *could* say, really, and definitely nothing she could do. Artemis's fancy healing trick only worked on injuries she'd caused herself.

The Goddess of Healing would be able to do something, but Kyana hadn't heard anything about Aceso since the Breakout. She only knew the goddess was making rounds across the world trying to heal the dying from the havoc wreaked by Dark Breeds, and in order to summon her, Kyana would have to return to Olympus.

She didn't want to leave Henry alone like this, and taking him with her wasn't an option. Without gods' blood, or special invitation from Ryker or Zeus, he'd be killed the instant he attempted to step through the portal to Beyond. She'd have to take him Below and hope the Mystics there could help tame him as they had Haven.

"You . . . saved me . . . too." He squeezed his eyes shut and as Kyana watched, his yellowish skin slowly lightened to a pale ivory. He was going to be okay. "Didn't know . . . I was strong enough to resist . . . till I saw you."

The lump in her throat was slowly becoming a

boulder. Time for chitchat would come later. Right now, she just wanted to make sure he'd stay okay. That he wouldn't backslide into whatever was wrong with him.

"I need to figure out where we are so I can get us home."

Henry twisted beneath her hand and sat up. "There is a park . . . less than a hundred miles . . . from wherever we are." His words were clearer now. He was getting a better handle on his old self. Relief swelled in Kyana and she sat beside him. "It's where he had my bones brought . . . where he raised us all."

Excitement steadied Kyana's hands. "Is that where Cronos is staying?"

Henry gave a brisk nod. "For now."

Kyana felt the weight of the night settle on her shoulders. If Henry was right, Cronos could pick up and move again before Kyana could assemble a group to hunt him down. Going alone would be suicide. She gnawed on her lip as she considered her options, which didn't take long given she really didn't have a single one.

She opened her mouth to say as much but Henry's icy hand cupping her cheek froze her lips.

"Beautiful," he whispered. "My daughter."

Tears stung her eyes, but she refused to let

them fall. Years of catching up and rebuilding bonds would have to wait. Henry could still swing to Cronos's side, and small glimmers of the man she knew weren't enough to convince her otherwise.

"I need time to . . . heal. Run."

There was no way she was leaving him to face Cronos and the consequences of saving her life alone, and there was no doubt in her mind that Cronos *would* hunt them down.

"No, we'll have to find a place to hide out until dawn. Then I'll figure out where the closest port is and get us home."

"No," Henry snarled, sitting so straight he looked as though he might shatter if she touched him. His fingers bit into the flesh of her arm, leaving instant bruises. "I've broken a vow . . . to *him*. He'll be able . . . to find me. Get away . . . from me."

"I liked it better when you couldn't speak," she muttered.

The hum of power inside her wasn't as strong as it had been a few minutes ago, but it was still alive. She'd use it to get as close to home as possible before it fizzled out completely. She had no idea if she could use her goddess speed with a passenger, but she was about to find out.

Before Henry could offer any further excuses, Kyana laced their fingers and pulled him to his feet. "Hold on tight."

Not knowing if it would work, but having no other options, she focused on their destination. Once she had a clear image of where she was going in her head, she tightened her grip on him and disappeared into the wind, trusting the huntress in her to get her home.

They fled from town to town, pausing long enough for Kyana to check on Henry before shooting off again. She didn't know how much time had passed, but her body ached like she'd been running for days. Her limbs felt like lead, and her body was turning blue from the combination of speed and March winds.

Still, once they crossed into St. Augustine, she didn't allow herself to break her pace until she finally reached Castillo Drive and the fort was within her sights.

Her strength gone, she collapsed onto a bench outside the drawbridge and took a minute to catch her breath. "I need to clear your entrance so I can get you to portal Below," she said. "I need you to stay put for a minute."

"Won't go . . . Below. Can't be trusted."

"Yeah, well, I'm certainly not going to leave

you up here with the humans, then, am I? Now sit tight while I go get help bringing you inside."

Gods knew she was too tired to do it herself.

Henry gave a soft sigh. "Still my daughter. Stubborn," he said. "I should be . . . taking care of you."

"I think I owe you a little taking care of."

Kyana stood and used the last of her strength to make her way to the sentinels standing guard outside the drawbridge.

As she strode down the wooden path, her insides spasmed at the thought of her close call tonight. Of the memory of Mehmet's mouth and hands on her. Of how close she'd come to being murdered by the people who'd stolen her life the first go-round. If not for Henry, Kyana—and the Goddess of the Hunt—would definitely be dead by now.

For the second time in her existence, Henry had given Kyana life.

And as she pointed the guards in his direction only to find his bench empty, she noticed with exasperation that, for the second time in her existence, he'd also vanished from her life without giving her a chance to say good-bye.

Chapter Seventeen

Kyana slumped against the drawbridge entrance to the fort, her gaze lingering on the vacant bench. She could go after Henry, but her sprint back to St. Augustine had exhausted her. She was feeling the withdrawal of ambrosia, and if she pursued him now, she wouldn't get very far before running out of the last remaining drops of steam she'd retained.

Besides, it wouldn't matter. The harder she looked for Henry, the harder he'd make sure she didn't find him. He'd done as much in his first life when he'd learned he'd become a target for the Vampyre hunters. If he really was traceable by Cronos because of a broken vow, Henry would stop at nothing to protect her from being close to the fallout.

Still his daughter? Yes. And he was still very much acting the part of her Sire.

But as much as she wanted to find Henry, her priority had to be Cronos. There was no telling how long he'd hole up in the park where Henry had said he'd be.

With a sigh, she pushed off the wall and made her way toward the fort's portals. She needed to eat, rest, and find Ares and the others. Cronos wasn't far away, and if she wanted to make certain it stayed that way, they were going to have to find his camp before he had a chance to move on.

"There you are!"

Kyana turned from her position looking out onto the sunrise lighting up Artemis's gardens to find Haven striding toward her, Ryker and Geoffrey in tow.

"Where the hell have you been?"

She allowed her gaze to slide over Haven's shoulder and settle on Ryker. Anger was radiating off him like steam, and she wasn't in the mood for a lecture any more than she was in the mood to deliver the sordid details of how she'd spent her horrifying night.

She plopped down at the table, helping herself to another handful of tangerine slices. "Don't start," she muttered. "I'm in a mood."

"Do you have any idea what we've been

through looking for you?" Haven demanded. "Your scent disappeared in Tolomato and Geoffrey couldn't follow it out of there, but hell if you were there! Hiding in a grave maybe? What gives?"

"Yeah," she said, rolling her eyes. "Hiding in graves, looking for shinies. You know me."

Geoff stood beside Haven, his arms folded and his glare piercing. "What happened to you?"

Kyana shoved another tart wedge into her mouth, wishing she'd had more time to collect herself before they confronted her. Time to prepare a story, maybe bathe. Anything.

"Leave," Ryker said, saving her from creating a diversion from the topic herself. "Both of you." He snapped his glare to Kyana. "Don't look smug. You're not off the hook. I want explanations, I just don't want witnesses when I throttle you."

Kyana glared right back. She wasn't about to be put on a leash or resort to answering to anyone. She wasn't a naïve fifteen-year-old girl, victim to the whims of an abusive husband anymore. What had happened tonight wasn't her fault, but all three of them were looking at her as though she'd done something stupid. More than that, like she'd done something stupid *again*.

"How 'bout *all of you* leave," she grumbled, pushing to her feet. "I'm tired and sore and really in no mood for a chat."

She thought she caught Haven staring at her face and remembered the blows she'd received. Surely by now they would have healed, but there was something in Haven's gaze that made Kyana wonder what her Witchy eyes could see that the others could not.

"You all right?" Haven asked, her tone softened with worry.

"I will be as soon as I talk to Ares." She needed to talk to all of them, to see which of them would look for Cronos at her side. But not now. Not until she'd fully calmed from her rendezvous with Mehmet.

"I said leave," Ryker repeated. Kyana looked up to find him glaring at Geoffrey, who finally nodded and whispered something to Haven.

A moment later, they were striding from the hall, Haven glancing back wearing a concerned expression on her face.

"I summoned Ares," she muttered when they were alone. "You might want to leave before he gets here."

After what she'd been through, seeing Ryker was indeed a comfort, and yet, that he was always there, every time she turned around, every time she had a moment of weakness, was grating on her nerves. She wasn't used to being watched over so carefully, which was exactly what Ryker had been doing since Kyana had been changed into the Goddess of the Hunt.

"I hear all summonses." He was behind her now, his arms reaching out to pull her toward him. She stepped closer to the window, silently letting him know that she was in no mood to be coddled, though truly, she was. "What the hell happened to you tonight?"

The chiding in his voice was replaced by such a real note of concern, Kyana's resentment quieted. She wasn't mad at *him*. She had no reason to be. She was pissed that she'd nearly been a victim tonight, but Ryker's concern didn't deserve bitchiness in return. She still couldn't believe how easy it had been to be terrorized by Mehmet. How easily she'd reverted to a frightened kid.

She swallowed back the bitter retorts begging to be barked. He didn't seem eager to press her for explanations. Likely, he could sense that this wasn't the best time for her to offer answers . . . he was becoming so good at reading her lately, that wouldn't surprise her in the least. "Long story. But I'm fine."

He took a step back and crossed his arms over his chest. The moment of tenderness fell away from him, replaced by granite again.

"What?" she asked, suddenly feeling like he was a mile away instead of a couple of feet.

The muscle in his jaw ticked. "I thought we were past all the secretive bullshit."

Her defenses rose, wiping away the need to cry and putting in its place the need to protect herself. She didn't owe him any explanations. She'd never promised him anything, and this was why. That look of entitlement in his eyes made her want to punch the shit out of his gorgeous face.

"I thought I was past a lot of things. Apparently, I was wrong."

"What happened?" Some of the anger in his voice disappeared.

They stood looking at each other in silence for a long moment as Kyana contemplated how much she was willing to tell, and how much he deserved to hear. Probably, he deserved to hear the whole truth, but that wasn't happening.

If she talked about Mehmet, even uttered his name aloud, she could break down, could become inconsolable. Could be weakened and pathetic. No. It helped no one to talk about Mehmet. That bit, she'd keep to herself.

But Ryker did deserve *some* explanation. If the shoe was on the other foot, she'd sure as hell want to know where he'd been too.

So what the hell could she tell him that would satisfy him for at least a little while?

"I saw Henry." Now why the hell had she said that? She'd already told herself that she wouldn't say a word about Henry until she was sure he was safe. The last thing she wanted was for Ares or Ryker to put him on the list to be hunted and killed.

"What?"

"Never mind." She dropped to her chair, propped her elbows on the table, and rubbed at her temples. "Why isn't your father answering my summons?"

"No clue. You saw Henry?"

She'd given him a bone that he'd fight to keep. Damn it all. "Leave it be. He saved me. That's all you need to know. Forget he's alive. For me."

He sat beside her, his gaze so intense she felt herself squirm. "What the hell did you do this time to need saving?"

She flinched. "Excuse me?"

"Can't stay put and do your damned job, can you? Let me guess. You went off half-cocked, forgetting that you're a goddess now whose powers haven't been fully siphoned. Forgetting that, should you die, the world will suffer."

His tone steady, his gaze never wavering. But deep down, he was seething, and Kyana was pretty sure it would hurt less if he just punched her and got it over with.

"I did not!" Lovely. Now she was sounding like the insolent child he seemed to think she was. She took a deep breath and stalked to the fire burning in the marble hearth across the room. Holding her hands over the open flame, she tried to calm herself. Confessing that she'd been stolen away in the night, caught off-guard like a naïve fool, didn't sit well with her.

Pride goeth before the fall.

"There are some things I had to relive in the last few hours," she said, deciding that was safe enough to say. "And you know enough about my past to understand why I won't talk about it again here and now. I'm only going to tell you that Henry saved me from that, and I want him saved now despite misgivings anyone, including you and your father, might have about keeping a Novus alive."

Ryker watched Kyana pull her hands from the heat and wring them in the skirt of her chiton. She was nervous, and the fear in her eyes made him regret lashing out so harshly. The mention of her past held his tongue from doling out more punishment.

There was only one thing from Ky's past, that he knew of, that would have her twisted in so many knots. She'd confessed some of her human life to him, confessed her murder, her rape. Was that what she referred to now? How could Henry possibly have saved her from the tormentors of her past who'd long since been dead?

Of course, if she'd really seen Henry . . . Perhaps Mehmet had been raised as well.

Anger surged through Ryker's veins like white rapids but he kept his composure. He'd attempt to let his own calm feed her until she could feel it for herself, if she'd just let him brush that damned chip off her shoulder.

He reached for her, and this time, she didn't back away. As he pulled her to his chest, he buried his face in her hair and kissed her forehead.

"I didn't go off half-cocked," she whispered.

"All right."

"You won't hunt Henry?"

"No."

"Thank you."

"He won't hunt Henry, but I sure as hell will." The barked words sliced through the momentary peace they'd found, and both Ryker and Kyana spun to face their intruder.

Ares stood in the doorway, his face wearing the normal scowl and intense look of concentration.

"Get lost, Ares," he said, pulling Kyana's back into his chest, sensing this could get ugly.

His entire body was tense at the sight of his father, but he wasn't going to add to the tension. The topic of Henry was going to be a sore one between Ares and Ky, and Ryker didn't need to add fuel to the fire. He'd been dealing with Ares for centuries. He knew how to work with him without letting familial issues distract him. Family drama part two could wait until later.

Ares tapped the hilt of the sword swinging from his hip and smiled. Ryker couldn't help but notice Ares's refusal to so much as glance his way. "Your Sire has risen like the others?"

Kyana stiffened in his arms. "Touch him and I'll slit your throat with your own sword."

She didn't look at Ares, but the promise hung in the air, leaving no room for doubt. Ares had ordered Henry's death once, the night he'd created Kyana. However, this time if Ares overstepped the bounds Ky had drawn, Ryker would have hell on his hands.

"Mm. Yes. Let's leave a Novus, unsigned to our

treaty, loose because you're a sentimental fool. We hunt all the others and leave him to wreak havoc." Ares fell into a chair by the fire and sighed. "Who raised him? Cronos?"

"Of course," Ryker said, running his hands up and down Kyana's arms, hoping to soothe some of the fury he could feel storming beneath her skin.

Finally, Ares looked his way. Something flickered in the cool blue eyes staring at him, then just as quickly, returned to the steely coldness Ryker was used to seeing there. "If you didn't call me here to do my job and hunt your Sire, why am I here?"

Kyana released a ragged breath before stepping out of his arms to face Ares. "I know where Cronos is. At least where he *was* a little while ago."

"Where?" Ares stood.

"I'm not sure. Close. In a park outside of Jacksonville."

"You're strong enough to accompany my guard?"

"Like I'd let you go without me." She grabbed a goblet of wine and ambrosia and took a long drink.

"Gather what you need and meet me at the bank of portals Below."

Without another word, he turned and strode from Kyana's temple, leaving a sudden tension hanging between Ryker and Kyana as they stared at each other. There was a silent understanding that passed between them that he wouldn't be going with her.

He wanted nothing more than to stay at her side and watch her back, but he'd fallen in love with a woman who could take care of herself. Despite his earlier demands to know where she'd gone and what she'd done, he had to let her do that now. There were people here, on Olympus, and Above on Earth who *needed* his protection. It was his duty to give it to them.

Losing the Goddess of the Hunt was one thing. Losing the God of Gods was quite another—a responsibility he didn't take lightly.

But at the same time, losing the Goddess of the Hunt didn't mean half as much to him as the possibility of losing Kyana, the woman.

"You won't play the hero," he said. "You'll let Ares and his guards do their jobs. Hell, Ky, there's no reason for you to even go. Ares can bring him in just as well as you could."

He knew the suggestion wouldn't fly, but it was worth a shot.

"Ares is good at arresting. *I* am good at hunting." She brushed her hair away from her face, tucked it behind her ear. "If Cronos isn't there when we arrive, there's still a chance I can follow and find him again. It would take Ares a lot longer to do that, *if* he was successful at all."

"Don't go." He hated the pleading he heard in the faint words, but could do nothing to make them sound less desperate.

Her gaze softened but her stance remained rigid. "One of the few things we have in common, Ryker, is our need to fulfill our duties. This one is mine. Don't interfere."

"This isn't just *your* duty, Ky. Stopping Cronos falls on all of us."

"My duty is not only stopping him, but keeping Olympus safe. That means keeping *you* safe."

He wanted to shake her. "I don't need you to protect me."

She gently tugged his arms around her waist and pressed her cheek to his chest. "And I don't need you to protect me either, Ryker."

Her voice was muffled by his body when she continued, "When you look at me . . . do you see the half-blooded Dark Breed you met ten years ago, the one you claim you want a lifetime with? Or do you see Kyana, or maybe just the Goddess of the Hunt?"

"You are the same person, Ky. There's no separating the three."

"Yes there is."

She tried to push past him, but Ryker couldn't let her leave like this. "You are a goddess, now. But you wouldn't be one if you hadn't been strong enough to defeat the Dark Breed that lived inside you for two hundred years."

He leaned down and buried his face in her sweetly scented hair, wishing he could make her believe him. Holding her like this was as natural as blinking. She was beginning to initiate such intimacies, which pleased him more than he'd thought possible. The idea of losing her now, when she was finally letting the walls between them crumble completely, was unbearable.

He squeezed her tightly before she stepped away. She offered him a soft kiss to his cheek and whispered, "I'll be careful," in his ear before making her way to her room and closing the door, a deliberate signal that it was time for him to go.

Chapter Eighteen

While she waited for Ares, Kyana sat on one of the marble benches outside the portal alcoves and rested her head in her hands. Her temples were pounding and her chest was painfully tight. How could she have lived for two hundred years as such a strong, independent Dark Breed, and in one night be so quickly reverted back to a human victim?

"Mind using that nifty trick of yours and painting me some of what you're wearing?" Haven appeared in front of her, her fingers playing with the gauzy chiton Kyana had lent her.

"What are you doing here?" Kyana asked, snapping out of her funk. She looked around for Geoffrey, who was supposed to be minding Haven.

"Don't worry. Geoff knows I'm here. He's starting to trust me a little, I think." The grin on Haven's face was genuine, even if the glint in her eyes was questioning whether Kyana could say the same.

"You can't come. Vampyre . . . sunlight . . . poof. Remember?"

"Yeah, 'cause that's something I'd forget." Haven shrugged and plopped onto the bench beside Kyana. "Sunlight doesn't affect me. I didn't realize that right away, but as time wore on, before I was brought in, but yeah, sunlight not an issue."

Kyana scowled. "How the hell is that possible?"

"You were two breeds . . . the Vampyre was prominent. That meant all the shit that came with your Lychen half wasn't as tuned as it could be. You know that. Same with me. I'm Witch. Then Lychen. Then Vamp. Other than strength and these . . ." She licked the small fangs that hadn't been there a few months ago before her Turning. "I don't have many Vamp traits. Not that you'll catch me sunbathing at the beach or anything."

Kyana studied her for a long moment. Granted, she'd known only one other Half-Breed, but Vampyre was Vampyre, and sunlight was the ultimate no-no.

Finally, Haven sighed. "Why the hell would I lie? Think I want to be roasted? I can help you,

Kyana. Don't be a stubborn ass." She lifted the skirt of the chiton and let it fall back around her legs. "Now can I have different clothes or not?"

"It's girlie," Kyana said. "You should like it."

Artemis hadn't liked Haven walking around her temple in the jeans Kyana had painted on her before, and had painted the new goddesslike attire on Haven herself. At first, Haven had seemed to like the soft material. But now she was looking at it as though it was, gods forbid, polyester.

Haven raised an unappreciative eyebrow. "Expect me to fight in this? Really? How 'bout some leather like yours?"

The Haven of old had worn plenty of leather and denim so the request shouldn't have saddened Kyana as much as it did. There was something about seeing Haven in light pink, nearly transparent flowiness that kept her from remembering every two seconds that Haven had changed so drastically.

With a sigh of regret, she ran her fingers down Haven's back, then down the side of her thigh, painting on a white blouse and a pair of leather pants the color of soft butter.

"Boots?" she offered.

Haven nodded and Kyana complied. The black thigh-high boots topping the ensemble sort of made Haven look like a bumblebee pirate. Kyana kept that opinion to herself.

"Thanks."

"Yep." Kyana looked up to find Ares approaching, decked out in warrior garb from head to toe. Sword, tunic, chest plate, and helm. He looked ready to take on all the Spartans by himself.

"Find a working port near Jacksonville?" she asked.

There were several hundred ports from Below to different locations Above in the human realm, but only half a dozen or so that provided a return trip. Since the breakout, however, many of the ports leading out had also been disabled to provide the gods better access to knowing who was going where at all times.

"There's one about twenty miles away that I ordered the Witches to reopen. We'll have to take a quick jaunt, but it shouldn't slow us down too much."

"Good. Let's go." Kyana moved to leave, only to be brought up short by Ares's hand on her arm. She glanced down at the offending appendage, then back at its owner. "What?"

He pulled her away from the portal alcove and motioned to his Elite Guard. "This location isn't controlled by the Order. They go through first.

Then, when I'm certain it's safe, you can pass."

"You? Overprotective? I never thought I'd see the day."

"You are a goddess now." He pressed his free hand against the mark of Zeus at the center of the gate. "Certain precautions must be seen to." His gaze jerked over her shoulder to land on Haven. "That includes your friend. She's *your* responsibility. She causes trouble, and she becomes mine. Are we clear?"

How many times was he going to tell her that? Asshat.

"Crystal." Kyana sighed, missing the days when she was the protector and not the protected. "And Haven won't cause any problems."

She looked at Haven for confirmation and received an eye roll in response. "Got a leash? You can stick it around my neck."

Haven's sarcasm wasn't appreciated by Ares, but Kyana bit back a smile.

"Let's just go," he grumbled, motioning for his guards to enter the portal.

Ares kept his hand on her arm, like he was afraid she'd rush the gate. The old Kyana might have. But goddess Kyana was becoming more responsible by the day.

It was a sad thing.

When his guard disappeared through the portal, Ares took a step toward the gate, and then faced her. "Step through immediately after me."

"Will do." She grabbed Haven by the hand and pressed as close to Ares's back as possible without touching him and waited for him to disappear.

She and Haven followed right away, the black wormhole turning to bright light. Her skin tingled with the chaotic energy as she traveled the portal. She was dumped on the other side, nearly toppling into Ares in her fight not to fall.

"As I said . . ." Ares gripped her arm to keep her steady as Haven rushed in directly behind Kyana, shoving her forward. "This is not our domain. The portals are a bit stronger."

"Uh-huh," Kyana muttered, already distracted by their surroundings. They were standing smack in the middle of a deserted main road across from a mall and a vacant Red Lobster. "Who the hell put a portal on a median in the road?"

"Someone with a death wish," Haven grumbled, taking in their surroundings. "I know this area. Drake's mom lived around here somewhere. This road . . . busiest around."

Maybe it had been, but right now, it was eerily still and quiet. While Kyana had grown used to seeing humans and Dark Breeds walking the streets of St. Augustine, here it looked as though no one had returned since the evacuations.

She pushed aside the unfamiliar wave of pity for the people who'd once called this area home, but she couldn't help but wonder what had happened to those who'd lived here.

"Which way?" Ares asked.

Kyana let her gaze roam over the destroyed restaurant and back across the street to the mall. She closed her eyes and drank in a deep breath, centering herself until a static charge slowly tilted her head toward the street that led to the mall's parking lot.

"That way," she breathed, a smile creeping into her voice.

Artemis had told her that her instincts would gradually become more alive. She hadn't been lying. She focused on Cronos, and a magnetic pull instantly grabbed her as though sucking her entire being toward it.

Ares took her arm, preventing her from taking off in that direction. "We do not know what we're going to walk into. I need to know that you'll stop when I give the word. We're not going to charge into Cronos's camp without scouting the area first."

In other words, Don't live up to your reputation and

go off half-cocked. Kyana nodded her agreement and gestured to the sentinels. "Can they keep up?"

Ares looked at his guard. "They'll be slightly behind us, but they've been given potions to help them accomplish their duties."

She looked to Haven. "And you?"

Haven grinned. "Cheetah."

It took a moment for Kyana to understand what Haven meant, then she remembered the tiny white kitten Haven had been in the Healing Circle.

"Wow. All right then."

"I'll need new clothes when we get there."

Kyana nodded. "Ready?"

She watched Haven kneel, placing her hands on the ground, much like the way Kyana always had when she'd shifted to Lychen form. Haven lowered her head and closed her eyes. Unlike when Kyana shifted, however, there was no growing and stretching of Haven's bones. Her body shimmered, then glowed as if her soul had captured the moon and was now oozing it from her pores. Gradually, the glow was replaced by tiny black splotches until the woman disappeared completely and an elegant cheetah sat at Kyana's feet.

"Impressive." Kyana sighed, suddenly saddened at the loss of her Lychen abilities.

"It's an abomination," Ares hissed.

Haven growled and Kyana chuckled. "Are we ready?"

As Ares gave the command to go, adrenaline spiked through Kyana's veins.

She followed in a blur of speed, glancing back occasionally to make certain Haven was still with them. She remained close behind, her golden fur glimmering beneath the sun as they sprinted down the middle of the road. Kyana held her focus, terrified she'd lose the faint scent she'd managed to grab as they passed a dozen chain restaurants.

The scent became stronger as they neared the end of the road and headed left down Highway 17. As they neared the Naval Air Station, the scent became so strong, Kyana had to stop to catch her breath. She was choking on a stench she knew far too well.

"He's . . . here," she managed, bending to position her head near her knees and gulping in oxygen, still unused to needing it at all.

While she worked on breathing, she and Ares waited only a moment or so before Haven and the sentinels caught up. Tents were still set up, fires smoldered, and ceremonial platforms lay cold and empty.

Two things were painfully clear: Cronos had been there and they'd missed their opportunity to stop him once again. Haven darted behind a bush, and a moment later, she stuck her blond head out and called for Kyana to clothe her. Kyana complied, then rushed to get back to Ares's side.

"What do you want to do?"

A little shocked that he was asking, Kyana swallowed. Other than get here and kick ass, she had no real plan of action. It was that half-cocked side of her rearing its ugly head again.

"I need to see if I can pick up a new scent. Or at least try to feel him again." She looked to Haven. "How 'bout you? Feel him?"

Haven shook her head. "But I do feel his . . . residue, I guess. He's definitely been here. It's like the place is covered in black aura. It's the same feeling I have when I wake up."

Ares reached for Kyana's neck. She jerked. "What are you doing?"

He slipped the necklace from between her breasts and fingered the whistle dangling on the end. "Release them. They have a better chance of picking up a trace than either of you do."

Feeling silly, she removed the chain, blew into the whistle, and set it on the ground. Her pups appeared in a glittery fog, yelping and wagging their tails in glee at their sudden freedom. They followed a path to the campsite and Kyana commanded the dogs to search. In a flash, the dogs bounded off in three separate directions. She hoped they knew to come back to her if they found anything since she didn't have any eyebright on her to watch them from her current position. She still wasn't quite sure how to use her new pets to their full potential.

While Ares issued the order for his guards to scout the area a mile in every direction, Kyana and Haven scavenged the tents. Knowing they'd find no one here didn't stop her from moving from one canvas roof to the next.

They approached the largest tent, presumably Cronos's, and Kyana glanced back to find Ares with his head inside a tiny tent on the far side of the camp and his guards scouting the perimeter.

"I don't really want to go in this one," she admitted, her skin already chilled just from lingering outside it.

"Me either. Definitely his though. I can feel it," Haven said.

"How long since he was here?"

She shrugged. "Less than an hour, maybe? I think . . . he knew we were coming." She looked to Kyana with a worried expression. "What if he feels me the way I feel him? What if he knew to leave camp because he could feel me approach? Maybe I shouldn't have come . . ."

Taking Haven's hand, not to keep her by her side, but to offer support, Kyana gave a light squeeze. "We can't change everything we've done in the past couple months, Haven. But we can fix it now. If he was here . . . if he sensed you coming and left, then he's scared. And if he's scared, then he's not fully strong yet or he'd welcome the confrontation. But I need you to stop feeling so damned guilty all the time, all right? I need your head clear and in the game."

Haven looked away, but gave a slight nod before she pushed open the tent flaps and stepped inside. Kyana followed, hoping she'd finally gotten through to her.

She stood in the tent opening, drinking in everything before letting the flap close behind her. Silver candlesticks atop a golden chest, which, to her dismay, was completely empty. A large, circular mattress covered in silk blankets sat in the center of the floor, rumpled and recently used. Even the tent's canvas was overlaid in gold. Hundreds of gold and silver pillows lined the walls for sitting. A tall, ornate chair divided the room and sat in front of the opening. From here, Cronos could look out over his minions, watch the entire campsite, rule from his damned throne.

A breeze ruffled the canvas, stirring up the scents of the now-dead Mehmet and Azime, and there was even the faint hint that Henry had once stood in this pseudo-temple. They'd all stood right here.

She shivered.

With Haven at her side, she made her way across the room where a diamond-encrusted table had been erected. On top of it lay a silver-plated dagger with an onyx hilt.

Geoffrey's dagger.

"How the hell did he get this?" she asked, picking it up and rolling it against her palm.

"Is—is that Geoff's? The one he left in your room?"

Kyana nodded, her mouth suddenly dry as she came to the same conclusion Haven seemed to. Cronos had stolen it right from under her nose. But how?

She must have asked the question out loud because Haven pivoted and answered. "Conjuring spell. He's surrounded by Mages. He could have had one of them summon this object to them."

"Or someone stole it and gave it to him." Despite her reluctance to do so, her gaze swung toward Haven.

No. She couldn't have. *Wouldn't* have. Not when she was trying so hard to redeem herself. Would she? And if she *had* somehow gotten the dagger to Cronos, she deserved an Oscar for the look of horror on her face now.

"Did . . . anyone go in my room after you and Geoff left it?"

Haven shook her head, her green eyes wide and unblinking. "I didn't see anyone. Stop looking at me like that. It wasn't me!"

"Okay. I know. I'm sorry."

For now, Kyana would believe that Haven hadn't betrayed them all again. At least until there was reason to believe differently.

"So . . . a conjuring spell?"

The look of hurt didn't quite leave her face, but there was no anger there. Kyana almost wished there was.

"It's the only thing I can think of. A traitor would be plausible if the dagger hadn't been in Artemis's temple. No one is there without Lachesis or Jordan's consent. If someone on Olympus was untrue to the Order, they'd know immediately."

Swallowing the disgust and frustration in her throat, Kyana flung the weapon onto the bed.

"Don't," Haven protested, seizing the dagger

and slipping it into her belt. "Cronos has Mages working for him, and more than likely Witches as well. We don't want to give them an opportunity to fuck with something so personal to Geoff. They can do some really sick magic with something like that."

"Right." Kyana turned slowly on her heels, taking in the rest of the quarters. Against the far wall, a small rectangular frame on a table caught her attention. She made her way toward it and froze when she saw the faces staring up at her. One belonged to Mehmet.

And the other . . . belonged to her.

Chapter Nineteen

"Kyana? What is it?"

Kyana felt Haven move closer behind her, but couldn't answer as she stared down at the cracked glass over her young, human face. The portrait had been painted on her wedding day.

Eyes filled with hope stared back at her from her own face. The naïveté that came with being a young girl who prayed for a loving marriage with a husband she'd adored. A face unmarred by hands that would soon strike her down daily. Eyes not yet hardened with the realization that she was a possession to be abused and misused. Blood not yet tainted with the gift of life Henry had injected her with, the blood of a monster she'd been fighting ever since.

"Bastard." She snatched up the portrait and tossed the glass aside, shredding the canvas into a dozen pieces. As they fluttered to the ground, they drifted toward one another as though carried on an unseen breeze. When the tiny pieces wove themselves back together, she let out a soft whimper.

She felt Haven's arm drape around her shoulders and leaned in toward her friend.

"Leave it, Kyana," Haven whispered. "He knew you'd come. That was meant to hurt you. Don't let it."

But Kyana couldn't pull her gaze away from the portrait. She could burn it, but what good would that do? Whatever magic had been cast upon it would likely just put the flames out before any real damage could be done.

"He's a sadistic prick," she whispered. The more personal this became, the more likely she was to fly off the handle and lose her cool. The more likely it was that she'd make a mistake. Cronos knew that. He was banking on it.

"Yes, he is."

She forced half a smile. No one knew that better than Haven. "Shall we leave him a message of our own?"

Without waiting for Haven to answer, Kyana gathered the portrait in her fist and smoothed it out on the table again.

She slid Geoff's dagger from Haven's belt and stabbed the heart of the mattress, dragging the blade all the way down the center to release a plethora of feathers into the air. She continued to gut the fabric until her hands were too weary to do more damage. Then she turned to the smoldering fire in the center of the tent. She pulled a small stick from the pit, rubbed it in ashes, and returned to the bed. With a sick sense of pleasure, she scrawled the words *FUCK YOU* in soot across the tent fabric, creating a headboard of sorts, and stepped back to survey her handiwork.

The sky outside rumbled as a warm feeling coated her skin. She was going to enjoy coming face-to-face with him. She might not make it out of the fight alive, but when she was done with him, he was sure as hell going to know he'd been in the fight of his life.

"Does all this mean something?" Ares appeared beside them, looking over what Kyana had done. He pointed at the new headboard design. "Did you do that?"

Kyana dropped the sooty stick and shrugged. "Did your guys find anything?"

"No. Call back your dogs and see if they have anything interesting to show us."

She blew into her whistle twice, but kept it

firmly in her fist so the dogs wouldn't return home. There was no sign of them, but not too far away, a loud howl sounded followed by a chorus of barks. Together, Ares, Kyana, and Haven sprinted from the tent and toward the ruckus.

Behind the campsite, all three dogs were jumping in place, barking and dancing in happiness when they arrived. Kyana stared at the horror the dogs had brought them to. How could she not have smelled this? The vulgarity of the sight before her made her want to turn her gaze away.

Bodies lay side by side and feet to head for at least the length of half a football field. Naked and bloody. Some nearly devoured, others seemingly untouched. All human. Kyana was no stranger to death, but the dismembered gore surrounding her made her swallow to keep from retching. Haven, however, wasn't able to hold back. She leaned over and vomited, her body shaking. When she stood back up, her face was pale, and she lifted her blouse to cover her nose, leaving her watery eyes the only visible part of her face.

"You all right?" Kyana asked.

Haven shook her head, then nodded. Kyana took that to mean she wasn't sure if she was going to puke again, and took a cautious step away.

Ares pointed to something in the center of the field. "What is that?"

Trying to get a hold on her queasiness, Kyana strained to see what was written on the white flag. They had to walk over the bodies to get to it, but as they got closer, a whole different kind of sickness washed over her.

Painted on the sign in blood read the warning: FAILURE TO FOLLOW. LEARN.

"He's sending a message all right," Haven said, glancing at the bodies at her feet.

No matter how she tried not to, Kyana stared at them too. Some were indeed human and fresh, but others were far too rotted to have been killed recently.

"Yeah," Kyana agreed. "This is what happens to those who choose not to follow him when given the chance."

"Pure evil." Ares let out his breath in a hiss that brought a whole new worry to Kyana. If this was freaking him out, they were probably screwed. "How could he call himself a god and do *this*?"

She was surprised at the softness in his voice, at the compassion she heard there. She'd always thought of Ares as an emotionless prick. She was glad to think maybe she'd been wrong.

A deep growl turned all three heads toward a

small structure just inside the hiking trails to the east. As Kyana and Ares exchanged a quick look, more growls were followed by a sad, loud yelp, then a thud.

"Shit." Kyana shouldered her way between Ares and Haven and sprinted toward her pets.

"Kyana!" Ares called out. "My guards are out there. Do not be stu—"

But she was already gone, tearing across the park and skidding to a halt only when she saw one of her dogs, the smallest of the trio, lying on its side, panting in agony. She spun in a tight circle, but there was no sign of the guards or anyone who might have done this. Hell, she couldn't even see the other two dogs.

Ares approached, his silver gaze sweeping the park before resting on Kyana.

"Where are your guards?" she asked, bending to place a hand on the dog's belly, willing it to understand she'd make sure it was going to be okay.

Haven stooped beside her. "I can help him. Go with Ares. Find who did this."

Kyana would have done exactly that, but there wasn't a single scent on the wind to give her any clue where the hell to look.

"They've got Mages or Witches with them," she muttered, breathing a little easier as Haven worked her magic on the dog. "They've got to be using Scent Removing Charms."

She could read Ares's expression well. He wasn't keen on leaving Haven alone and unsupervised. But this wasn't exactly the time to remind him that the bigger threat was Cronos. He'd have to figure that out for himself.

The sound of footsteps coming from behind spun her around. There was no one there, but they didn't quiet, sounding as though a group of something was fleeing in the opposite direction. Kyana didn't wait for Ares. She took off after the sound, desperate to hold on to it in case it disappeared like the scents.

She felt Ares behind her as she sprinted, leaving Haven behind to tend the wounded pup. The sounds were moving as fast as she was, and she was forced to tap into her goddess speed and use the last of her store of ambrosia to keep from slowing down.

Something white caught her eye, sending her around a tree. She leaped, caught a branch in her hands, and swung out and over the fleeing object. She caught a robe in her hands, her body landing hard on top of her prey, and she found herself looking into the decomposed face of a grinning lunatic.

Dark, congealed blood glued the creature's mouth closed, and the foul odor emitting from him gagged Kyana, but she held on as he squirmed beneath her, reaching his gnarled fingers outward where she saw a twiglike wand just out of his reach. She grabbed it, snapped it in two, and rolled away from the Mage as he howled at the loss of his only weapon, just before she slammed her boot into his head, shattering his skull like a thin sheet of glass.

Magic killed Mages, but this one wasn't getting up again. It was too newly born to reconstruct itself, thank the gods.

She could hear Ares in a scuffle of his own and turned to find him warding off flashes of blue and red light with his sword, reflecting the spells back to their owners as a trio of Mages circled him. None looked smart enough to recognize they were up against gods. They looked hopeful that they might actually end the day alive. With any luck, one of them would. They needed information, even if it came from half-dead fuckers like these.

Behind Ares, a flash of green light soared at his head.

"Ares! Duck!" she screamed, rushing to his side.

He bent, and the green light shifted slightly to the right, smacking Kyana in the center of her chest. She was lifted off her feet and thrown into a tree where the green light slowly ate its way through her flesh to rest inside her.

Hands gripped her beneath her arms and dragged her backward. The agony of her insides being invaded nearly made her black out. It was Haven. She and the dogs left her there, running toward Ares as he played baseball with his sword and those damned lights.

Her legs and arms wouldn't obey as she ordered them to stand her up so she could defend herself. But no one was paying her any attention. They were all focused on Ares.

She tried to open her mouth to warn him again as branches overhead came to life and reached downward toward his head, but her mouth wouldn't work.

Haven saw them, reached up and snapped them from the tree before they could do any damage, then pulled something from around her neck and slid it over Ares as he drove his sword through a Mage's belly, lighting up its torso like a Christmas tree as magic wove itself from the sword to the wound.

The amulet around Ares's neck glowed, and

Haven's words were indecipherable as she spoke her spell.

"Get to Kyana!" she screamed. "They can't see you. Port her to safety now!"

Ares grabbed Haven by the arm, dragging her to Kyana's tree, and in the next instant, all three of them and the three dogs were soaring through the wormhole of Ares's port toward safety.

Kyana closed her eyes and hoped she'd survive to land on the other side.

Chapter Twenty

Ryker felt Kyana's return to Olympus while in the middle of a meeting with his guards—and knew immediately something was wrong. Without explanation, he ported to her temple, his racing heart having nothing to do with the magic required to do so.

"Where is she?" he demanded the minute his feet touched marble.

Artemis stood before him, her face pale as she pointed toward Kyana's rooms. "The Healers are tending her."

"What the hell happened?" Though he desperately wanted to know the answer, he didn't linger to hear it. Instead, he sprinted to her rooms behind the stairs and flung open the doors.

Kyana glanced up at him from where she lay on the sofa in her sitting room, pale and drenched with sweat. She tried to sit, but he was kneeling at her side in an instant pressing her back into the sofa.

He smoothed her damp hair from her face. At the sight of the blood staining her vest, his heart constricted. So much blood. "What the hell happened?"

"I'm all right," she said. "Just hurts like a bitch."

He looked up to find Haven perched on the windowsill chewing on her lip. "Start talking."

"Mages," she said. "They managed to get in a good hit before we took them down. A paralyzing spell of some sort that incapacitated her for a while, but it won't last. She's already coming around."

He placed a hand to Kyana's brow, which she immediately shook off, but not before he felt the cool clamminess of her skin. "Where the hell is Ares? He was supposed to make sure you were kept safe."

"He did. He's one kick-ass god," Kyana muttered. "Remind me not to piss him off anymore." She slipped her hand in his and tried once again to sit up despite the protests of the Healer tending her. "He needed tending too, Ryker. He didn't abandon me and we're all fine, so stop scowling."

"You don't look fine," he grumbled. "You're bleeding. A lot."

"I'm a goddess," she said, smiling. "I'll heal."

He eased beside her on the sofa and took her in his arms, making her half sit on his lap. "I'll send the Nymphs for food. Ambrosia will speed things up."

The Healer sighed and gave up trying to clean the wound he hadn't yet seen. "She's clearly not going to let me finish here. I'll see to it she gets ambrosia."

When the door shut behind her, Kyana sighed and closed her eyes. "I'm exhausted. Haven, tell him what we found."

"We found Cronos's camp. He left some nice . . . gifts there for us. Knew we were coming. One of which was Geoffrey's dagger," Haven said.

"The one he left in here? That would take some powerful magic to call it off of Olympus."

Haven nodded. "Yeah, apparently some of the Novi he's raised are pretty damned powerful." She stood and started for the door. "You'll stay and take care of her?" she asked Ryker. "I need food of my own. Think Artie will mind?"

Kyana shook her head. "Help yourself. She won't care."

"I hope Ares doesn't show up and throw a fit," he said. "She doesn't look up to a fight with him."

Kyana gave a slight smile. "He won't. Haven

could have run back there. She didn't. She saved our asses instead. I think Ares will lay off her a bit now."

She lay back and closed her eyes. "Look in my boot? I put Geoff's dagger in there. He'll want it back pronto."

"I'll make sure he gets it." Ryker leaned over and carefully unzipped her boot, pulling it from her foot with care, unsure what parts of her body had been injured. He turned it upside down. Nothing. He tried the other boot and got the same result. "It's not here."

Kyana sat up. "What . . . oh shit. Geoff is going to kill me."

He watched her frantically jiggle the boot for a moment, her expression worried.

"I think I lost it in the fight."

"It's all right. I'll get him a new one."

"He loved that dagger. A tracker's weapons are very personal."

"He's not a tracker anymore, Ky. He'll deal."

And if he lashed out at Kyana for this, Ryker would make him deal. Period.

The pain began to ease that evening and she found herself alone, waiting for Ryker to be done with his meeting with Atropos, who'd summoned him shortly before she'd finally fallen asleep. Kyana contemplated seeking him out instead. But as she swung her feet out of her bed and onto the floor, the jarring motion made her ribs burn all over again, and the thought of riding a bouncy chariot down the mountain was about as appealing as letting someone kick her in the teeth.

Instead, she hobbled her way across the temple, ignoring the Nymphs lying about and the sentinels standing guard at every door. What was keeping Ryker?

She was tired of thinking. All she wanted was to feel strong again, and maybe find something to help her forget this horrible day and grant her the ability to have dreamless, peaceful rest so she'd be alert for the meeting to come tomorrow. She sighed and entered the dining hall.

"You are hungry, Mistress?" A Nymph stretched out before the fire stood the instant Kyana stepped into the hall.

Kyana eased into a chair beside the fire and contemplated the beautiful creature. She *was* starving . . .

"Yes," she said. "And thirsty. Fruit and something strong to drink, please."

"Of course."

The Nymph bowed and disappeared in a glittery spiral of green lights, reappearing a few heartbeats later. She had to be at least six feet, seven inches tall, and towered so high over Kyana's chair, looking up at her caused Kyana's neck to cramp.

She placed a platter of strawberries and kiwis, pineapples and some fruits Kyana didn't recognize in the center of the table, then produced a porcelain jug and proceeded to fill a goblet with a deep golden liquid.

"What is this?" she asked the Nymph.

"Dionysus's special harvest of wine. You did ask for a strong drink?"

Kyana nodded and took a tentative sip. Yes, this was far better than the alcohol-free cider she was usually served on Olympus.

"You're wounded and exhausted," a voice said from the doorway. "You think becoming drunk is wise?"

She had to peer through the shadows of the dim room to see Ares scowling at her from the other side.

"I can hold my liquor."

He gave a short bark of laughter, then strode into the room, lifted the pitcher, and sniffed. "You must not have imbibed since becoming a goddess." He pointed to the pitcher. "That wine will muddle your mind."

"Let's hope so," she said, her fatigue seeping through her bloodstream to penetrate her marrow. "What do you want, Ares?"

She took a deep swallow of the wine. Because she wanted it, she told herself, and not to prove to Ares that she could.

The room was getting warmer. Kyana felt flushed and reached for the tray of fruit, too late realizing that Ares was right. She shouldn't have had the wine. She'd seen Ryker drunk once, and he'd been really freaking plastered.

From one shot of Jack Daniel's.

"What do you *want*, Ares?" she repeated.

As he made his way closer to the fire, she was better able to see his face. He looked as tired as she felt, and a momentary wash of pity for him softened her defenses. After all, she was pretty sure he'd saved her ass at least once today. She supposed he deserved a little civility in return. A little compassion, even.

She knew the burden of responsibility. Had lived with more than her fair share the last few months. But for what was coming, the responsibility was not truly hers. It was Ares's. The God of War would be charged with keeping the residents and defenders of Olympus alive. If they won, it would be his name called out among the cheers. But if they lost, his name in history would be forever tainted—*if* there were any survivors to remember it at all.

"I was hoping to find my son here," he said.

"He's not." She bit into a pineapple and sucked the juice. "Atropos asked to see him over an hour ago."

"Ah. That explains why he wasn't at his temple either." Without invitation he sat across from her and plucked a bunch of grapes from the tray of fruit.

"Please," she said sarcastically. "Join me."

"Any idea what she wanted him for?"

"Nope." But she wished she did. Atropos was the Fate of death, or at least she had been before her Chosen had been found. Whatever Atropos wanted with Ryker couldn't be good news, which was just lovely. All they needed was more to stress about.

Ares picked a grape from its stem with a delicate touch that surprised Kyana. Such a big brute of a man, best known for how well he killed.

"We have a lot in common, Ares," she said, pushing Atropos to the back of her mind.

His blond brow rose. "Do we?"

She nodded and took another tentative sip of wine. "We are both revered and loathed for what we're best at."

He leaned his elbows on the table and popped the grape into his mouth. "There is more we have in common, but you're too fool to admit it."

He had something he wanted to say, which made Kyana highly uncomfortable.

"Oh?"

He chewed, watching her as firelight danced across the table, warming her wine-flushed skin. "I do believe we both love my son very much, but we are both too stubborn to make certain he knows it."

Chapter Twenty-one

Kyana sucked in a breath, feeling as though Ares had just punched her in the stomach. "You're an ass."

He smiled, and she decided she liked his smile quite a lot. When it was genuine, it met his eyes, and the gray depths twinkled with merriment and lent a softness to his features that reminded her of Ryker.

"Am I? Are you saying you *don't* love my son?"

Her stomach clenched again, but this time it felt as though a net of butterflies had been torn and the creatures were fluttering about her belly.

"He's all right," she said. "Do you? Love him, I mean. Your history together would suggest otherwise."

"Ah. Averting my question by firing your own at me. My relationship with Ryker isn't nearly as interesting as yours so let's return to that, shall we?"

Her mouth was too dry. She sucked on a chunk of pineapple in hopes of moistening her tongue. It didn't work.

"I'm not playing tit for tat with you, Ares."

"No, that's our game."

Kyana looked up to find Ryker striding inside. He swung his cloak off his shoulders and passed it to the Nymph at the door. "Impromptu meeting?"

Ares reached across the table and took her goblet, drank a deep sip, and returned it to her.

It was Kyana's turn to raise her brow at him. "Thought you didn't drink."

Ares cleared his throat as Ryker took the seat beside Kyana. "I think I'm due."

"So?" Ryker asked, stretching his arm out to let it fall around Kyana's shoulders. He turned to Kyana, his expression one of worry. "How are you feeling?"

"Better," she lied. Her wound wasn't hurting so badly at the moment, but Ares's topic of choice was making her stomach cramp.

"Good." He looked to Ares. "Why are you here so late?"

When Ares didn't answer, Kyana cleared her

throat. "He was looking for you. What did Atropos want?"

His gaze shifted back and forth between his two audience members. "Some of her souls are missing now too."

Kyana blinked. "What? Why would Cronos raise anyone who hasn't been sent to Tartarus? They'd be less likely to join him."

"There are more important things to concern us now than the whys of it all," Ares said. His words were beginning to slur and Kyana regretted requesting the wine. If Ares pricked Ryker's temper sober, she could only imagine how ugly things could get when he was drunk.

Ryker took the pitcher of wine and held it up so the Nymph could take it. "I don't think it's wise to be drinking."

Before the Nymph could disappear with the spirits, however, Ares stopped her by grabbing her arm. "Leave it." His stony expression fixated on Ryker. "You might want a cup yourself before we're done here."

Watching her with a scrutiny that made her shift in her chair, Ares rubbed his chin. "I see no reason to stop our conversation just because Ryker is here. It has to do with him."

Ares waved his hand in dismissal at the

Nymph and set the pitcher back down in the center of the table. "We have tough days before us. One night of indulging ourselves might be in order."

Kyana scowled. He'd as much as told her she was foolish for drinking when he'd arrived. Ares was even more responsible and duty-bound than Ryker, and that was saying a lot. What was he up to?

She was suddenly overcome with trepidation that whatever was on his mind would get spoken, regardless of the regrets they might bring in the morning.

"Ares, maybe you shouldn't—"

"I'll do what I damned well please." He leaned back, his eyes so like Ryker's in the way they could pin her wherever she stood or sat. Powerful eyes. "Soon we will either be victorious in ridding ourselves of Cronos, or we will all be dead. I think the time for truths left unspoken is over."

"Ares—"

He waved off her second attempt at a warning. "Whatever you're doing to or have done to my son will cease at once."

Not at all sure what Ares meant, she looked to Ryker. "Have I *done* something to you?"

Ryker's expression was just as puzzled as Kyana knew her own was. "I don't know. Have you?"

"I don't think so."

"He isn't as focused as he should be," Ares continued. "Without focus, he'll be a, what do they call it? A sitting duck when Cronos arrives. I don't like seeing my son so distraught."

Kyana snorted. "Distraught? You make him sound like a weepy woman."

"My son does not weep. But he has taken up moping and staring out his temple window toward yours when he should be concentrating on strategies and preparations."

"I'm sitting right here," Ryker grumbled. "And my relationship with Ky is none of your business. I've been your lackey for centuries, Ares. Don't need you running my life anymore."

Being alone was looking appealing again. Kyana sighed. "So, what?" she asked. "You want me to leave him alone so he can focus?"

"Precisely."

Suddenly, the last thing she wanted was food. She pushed the platter closer to Ares before leaning back in her chair. "You're really protective for a guy who's never acted like a father."

"All right." Ryker stood and took Kyana's hand to help her to her feet. "We're done here."

But Ares didn't seem to hear him. Angry lines furrowed his brow as he scowled up at Kyana. "Who are you to judge me as a father?"

"Who are you to tell Ryker who he can and can't be with?"

She felt Ryker tense beside her. The last thing she wanted to do was stir up another fight between them. "Never mind. We're supposed to be fighting Cronos. Not each other."

His bronzed complexion paled and his eyes turned near black as they shifted toward his son. "Why stop now? I said I had truths to tell and I mean to speak them."

"I'm not having this conversation. Ky, I'll be in your rooms."

Kyana grabbed his hand, keeping him from storming out. Getting it all out in the open might do them both good, and if it was under the guise of wine, so much the better.

"Sit," she said. "Drink the wine, and you two have it out right here and now. Ares is right. We're about to go to war. You might never get this chance to have your questions answered again."

He jerked his hand free. "I don't need my questions answered. What good would come from finding out why he raped my mother? It only matters that he *did*."

"Go or stay." Ares stood, looking formidable in his stark white tunic and bloodred cape, his sword glimmering in the firelight as it clinked against the table. "But before you walk away from me, I will say this: I have enjoyed many perks of my godhood, Ryker. But never have I taken a woman to my bed who didn't beg to be there."

Kyana wasn't surprised. She'd had trouble believing Ares to be a rapist since Ryker had confessed that bit of his past in their game of tit for tat several weeks ago. He was nothing like Zeus, who played human women like a game of checkers.

To her surprise, Ryker sat back down, his face red and his fists clenched. "You're a liar."

Ares shook his head, the pained expression on his face pulling at Kyana's heart, though her loyalty and concern here fell fully with Ryker. What if this didn't turn out well? Was he going to blame her for not allowing him to walk away?

Well, so what if he did? It was unhealthy to live under a roof made of lies. He might be angry with her, but at least he'd know more about himself. "Go on, Ares."

"It is long past time that I stop protecting false memories of your mother. You are no longer a child to be coddled and she . . ." Ares shook himself. "Have you not ever questioned your eyes?

How they shift to red when you're angered? Or how that shift gave you the power of telekinesis? Have you ever seen mine do such a thing?"

Ryker wanted nothing more than to stand back up and walk the hell out of the hall, but he couldn't make his legs obey. Beside him, Kyana was eerily silent, a witness to what was to come. He wasn't sure if that made him more comfortable or less as he considered Ares's question.

Of course he'd thought about his eyes. The strange way they shifted colors when his ire had been pricked. So what? They didn't mean anything. All demigods were different. He'd just always assumed they'd come from his mixed heritage.

"You're saying I got my eyes from my mother?" he asked, struggling to remember the color of her eyes. He couldn't. There were many other things he remembered about her in great detail, but not her damned eyes.

Ares nodded. "She wasn't human, Ryker."

"Fuck you." He felt Kyana's hand squeeze his, but it did nothing to calm him. That he was half human was the only part of his bloodline he was proud of.

"She was a Mage with powers I'm ashamed to say intoxicated me. It is her blood that gives you the power to move things with your mind. It made you the most powerful soldier in my ranks, fighting without ever having to lift a hand."

Ryker's hands were trembling. Kyana reached around him, filled a goblet with wine, and pressed it into his hands. He took it and without thinking, downed the whole cup.

When he was done, he slammed the goblet on the table. "You're a lying bastard."

"Believe what you will, but it is the truth. And while I am spewing truths that should have been spoken long before this night, I did not claim you because of your powers as I know you believe. I claimed you because I needed to, as much as you needed me to. She wasn't kind to you, Ryker. And she did everything in her power to keep me from you."

Ryker's brain latched on to the words coming out of Ares's mouth and the memories they'd triggered. He'd been ten when Ares had come for him. It had been winter and the third day in a row that he'd spent locked inside his mother's herb closet, the scent of leaves and poultices gagging him as he'd stuck his nose to the cracks in the wood in an effort to breathe.

He could have gotten out, but doing so would have earned him even more of his mother's wrath, so he'd stayed, stilling his mind against breaking open the doors.

It wasn't until he'd been moments from blacking out from lack of air that he'd given in and used his mind to set himself free. She'd come home to find him sprawled on the floor, covered in his own filth, and had proceeded to beat him until he couldn't walk.

She would have killed him if Ares hadn't shown up to take him away, and as hard as it had been to leave with the man Ryker had believed had raped his mother, it had been a relief to watch her grow smaller as they'd disappeared.

"I'm sorry," Ares said. "I never wanted you to hate her, Ryker. I was hoping you'd forget all she'd done."

He nearly had, or the bad parts anyway. But now, as his mind wandered back over those first ten years, he could see her green eyes turn to red, swirl each time she lifted her hand to him and screamed at him for destroying her life.

"Why?" he heard himself whisper. "Why did she hate me so much if I wasn't a child born of rape?"

Ares closed his eyes, his chest rising as he drank in a deep breath of air. "She seduced me. Gods save me, I was weak to it. She thought that begetting me a son would give her a powerful place among the gods. When she was told after your birth that she could not accompany you to Olympus, she went mad. I thought if I left you with her, it would lessen her hurt. I was wrong, and you paid the price for it. I can never tell you how sorry that has made me."

Somehow, by the blessings of the gods, Ryker managed to find his feet. His head was spinning from the wine and from everything Ares had told him. He didn't want to believe a word of it, but he knew if he didn't, he'd be a fool. It all made sense to him now. His mother's hatred and abuse.

"Ten years," he said, moving away from the table, finally breaking his hold on Kyana's hand. "Why did you wait so long to come for me if you knew what she was doing to me?"

Ares swallowed, and for an instant, Ryker thought he saw his eyes turn glassy. "When your mother learned she'd never be allowed on Olympus, she disappeared. The magic she possessed was very powerful. I'd never seen you, but you are a part of me and I loved you because of it, not because of what you were, but because of *who* you were. It took me ten years to find a way to break through her spells. The instant I did, I brought you home."

Ryker stood frozen for a long moment before finally giving Ares one curt nod of understanding. Something had shifted between them tonight and a burden had been lifted off Ryker's shoulders that he hadn't known he'd been carrying all these years.

Unable to speak, he turned and left the room, realizing that for the first time in his life, he'd finally heard someone tell him he loved him.

Chapter Twenty-two

"Still awake?" Kyana muttered beside Ryker, curling against his side, her warm breath coating his neck.

"It's not as if he's spent the last centuries being father of the year," he murmured, not caring that he was forcing her into the middle of a conversation he'd been having quietly with himself. "He never even *tried* to make me like him."

"You heard what he said. He was protecting your memories of your mother." She sat and twisted to look down at him, her mouth stretching open in an enormous yawn as the sheet fell away from her breasts, finally giving him something to divert his thoughts. "I think he trained you to become his general and that was his declaration of love. I'm only sorry the real words took so long to be said."

He reached out and rubbed his thumb over her exposed nipple. "It should have been you."

Leaning into his hands, Kyana gave a soft moan. He had been in too foul a mood to make love to her when they'd gone to bed, and she'd been too tired from her injury. Now, however, it was all Ryker could think about.

"What should have been me?"

He kissed the dark peaks before tilting her head down and placing a soft kiss on her lips. "Ares told me he loved me tonight. Real or not, it was the first time I've ever heard those words. They should have come from you."

She pulled away, suddenly rigid. "You think I love you."

He nodded.

Kyana sighed and gave her head a light shake. "Ares wanted you to know how he felt in case he doesn't make it through this war alive. I believe he wanted to wait until you accepted him. He ran out of time."

"We're all running out of time," he muttered, slipping his fingers through her hair.

"Yeah, well, I don't plan on dying. No need for any huge declarations from me."

He smiled, taking no offense. "I know you love me whether you want to say it or not. I can say it enough for both of us." Ryker leaned down and pressed his mouth to hers. "I love you, Ky."

Kyana chewed her bottom lip and watched Ryker watch her. "Thanks. I think."

He grinned, flashing his dimples and making her all dizzy and hot in one crazy instant. "You're welcome."

He trailed his lips down her neck and she turned her body, shimmying along the mattress until she sat facing him so she could wrap her legs around his waist. As she let him rain kisses along her shoulders and throat, she sighed and tried to find some small thing to give him in return.

"I don't want you to die" was all she was willing to concede.

"Why not?"

She leaned in enough to let the heat of her hover just above the bit of him growing hard against her thighs. Her whole body was far too warm, but as much as she didn't want to have this conversation, she wasn't going to run from it. While she couldn't give him exactly what he wanted, she had to give him *something*. Ares had taught her a lesson tonight—that the threat looming over all of them was too real to allow so many loose ends to be left untied.

But how much was she willing to give Ryker right now?

"I don't want Geoff or Haven or Silas to die either. I'm not wanting to commit my life to any of them, but it doesn't mean I don't care."

"You already have." His smirk irritated the shit out of her.

"Excuse me?"

"You've already dedicated your life to them because you love them. You'd lay down your life for any of them and nearly have because you . . . Love. Them."

Kyana swallowed. "So?"

"So . . . you've already risked your life for me once." He slid his hand beneath the sheets, his thumb caressing the sensitive skin below her hip, just inches from where she really wished he'd play. That part of her was aching, burning for just one brush from him. Anything. "I think you'd take a bullet for me because you . . . Love. Me. Too."

It was all she could do to remain focused on the conversation and not impale herself upon him right then and there. He looked so damned sexy and sure of himself she wanted to eat him alive.

"I'd take a bullet for you because a bullet wouldn't kill me."

"You'd bathe in pure undiluted ambrosia for me, then." He slipped his finger inside her and she cried out before she could mute herself, her body folding against him.

"No," she whispered, raising her hips slightly to give him better access.

"Yes." His thumb flicked her clit and she bucked, her whole body seizing as it broke into a buffet of tingles and gooseflesh. "And since you can't say the words, you're going to show me. Now."

He dipped his head and caught her nipple in his mouth, stealing her words and her breath in one suckle.

"Ryker!" But her protest sounded weak, even to Kyana.

With a moan, she pressed her hands to his shoulders and pushed away, leaning backward so she could see him more fully and watch what he was doing to her body.

His broad shoulders and well-toned arms looked all the more muscular as he worked his hands between them, penetrating her with first one, then two fingers while she watched. He slid them back out, covered with her slick need, and Kyana thought she might pass out.

The mere sight of him, naked and powerful,

dried her mouth and dampened her thighs. Broad chest and narrow waist, all kissed by the sun. The fine trail of golden hair that slinked its way from his navel to his groin, where it encircled the part of him that pulsed for her now.

Strong thighs, dusted with small blond curls, pressed against the inside of her smooth ones. He was hard, she was hot. They were ready.

Using his shoulders, she pulled herself to her knees and pushed him backward. She straddled him, buried her face in his neck as she suckled his ear.

Could she do this? Having sex with Ryker was no problem. But could she do what he'd suggested she might and show him all she felt for him right now? Tenderness wasn't exactly her specialty, and while she wasn't ready to confess her love for him, she did truly want to show him that she cared deeply for him, that she was on the verge of something more than that.

This time, it couldn't be a screw. A good lay. This time, she had to make love to him.

Closing her eyes, she forced her heart to slow and her body to calm. Her need for him was going to drive her mad, but she had to keep control. Had to take this slow and fill every second with a realness she hadn't given him before.

She trailed her lips down his neck, her stomach in knots. What if she was no good at this? What if she didn't know how to communicate with her body any better than she did with her words?

Ryker could feel Kyana's tension grow by the second. He didn't know what was bothering her so much, but if he didn't make her relax, she was going to bolt. He could feel it in her tense muscles, in the stiff legs that now straddled him.

He found her mouth and kissed her as gently as he could, which was no easy feat since all he wanted to do was devour her. Slowly, blessedly, she relaxed the tiniest fraction and opened her mouth to him. Her tongue was warm and slick, her breath sweet. The long curls that tumbled across his face and chest were like silk, and as he ran his fingers through them, he paused long enough to cup her face.

Gently, he slid his arm behind her to cradle her and slowly lowered her onto her back. The moment he took over, he could feel the tension in her drain.

"You all right?" he asked, dipping his head to suckle her breast as she arched toward him.

"Mm hmm."

He lifted her leg, settling it atop his shoulder, and turned his kisses to her calf. As he inched lower and lower toward her thighs, Kyana's breathing became erratic.

She lifted her hips off the bed toward his seeking mouth and he granted her wish, tasting her, licking her, making her ready for him.

He wasn't going to fulfill her, though. When she came, he wanted to be inside her, wanted to feel her tighten around him and call out his name. Instead, he lapped until her breath became soft hiccups, then trailed his tongue to her navel, then breasts, then neck.

He'd be willing to bet that the word *love* hadn't been any more in Kyana's lifetime than it had been in his. It was going to be up to him to teach her what it meant and how to say it.

"I love you," he whispered into her ear, nudging her thighs apart and placing the tip of him against the center of her. "I love you, Kyana." He pressed slightly, the head of his dick pushing her open as she moaned against his throat and nipped at his Adam's apple. He slid inside, pulled out again. Repeated the whole process until his body trembled with the need to go faster, deeper. "I love you, Kyana."

Her nails raked his ass as she lifted herself toward him and wrapped her legs around his hips. He drove into her, whispering his mantra into her ear with each penetration as he felt her body tighten a bit more with each plunge.

Kyana kept her face turned into Ryker's neck and dug her fingers more deeply into his flesh with each word he muttered. With every confession of love, another hot tear broke free to streak her cheeks. With every movement of his hips, her body ascended into another realm. Her emotions and her physical being were at war with each other. Her heart wanted to beg for him to stop but her desire for him wouldn't dare tell him to.

Please shut up. Shut up shut up!

But as he said those damned words again, her heart silently begged him to keep going. Something inside her was breaking. Crumbling. Dissolving. With each quiet tear, a fear escaped and she was able to breathe more deeply. Her body was spiraling out of control and she clung to Ryker, thrusting against him, loving the way shivers rose upon her skin each time he moaned her name.

He forced her to look at him, rubbing his thumb along her face to wipe away tears he would never dare mention, then kissed her as her body sprinted for release.

"I love you, Kyana," he said again, and she lost it.

Her body came off the bed as her climax stole her breath. She bit into Ryker's shoulder to keep from screaming the angry words that were on her lips.

I love you too, damn it! I fucking love you too!

Chapter Twenty-three

Kyana had been so close to telling Ryker what she might be feeling for him and was still quite unsettled that the notion had come to her at all. Love Ryker? Did she truly? Or had it merely been her desire for him and the tenderness of the moment that had prodded those thoughts? She certainly didn't want to confess something as major as love only to discover later that it had been false. The last thing she wanted was to be the cause of more heartbreak for—

"Ryker!"

Ares's booming voice shook Kyana's temple, delivering the blessed interruption to her thoughts she'd needed. She tried to pry herself out of Ryker's hold, afraid Ares would barge in and catch them like this. But Ryker held her tight, pulling her so she was forced to lie pressed against his chest.

"He's had enough of my evening," he said, nuzzling her neck. "He can wait."

The bellow sounded again. Closer this time.

"With what's going on, we can't ignore him."

With a heavy sigh, Ryker released her and Kyana stood on shaky legs to redress herself in an apricot chiton. She'd just finished magically applying golden sandals to her feet when the doors to her private sitting room burst open.

"Have you lost your bloody mind?" Geoffrey's voice boomed from the other room. "First time I've closed my eyes in days and you storm through shouting about like a lunatic!"

A half second later, her bedroom door burst open and Ares charged inside, bloodred cape billowing behind him.

Still naked, Ryker unashamedly stood and zapped his clothing back into place before turning to face his father.

"This is not your temple, Ares," he barked.

Ares's gaze was hard, and the tenseness in his stance set Kyana at unease. "Has something happened?"

"I've already sent word to everyone. The council is meeting *now*."

"What's going on?" Kyana's heart raced. If Ares was worried enough to move the council meeting up several hours, something big must have happened since he'd left her temple.

Fingering the hilt of the sword on his hip, Ares backed out of the room slowly. "Ready yourselves," he said. "Cronos is making his way here even as we speak."

Whispered discussions reverberated throughout Ryker's council room as Kyana, Haven, Geoffrey, and Ryker made their appearance. They'd wasted no time in rushing back to Ryker and Zeus's temple, Ares's words leaving no room for talk among themselves. But if what the god had said was true, everything they'd been afraid of was about to come down upon their heads. Some in this room—if not all—were going to lose their lives today, and that thought alone kept Kyana somber and quiet as she took her seat between Ryker and Geoffrey at the long table.

Ares was already addressing the council, already being questioned by each and every deity who stepped into the room.

"Please," he said, raising his hands in an effort to quiet the hall. "I'll try to answer all your questions, but for now, just know that my informant has assured me that Cronos is indeed marching in our direction as we speak. He's found a way to breach the portals to Below, and from there to here, Beyond."

"Who is this informant? To know such things, he'd have to be close to Cronos! How can we trust such a person?"

The disembodied voice seemed to have hit the proverbial nail on the head with his question. Everyone shut up to hear the response.

"You can trust him because I say so!" Ares roared. His patience had obviously been pushed to the limit, his cheeks red, the veins in his neck bulging and purple. Then he pointed to the guards at the door and nodded. "Bring him in."

The large doors of the throne room burst open and an eerie hush fell over the room. As one, the gods and goddesses stepped back like the parting of the seas, offering those at the council table a clear view of their intruder.

All thoughts of impending doom evaporated as Kyana found herself staring into Henry's eyes.

She tried to stand and failed. Instead, she gripped the edge of the table so tightly, her knuckles cracked under the pressure.

Her Sire stepped completely into the room.

"Dark Breed!" someone screamed, quickly followed by "The attack has begun!"

It seemed to Kyana as if everyone regained his

senses at once and turned on Henry. The air crackled with electricity as weapons were unsheathed and Henry was encircled.

"Don't let them hurt him," she breathed, looking to Ryker.

But before either of them could move to protect him, Henry held out his arms and spun in a slow circle. "Do you not wish to hear what I have to say?"

These people wanted to kill him. Wanted him to pay for all those marching toward them now. Yet there wasn't so much as a flicker of concern in his eyes. Was he counting on Ares to protect him now? Didn't he know how much Ares had always loathed him?

It was madness.

"Step away," Ryker said, addressing the crowd. "Let him speak."

Henry stopped at the raised dais and looked at Ryker. "Ares speaks the truth. War *is* heading your way."

"We're aware of that." Though his voice was calm, the stiffness in Ryker's body suggested he was anything but. "But which side of it are you on?"

Ares moved to stand beside Henry. His gaze on Ryker, he said, "He is on mine. On ours."

Certain she was as white as the marble table-top, Kyana was only able to emit a hoarse croak.

"What's going on, Ares?" Geoffrey demanded.

"Henry is the one who informed me of Cronos's approach."

As he folded his arms over his chest, Zeus's ice blue eyes narrowed with suspicion. "And you believed him?"

"I did—and do." Ares didn't back down from the scrutiny of his peers. He gestured to Henry. "He has been working to defy Cronos since he was raised from his grave. I believe that proves his allegiance, and for it, he has mine."

"He is a Dark Breed," someone seethed from near the door.

Kyana shook off her shock as anger revitalized her. "So was I," she said. "As was Geoffrey. This man is my Sire and you will treat him with respect unless given reason to do otherwise."

"Thank you, daughter," Henry said, turning his back to her and facing the crowd. "But the only thing these people need to hear today is my advice to pull every member of the Order you can reach here to Olympus, because this is where Cronos means to have his battle."

From the corner of her eye, she saw Zeus twitch beside Ryker. He obviously had something he

Chosen 267

wanted to say and was finding it difficult to leave the podium to Ryker. He caught her staring, and his jaw tensed as the soft skin beneath his eye twitched with annoyance.

"You have something you wish to say, Zeus?" she asked.

The old god stood and rested his weight against the table, his white robes blending in with the marble all around him. "Why, in our names, should we call every member of the Order here to Olympus and leave the rest of the world unprotected on the word of a Dark Breed? Or perhaps that is the goal here? To leave another place weakened based on a false threat to our mountain? Please, Dark Breed. Give us one good reason why we would heed any warning you might deliver."

"Because," Ares said, motioning for Henry to follow him onto the dais where they could peer over the crowd. "Henry speaks for me now. He is my Chosen. *He* is the new God of War."

Chapter Twenty-four

Grateful to have been already seated, Kyana struggled to still the tremors in her legs and arms. She could see Ryker arguing with his father. Ares wasn't fazed by the anger coming off his son like a sunburst. The ringing in her ears prevented her from hearing what they were saying, but truly, she wasn't sure she even cared.

Henry.

The God of War.

"You never wanted to join the Order before," she accused, not sure why she was having such a difficult time wrapping her mind around this announcement.

Henry met her gaze. "I never had anything to offer before."

"And you do now?"

"Yes."

He said nothing more, instead turning his attention to the argument still raging between Ryker and his father. Kyana took a deep breath, ready to stop their bickering. There were more important matters right now. Their power struggle was going to have to wait.

". . . can't just lay something like this on her," Ryker was saying. "You could have warned her. You had plenty of time."

"He only decided to take my offer this morning. I wasn't going to say anything until I knew for sure. Your opinions wouldn't have swayed me—it is my right to pick *my* Chosen, so I found someone worthy of the title I wanted to bestow *on you*."

"Worthy?" Kyana asked, a sudden rush of anger curbing her desire to shut them up. "You sent tracers out to kill him. You ordered his death!"

"He broke our laws when he turned you and had to be punished for his actions."

"So what has changed?" Ryker asked. "He is still now what you hated then."

"Henry was raised by Cronos and was able to not only go against the dark god, but to survive it. That takes enormous strength and proved to me that he's capable of containing the power that comes with being the next God of War. More than that . . ." Ares looked at Kyana. "His loyalty to *you* makes him loyal to the Order of Ancients."

"He was *always* loyal to the Order, damn it. He may not have been an official member but . . ." Kyana said. "You were just too—"

"Pigheaded to notice. Yes, I am aware of my faults, Kyana. It seems getting to know other *Dark Breeds* has swayed my opinion that they aren't all the same."

Was that a compliment? Kyana snapped her mouth closed, unsure how to respond.

"You do realize I'm standing right here?" Henry said, his jaw giving a slight tic.

"They tend to do that," Haven muttered.

Kyana shot her a warning look, and Haven rolled her eyes and settled herself on the bench.

"He's a Novus—not a mere Dark Breed," Ryker hissed. "One of *Cronos's* risen. We don't know that he can be trusted."

"Yes," Kyana said, smiling up at Ares. "We do." Turning to Ryker, she placed her palm flat against his chest. "I trust him with my life."

"We can discuss trust later," Henry said, pulling all eyes back to him as he held out his hand to Kyana.

He looked so much stronger than the last time she'd seen him. The blackness was completely gone from his eyes, the mossy green shade she'd once known so well returned.

Her Sire. The God of War.

Holy shit in a Tartarus toilet.

Standing on shaking legs, she took Henry's hand.

"Cronos's numbers are no longer a problem." Henry gestured for the door. "I wish to show you something."

He led Kyana out of Ryker's temple. The bright moon lit up the acres surrounding the mountain and a soft gasp escaped her as she peered into the night. There wasn't a single square of grass left to be seen, every inch occupied by a body shining in silver armor and red cloaks. From the steps of the temple, a sea of heads disappeared over the horizon, their numbers far too many to count.

"What the hell?" She stepped farther outside to stand between Ryker and Henry. "Who are they?"

"My army," Henry said. "In service to the Order of Ancients."

As Kyana took in the decrepit faces staring back at her, her heart hammered with understanding. Cronos hadn't been the only one digging up graves. No, the souls missing from Atropos's domain had been raised by Henry. Brought here by Henry.

Past presidents, generals, czars, and soldiers. Farmers, peasants, wives, and fathers. They were massive in numbers and ready to fight for good, just as they had in life.

"How did you do this?" Kyana whispered in awe.

"The same way Cronos did."

"You extracted some kind of vow in order to get them to serve you?"

"No, they've joined the Order of their own free will. When I explained why I'd interrupted their sleep, they willingly offered their skills."

"Holy hell," a voice said behind Kyana. She looked over her shoulder to find Silas staring bug-eyed at the scene in front of him. "We just might stand a chance."

Kyana squeezed Henry's hand, a bubble of joy building until she couldn't contain it. Henry was a Chosen. She wouldn't have to lose him to some Vampyre hunter again. Nor would she have to fear the Order demanding he be hunted down and killed. He would be here with her, on Olympus, for all eternity.

For the first time since Haven raised Cronos, Kyana felt a wave of relief and hope that they might not be doomed after all.

She looked up to find Ryker grinning from ear to ear.

"Henry," he said, "welcome to Olympus."

Ryker led the group to the armory beneath his temple and opened the massive wall of weapons for the others to see.

"Take what you're able to use, but no more. I want to make sure everyone is armed," he said, passing two of his guards a box of little blue spheres that lit up the otherwise dark armory.

Beside him, Kyana stared up at the wall, her face haloed in the blue light making her look positively stunning. The frustration and determination on her face made him smile. Gods, he fell harder for her every damned day. He'd never in his life met anyone with as much tenacity as she, and could think of no one he'd rather have fighting at his side, or anyone he wanted to protect from the fight so badly.

"What are those?" she asked, running her finger over one of the spheres.

"Ambrosia casings." He lifted an orb and twisted it, and the blue light immediately turned bright pink as he revealed the thick liquid inside. "For weapon coating."

She raised a black eyebrow at him and pursed her lips together. "Is that smart? Having weapons on the field coated with this stuff? If one of Cronos's lackeys gets their hands on it, they have a good chance of using it on one of us."

"They'll keep one coated weapon on them at all times in case they have the opportunity to use it on Cronos. But for the majority of the fight, they'll be using silver-plated arms."

He slipped his hand to her lower back and ushered her from the room to give others the space to grab the weapons of their choice. Upstairs, they found Ares and Artemis sitting at the long table below the dais where his throne sat.

Feeling the light touch of fingers on his arm, he turned to see Kyana looking worriedly up at him. "What can I do?"

Kyana never waited for instruction or asked permission for anything. That she was doing so now suggested she was far more afraid than she'd ever admit.

If he didn't know that she was completely focused, his own ass would be in serious trouble, because there was no way in hell he'd be able to keep his head in the game.

He wanted badly to pull her into his arms and reassure her that everything was going to be all right, but he couldn't. He didn't know what was going to happen to all of them, and wouldn't lie to her.

"Just survive, Ky. That's all I need you to do."

Chapter Twenty-five

Ares led them around the back of the temple toward a small army of sentinels guarding the path to the Oracles' caves. Kyana noticed his fingers tap, tap, tapping the hilt of his sword as though he was eager to get the fight started, eager to kill those threatening his world.

She knew exactly how he felt.

She was looking forward to driving her dagger through as many Novi as possible. Never in her life had she been afraid of a fight, but if she was honest with herself, she'd have to admit that the thought of coming face-to-face with Cronos today had put her stomach in knots. With any luck, none of the major deities would ever step foot on the main battlefield today. Hopefully, Henry's front line would keep the bastards back.

But she couldn't count on that. She was going

to get her hands dirty today, just like everyone else, and as she took in the faces around her—Geoffrey, Ryker, Henry, Haven, Silas, Artemis, Ares—she wondered what the night would bring. How many of them would be injured, or worse?

Would Kyana even be alive to find out?

She shuddered, jolting out of her thoughts as Henry's voice broke through her suddenly fogged head.

"We have to prepare a strategy now," he was saying.

"We need to gather everyone here and shut down the portals," Kyana insisted. "If there's no portal, there can't be an attack."

Ares cast her a scathing look that suggested he thought she might be a little stupid. "We gather all the Order here and shut down the portal . . . that's your solution? And when are we to leave Olympus again? Never? The moment that portal works again, the threat returns as well."

"I don't hear any of you coming up with anything better," she replied, fighting the urge to poke out his eyes just to squash the glare aimed at her.

"We don't have time for this," Geoffrey said, stepping between them. "We don't know how long we have—"

"Less than an hour," Henry interrupted, his gaze fixated on the moon. "They plan to attack well before sunrise so the Dark Breeds who are vulnerable needn't fear sunlight."

A pity. If the bastards waited just a few more hours, they could just wait and let the sun do all the dirty work.

Taking a deep breath, Kyana exhaled all her doubts and insecurities. "Have we left enough Order members Above to protect the humans from those not planning to attack Olympus?"

"Our priorities must be *here*, Kyana," Henry said, taking her hand and giving it a gentle squeeze. "Humans have become accustomed to boarding up tightly until sunrise. We'll have to trust the majority will remain safe."

A quick, burning wash of regret rocketed through her blood. She'd spent the last eighty years protecting humans from her own kind, without caring about their fate one way or another. Now, however, she'd seen the humans' ability to rebuild a world devastated by monsters, and she admired their resolve. It bothered her to no end that, should the gods fail here today, all their efforts would be for nothing.

But this was war. People were going to die. *Gods* were going to die. She just had to hope the numbers wouldn't be as staggering as when Tartarus had opened.

"Where do we even begin?" she whispered.

"All the gods are to stay inside Zeus's temple," Ares said.

"Yeah, that's not going to happen," Kyana mumbled. She glanced up, certain she'd see the same "yeah right" feeling in her gut expressed on Geoff and Ryker's faces.

It wasn't there.

In fact, both gods seemed to be in complete agreement with Ares's command.

"You can't be serious," she said. "You expect to go to war and keep me locked inside the temple unable to do anything to help?"

"It is not your job to dictate policy on strategies," Ares said. "Let me do my duties without interference."

She held his stare, refusing to back down. "Fine, then. What about logic? If every god, goddess, and Chosen is in one place, it's like mass suicide. If the temple is breached, everyone will die."

"Then what do you suggest?" Geoffrey asked.

"Separate everyone by their status. Those who have their Chosen already. Those who've completed their siphoning. Those who are most vulnerable because they have neither." She looked at Ryker. "Those are the ones who need to be as far away from your temple as possible, as well as the Chosen who've been found in the last couple of days. Without proper training, they're sitting ducks."

"She's right." Ryker pointed to the Oracle caves above the temple. "The same goes for the Oracles. Cronos can't get his hands on them. If we don't win this, they must be as far away from him as possible."

Henry waved his hand as though swatting a gnat. "It will be taken care of."

Somewhat relieved that the weakest would be taken to safety, Kyana turned her gaze toward the distant, unseen portal at the foot of the mountain. Something in the air changed. The very wind hummed with an electrical charge.

"Take your place atop the turrets, Kyana," Ryker said, moving to follow Geoff and the others inside. He'd felt it too. The worried gleam in his eyes said as much.

Kyana trailed behind, knowing it was going to eat at Ryker and Geoffrey to stay out of the fray. But as much as it pained her to admit it, Ares was right. It would take the force of the gods to bring down Cronos, and they couldn't risk losing any of their number on the buffoons who'd come through first.

"How will they get through the portal?" she asked, the loud bang of the temple doors shutting and being magically sealed making her jump.

"The only way they can pass through is if Cronos gave each of them some of his own blood." Ryker turned and pulled her into his arms, placing a kiss on the crown of her head. "When you get up there, Ky, stay the hell down. Do you hear me?"

She nodded, wishing he could go with her so she could keep an eye on him. But his place was here, and hers was with the tracers and Artemis, who were already in position to fire.

She watched him move through the crowd, awed by how confident and strong he seemed. His broad shoulders held no slouch, his lean, solid physique a totem for the weight they'd all placed on him. She wanted to go to him, to slide her arms around his waist and make him hold her. She wanted to crawl into bed with him and stay there forever.

Forever?

Gods save her, *yes. Forever.*

If there was ever a time to tell Ryker she loved him, it was now.

But she couldn't do it. If she said the words, it would be like admitting they were going to die.

And that was one fear Kyana would never allow herself to voice. Not when it was too easy for it to come true.

Chapter Twenty-six

From Kyana's position atop the turrets of Ryker's temple, the shimmering portal at the foot of the mountain was no more than a glowy, white-hot speck in the predusk gray. A bright, shimmering light, much like a halo, fell from the darkening skies as the constellations, led by Kheiron, Orion, and Leo, were led out onto the battlefield. Tracers and sentinels who'd been trained with bows and arrows filled each marble slit on the tower, poised and ready to fire on Kyana's command the moment the sun set and the portal was breached.

In the center of the turret, the Nymphs encircled Artemis, each so skilled with a bow they didn't need the raised aid of the ledge. Four cauldron-sized bowls of ambrosia lay spread at their feet, dangerously close to both Artie and Kyana, ready to be used the moment Cronos showed his evil face.

She squinted trying to see through the growing shadows, waiting, hoping, fearing Cronos. The last remnants of pinks and yellows lowered over the horizon. Down. Down. Down. "Focus on the portal! We need to prevent as many as we can from gaining ground."

The glowy white hot speck of a portal shattered like a thousand shards of glass. The sun vanished and the gray dusk cloaked the grounds as a dozen black shadows stepped through the shimmering gates.

She clenched her conduit in one hand, took the bow Artemis handed her in the other, and whispered, *"Separo."*

Three arrows appeared in her hand, and as Artemis shoved the quiver onto Kyana's back, they disappeared and filled it. She was ready.

The slow swoosh of stretched bowstrings were the only sounds Kyana allowed herself to hear as archers all around her took their positions. She removed the conduit from her neck. Wrapping the chain around her wrist three times, she struggled with the closure.

"Here, let me." Artemis stepped back out of her circle of Nymphs and secured the clasp. She turned the chain so the tiny arrow rested against the inside of Kyana's wrist, falling into her palm when she lowered her arm.

Artemis's stare was penetrating, and the slight glimmer of fear Kyana glimpsed within her amber eyes increased her own growing anxiety. "Lead us with courage, but don't be stupid. Our duty is to protect you. We're prepared to lay down our lives so that you may live on."

Kyana resisted the urge to hug her, though at the moment, it was all she wanted to do. "Stay at my side. If the temple is breached, I'll get us out of here."

"There's nowhere to run, Kyana." Artemis turned to watch the portal.

Unease boiled Kyana's stomach. "Don't *you* do anything stupid. My siphoning is done. Your life is just as important— What the hell is that?"

A blinding white light coming from the direction of the portal lit up the night. She eased the bow off her shoulder and slotted three arrows, her gaze fixated on the pulsating light.

A heartbeat later, the light was shattered as dozens of bodies rushed through the portal and onto the temple grounds. More followed, and more, making the gardens and pathways move with enough shadows that they appeared to be alive.

"Fire!" she screamed, terrified now that there were far too many of them getting through for her archers to handle. She aimed, letting loose her arrows directly at the portal's heart. Hundreds of arrows shot off around her and over her head, filling the night with the chilling sound of high-pitched whistles.

Kyana took aim, targeting a Hatchling that broke through the crowd to soar toward the towers. She fired, her arrow striking the beast between the eyes, sending it tumbling back to earth with a ground-trembling thud, and the arrow reappeared in her quiver. She fired again, this time striking the heart of a Leech, mindlessly wandering away from the crowd to feed on the fallen. It fell beside its dinner, its skull crushed by the weight of her blow.

They managed to clear a five-foot radius in front of the portal, but the front lines had no time to drop their guard as another wave of Cronos's army surged through. Screams sliced through the darkness, both, Kyana knew, from the invaders as well as from members of the Order.

From this distance, it was hard to make out which of the fallen bodies belonged to which side. The faint sound of metal cutting against metal as sentinels wielded their swords clashed with the sporadic orchestra of magic sparking and hissing.

It was a horrific sound track playing for them tonight.

The tables in the throne room sat empty of bodies. Every soul in the room stood pressed to the windows, watching the fight outside. Ryker watched as the night lit up with fiery arrows. His gaze kept sweeping from the rush of horrors penetrating the portal and to the turrets in hopes of glimpsing Kyana.

She never appeared.

He'd have to trust that she was all right, otherwise, he was going to go out of his ever-loving mind.

He turned from the window, sick of watching one body after the other fall . . . Dark Breed, sentinel, Witch, tracer. It was growing harder and harder to distinguish the bad from the good. All he knew was that the beings in this room needed to be guarded with every arm they had. They were putting their trust in a front line they couldn't even see anymore, and most of them were silent with worry.

Geoffrey, Silas, Zeus, and Hades huddled in the corner in whispered conversation. A trio of

Witches in charge of keeping the throne room sealed sat in silence by the door as they waited for their skills to be called upon again.

And from there, his gaze traveled to the chair by the window where Haven had been curled up. His chest tightened.

She was gone.

His gaze swept the sea of faces around him. She was nowhere to be found.

Though he feared what he might find, he turned back to the window and saw the wisp of blond hair disappear around the corner. She must have slipped out before the Witches had resealed the room.

He was going to have to order the barrier broken again and hope he could bring her back.

Chapter Twenty-seven

The whistle of arrows continued to fly, but Kyana could no longer tell if they were making a difference. Below them, the battlefield had become so chaotic that they might have slaughtered their own people if not for the magic placed upon their weapons.

Kneeling behind the wall, she removed the whistle from around her neck and gave it a quick blow. As the dogs bounded from their tiny home, she pulled the small pouch that contained vials of ambrosia-laced lemonade from the small slit in her chiton and dug around for the few leaves of eyebright she'd placed inside after she'd returned from Cronos's camp.

"Scout," she commanded, and slipped a leaf onto her tongue.

With three soft barks, the dogs turned and

leaped from the roof. Kyana reached out her hands to grab at them, her heart pounding at their suicidal jump, but when she reached the turret and peered over the edge, she saw them dashing gracefully between warring bodies, alive and unscathed.

"Artemis," she whispered, sliding to the cool floor as the eyebright began to work, "Take over."

She heard Artemis say something, but her words were already muffled and distant as Kyana's mind split into the three visions of the dogs separating, moving closer to the front lines as Kyana silently instructed them to. The bitch, healthy again from Haven's ministrations, kept low to the ground, lifting her head only when she was required to bound over a fallen body.

But the two boys weren't so cautious. As one pressed his hind legs to the ground and shot upward toward a Novus struggling with a Witch, Kyana watched the foulness of the Novus's throat being ripped from its body.

The pup's brother was just as brutal, taking out three Novi, Lychen by the looks of them, as he sped toward the back of the portal to the few sentinels who'd managed to push a wave of intruders off the temple grounds.

Kyana's stomach twisted as her vision switched

to focus on what the bitch showed her. It was like watching a horror movie. Thousands of bodies beating against one another in a struggle for survival. Skilled members of the Order holding their own, and fresher ones being torn apart by their unforgiving enemies.

She caught a glimpse of a familiar head of blond hair about two feet away from where the bitch lay pressed to the ground.

Haven.

What the hell was she doing out there? She was supposed to be glued to Geoffrey's side. Gods, he'd better not have left the temple too.

Her heart racing, Kyana's mind searched for potential ways to get to Haven—to watch her back. But there was nowhere to go from here except down, and she was pretty sure her landing wouldn't be as painless as the dogs' had been. Instead, she was forced to watch in helpless horror through the dog's eyes as Haven emitted a bright light from her body, sending four Novi back through the portal before spinning to take on three more.

She truly was good, kicking one, punching another, that aura around her keeping the beasts from piling on top of her.

But then the aura splintered, keeping her left

side protected and her right vulnerable. Kyana opened her mouth to scream a warning, but knew Haven would never hear her. As a Dark Mage approached Haven's weak side, Kyana willed the bitch to come out of hiding and attack. The dog wasted no time. She soared into the air, knocking the Mage to the ground as Haven turned to face her attacker.

Haven raised her arms, her mouth moving in an incantation Kyana couldn't hear over the bitch's growls. Before she could finish the spell she was weaving, another Mage appeared behind her, lifted his wand, and shot a bolt directly at Haven's back. She went down hard, the remaining aura shattering as she hit the dirt path beneath her.

Kyana watched in horror as the bolt that had struck Haven seeped back out of her body and slithered to the feet of its owner. With a flick of his wrist, the Mage jerked the wand toward the ground, and the light vanished into its tip.

Kyana gagged on fear. Haven wasn't moving. The Mage stepped over her prone body toward the bitch, ripped her from her foe, and tossed her beautiful golden body into a nearby tree. The loud yelp pierced Kyana's heart.

"Return," she whispered, both aloud and with her mind. "Come back!"

But at the same time, she feared their return, knowing it meant she'd no longer be able to watch Haven—to make certain she was alive.

"Bring her," she whispered. "Retrieve!"

She had no idea if either command would work, but when the dog clenched Haven's robe in her teeth and began to drag her back toward the temple steps and away from the screaming portal, Kyana allowed herself to exhale. Haven was still helpless, lying several dozen feet away from the temple, but surely someone could get to her now, could make sure she was all right—

A bright light filled the grounds below, just beyond the temple steps. Kyana's chest clenched again as the dogs showed her the image of Ryker marching down the steps, his staff lifted over his head as he shot off bolts of crisp energy, temporarily clearing the field around him. With each step he took, another bolt flew from the conduit, keeping him in its protective circle.

Closer to Haven.

He was going to save her!

She watched, her body filling with renewed hope as Ryker scooped Haven into his arms and disappeared back inside the temple.

If she hadn't loved him before, she certainly did now.

The effects of the eyebright began to fade, filling Kyana once again with a searing heat and a wave of nausea. As her eyesight became her own, she blinked to clear her vision and found the two boy pups panting at her feet.

The wounded bitch, however, took a few moments longer, appearing on the turret and collapsing in a heap just out of reach.

"Put them away and the magic of their containment will heal her," Artemis said. "It'll be slow, but it's all we can do right now."

Kyana obeyed, wishing she could do the same for Haven. Her throat raw with the need to scream, she blew into the whistle and set it on the ground. The dogs vanished within, and Kyana fumbled to her feet.

"Haven was hit by a spell," she said. "Ryker got her but I don't know if she's all right! I need to go see—"

"You won't!" Artemis's hand reached out to grab Kyana by the arm. "Could you see anyone else?"

Kyana closed her eyes and shook her head. "No one I recognized. The other gods are still inside the temple—I didn't see any out there."

"Thank Zeus."

The look of worry etched on Artemis's face

did nothing to ease Kyana's fears. Artie was worried about her family—her father, Zeus; her twin, Apollo. Everything and everyone she loved was right here on this mountain so close to the horrors coming at them.

Kyana knew how the older goddess felt. Everything *she* loved was here as well, and one of them was already injured or possibly worse.

Silas, Henry, Haven, Geoff, Ryker . . . all of them could die here today.

But not without a fight. Ryker's show of heroism with Haven reminded Kyana of a spell of her own. One she'd cast only once before, when she'd first fully turned into a goddess. If there was ever a time to try it again, it was now.

"Stay down," she said, regaining the ability to work her legs. She climbed the nearest turret to stand atop it. She might be a goddess, but that didn't mean she was invincible. If the fall didn't kill her, the Dark Breeds below would.

She closed her eyes, both to stop from looking down at the ant-sized people fighting below her, as well as to focus. She raised her arms to find her balance and dug so deeply within herself that she became dizzy. Not good so high up. But there it was. That lovely little tingling she'd experienced once before.

It wouldn't last long, but perhaps long enough to prevent any more enemies from crippling the Order until the current ones were dealt with. At least it was something.

Blocking out Artemis's screams for Kyana to get down, she lifted her arms until they burned with the heat trying to escape them, then thrust them before her, covering the night with a light layer of gold. The bubble crept from the front to the back of the battle, covering them all in a dome-like sphere of protection that no new enemies would be able to penetrate.

If she could hold them off for just a little while, the Order might be able to regain some ground before Cronos decided to show up—*if* he decided to show up.

Order members paused only a second to glance at the bubble encasing them, but they found their advantage when the Novi took a bit longer to drink it in. The sphere acted almost like a magnifying glass for Kyana, allowing her to see in more vivid detail as one Novus after another was downed by the men and women who were proving to be a source of pride for Olympus.

So much blood muddied the pristine grasses of the grounds that Novi and Order members alike slipped and slid their way toward one another. So many on both sides were now dead that half the battlefield lay empty of any moving bodies at all, and the few Novi still slipping through the portal desperately sought to find a way to penetrate the bubble.

Kyana could feel her strength weakening. Could feel the power slipping away from her as the protective barrier began to fade.

"Finish them!" she screamed, tense with trepidation.

Something in the air was changing, thickening. It was as though she could feel Cronos's approach with each passing moment.

The barrier shattered, raining golden dust upon the heads of the living, and the battle commenced with fervor.

Shaking, Kyana reached into her pouch and opened a vial of her lemonade ambrosia, downing it as she tried to catch her breath.

"Do you feel that?" she asked Artemis when she was finally able to work her tongue again.

"He's coming."

Kyana nodded, relieved she wasn't the only one feeling as though Cronos's approach was a tangible shroud.

She turned to the hooded archer posted behind

her. "The moment you see anything change, you yell for me, understand?"

The archer nodded, keeping his gaze on the grounds below. Kyana handed her vial to Artemis, letting her finish what little remained. The old goddess didn't have a real need for the magic anymore, but it certainly couldn't hurt.

Pressing her back to the wall, Artemis squeezed her eyes shut. "I can't watch anymore. I want this to be over before the people I love are harmed. Just . . . make it all stop."

"As you wish, *Goddess.*" The archer turned, and before Kyana realized what was happening, he thrust his arm around Artemis's neck, kicked over the silver tub of ambrosia, soaking Artemis in the deadly pink liquid. In one swift motion, he lifted her off the ground and threw her over the side of the turret.

Kyana's ribs slammed into the rough ledge, her arm flung out in a fruitless effort to save Artemis. But it was too late. The soft crash of Artemis's body on the grounds below was followed by a chorus of hungry wails from the Dark Breeds who discovered her.

Blinded by rage, Kyana threw herself toward the archer as he moved to grab her foot, likely wanting to deliver to her the same fate he'd delivered to her predecessor. She caught him around the middle, slamming him to the ground, but as her body fell toward him, he rolled out of range and was on his feet again. She swayed off balance as she attempted to steer her body away from the flowing ambrosia, giving the bastard the advantage.

He grabbed her by her hair and swung her around, dragging her toward the stairs. Kyana screamed for the guards, who all appeared too stunned by Artemis's death to remember that they were fighters assigned to the job of keeping Kyana alive. But at her scream, the dozens of men and women atop the turrets snapped out of their momentary paralysis and broke into action at once, lunging at Kyana's attacker—Artemis's murderer.

Keeping his hand tightly wound around Kyana's hair, he thrust his free arm upward, releasing a ray of electrified energy that lifted Kyana's saviors up and over the side of the turret. So many screams tore through the wind, and the next thing Kyana knew, she was alone with a madman.

It had all been so swift, so damned fast, that Kyana couldn't catch a coherent thought that might save her sorry ass.

Kyana kicked out but the hands holding her were too strong. Even with the ambrosia coursing through her veins, she couldn't break his hold around her neck. She twisted her wrist, desperately trying to swing her conduit back toward her fist where she could grip it for power, but the stubborn jewelry just flopped against her arm, useless.

She clawed at his face, and as he threw her onto her back, her spine colliding with the sharp edge of a step, she took his protective hood off with her scrambling hands and found herself once again looking into the face of Mehmet.

Chapter Twenty-eight

This time, seeing her twice-dead husband caused a strange sort of empowerment to override Kyana's numb panic. The need to avenge Artemis's death propelled her back to her feet. She'd faced the bastard twice now, and both times, he'd ended up dead. Confident this outcome would be the same, she lunged, curling her fingers into claws, determined to rip out his eyes and feed them to his asshole.

But as Kyana collided with him, Mehmet ripped his wand from his sleeve.

"Püskürtmek!"

Kyana flew backward, slamming into the wall and smashing the back of her skull against the stairs. Stars burst before her eyes, and before her vision could clear, Mehmet had her by the throat again.

"This time, *you* will die."

Her lungs burning, Kyana released an angry hiss. The image of his burning face the last time they'd met fed her courage and she lifted her hands, summoning the same strange energy she'd felt when she'd sent him through the brick wall. A light burst from her palm, pummeling him in the chest and lifting him off his feet. She thrust her hand forward, forcing his grip to slip from her throat, then sent him sailing over the side of the turret. Let him find the same fate he'd given to Artemis! Let him be torn to pieces by the beasts below!

But as his body hovered in the air and she prepared to release him to his fate, he grinned, snapped the tether, and *flew* right back over the ledge to land in front of her.

Mages couldn't fly. Kyana couldn't process what she'd just seen.

One stumbling footstep backward was all she could manage as Mehmet tossed her down the steps like a rag doll. She rolled to a stop, her head cracking into the iron banister. Too late, she saw the boot heading for her face. Pain exploded in her jaw. Blood filled her mouth and pooled from her hair to stream over her eyes and cheeks.

"Where's all your fight now, *hanim*?"

Her hands finally free, she gripped her conduit and tried to block out Mehmet's menacing stare to find her center, her strength. As he lifted his boot once again toward her face, she grabbed his leg and twisted, listening with pleasure as bones crackled and snapped and she knocked him to the floor. She was on top of him in a blink, pinning him to the marble steps.

"Don't you ever call me that again, *pislik*."

That was precisely what he was. Filth. An insignificant asshat who didn't own her anymore. Kyana reached deep inside, searching for the power to send Mehmet to his death for the third, and gods willing, final time.

"You waste your time." With almost no effort, he broke free of Kyana's weight and slithered to the bottom of the stairs like the snake he was. As he rose to his feet, he summoned his newfound magic to send her onto her back. "I am prepared for your tricks this time, Kyana."

She fought with everything she had, both as the Dark Breed she'd once been and the goddess she'd become. But nothing in her small arsenal could help her break the magical bond pinning her to the floor. The same magical bond that she'd used on him when she'd killed him for the second time only days ago.

The more she struggled, the tighter his hold on her became. She couldn't breathe, couldn't think, couldn't break free. He came at her, rushing the stairs as though riding the wind. As he reached for her throat, she gripped his arms, trying to shove him away. He didn't budge. The hall began to fade. Her vision clouded. Her muscles went numb from lack of oxygen. Her brain slowed, and her struggles finally stopped.

Kyana accepted death. She wouldn't give the bastard the satisfaction of seeing her fear this time.

As she gave in to the inevitable, the tingling began in her fingertips and slowly climbed up her arms. The conduit at her wrist pulsed. Heat pooled in her chest and exploded outward until her entire body danced with electricity.

Opening her eyes, she stared at the tiny arrow. The amber glowed bright orange, floating off her wrist like a snake charmer's cobra, the sharp, pointed tip dipping toward Mehmet's hand, calling her attention to a familiar ring that glowed with the same intensity as Kyana's conduit.

Cronos's ring.

Was that what was making him so much damned stronger than last time? Had Cronos given it to him just so Mehmet could be the one to send Kyana to her grave?

The power of her own conduit surfed her veins, and Mehmet's hold on her loosened. She seized his arms, running him backward into the wall, then concentrated on one word.

"Sino in nex."

Mehmet's pale arms grew yellow as the veins beneath the thin skin blackened, disease spreading through his body. The fine black lines chased one another up his arms, to his neck, covering his face. He gripped his throat, his eyes wide. His features shifted, morphed before returning to place.

The disease should have stopped his newly beating heart. That it hadn't was proof that Cronos's ring was giving him more power than he should rightfully possess.

"You bastard!" she screamed, pressing her foot to his belly as she gripped his finger, wrenching the offensive jewel from his hand as she sent him tumbling feet over head to land belly down at the foot of the stairs.

Satisfied that she'd stolen his source of strength, she took each stair toward him slowly, using each step to regain a fraction more of her strength and power so that when she finally reached him, she was nearly coming out of her skin with the energies resurfacing.

When he finally stood, his back to her, she froze in a moment of hesitation at the slight shake of his shoulders. He was laughing.

Laughing!

Seizing his arm, she spun him around, determined to give him his final death this time.

But it wasn't Mehmet glaring down at her now. It was Cronos.

Chapter Twenty-nine

The fight outside was becoming dangerously close to the temple. So close in fact that everyone inside the throne room now had his weapons out and at the ready.

Ryker fondled his conduit and stepped out of the crowd, tired of watching and standing still. He made his way to the corner of the room where Geoffrey sat holding Haven. She was finally coming to, whatever spell she'd been hit with wearing off.

"How is she?"

Geoff glanced up, readjusting Haven in his arms. "She'll be fine. You should have let me fetch her, though. You could have been killed."

"You're not immune to that threat either."

Geoff was too emotionally involved with Haven to have been rational enough to make sure he remained protected if he'd gone after her. He would have rushed to her, forgetting the need to protect who and what he was now. Gods knew, Ryker would have been as mindless had it been Kyana lying injured on the battlegrounds.

"Is she strong enough for you to leave her now?" Ryker asked. "I need you to gather yourself. The fight is being brought to us."

Geoff nodded, though he looked reluctant to let Haven go. He settled her in the corner, propping her so that she'd be upright as she became fully awake.

"I might be able to buy us some time. Can you get the Witches to unseal one of the windows?" Geoffrey asked.

"What do you have in mind?"

Geoffrey lifted the amulet from around his neck and palmed it. "Stand back, mate."

Ryker obeyed and watched black light flicker from the cracks in Geoff's fist and drop to the ground. The marble floor shook, cracked, and between the split stone, thick oillike ooze crept into the room and pooled around Geoff's feet.

"*Meus pets, ego liceor vos venire contra vestri vinco!*"

The ooze stretched and lengthened, taking the shape of three massive, red-eyed hellhounds and three dead, eyeless soldiers.

"My pets," Geoffrey said. "Open the window. Let them out and they'll cause enough diversion to give us a bit more time to ready ourselves for their attack."

More than a tad impressed, Ryker backed away, his gaze riveted on the waist-high dogs with six-inch fangs. He'd never seen Hades call forth anything like that, but then there'd never really been cause before.

"Unseal the eastern window," he instructed the trio of Witches watching from the opposite corner of the room. "One of you needs to be ready to seal it again the second I tell you."

"We can try. It takes time to regenerate that spell and you just had us unseal the room to save that Witch—"

"Just make it happen," Ryker snapped.

They nodded, the smallest among them stepping onto a table, readying herself to cast the sealing spell at Ryker's command. He motioned Geoffrey and his pets over. The instant the blue light around the windows vanished, Ryker threw it open and Geoffrey gave instructions to his minions. They leaped over the sill and into the night air outside, and as the window was resealed, the screams outside intensified.

Geoffrey's pets were doing their jobs.

"How long will they give us?" he asked Geoff.

"Thirty minutes. Maybe le—"

A scream split the air, turning all eyes toward the door. Ryker shoved his way through the crowd, his heart suddenly pounding.

"Kyana."

He glanced at Geoffrey, and together they sprinted toward the door leading to the stairs outside. Silas quickly joined them and Ryker glanced back at the Witches. "Unseal it! Now!"

"We can't!" the smallest girl wailed. "We have to wait for the residue of the last cast to fade. Ten minutes, tops!"

They didn't have ten minutes. Kyana screamed again and it sounded like she was halfway up the staircase, the noise muffled but noticeably above them and behind the door. He slammed his shoulder into the door, joined by Geoff and Silas, but no amount of pounding, pushing, or cursing had any effect on the magic.

Ryker ripped the staff from his side and snapped it to its full length. "Stand back!"

Geoff and Silas barely had time to dive out of the line of fire before Ryker shot an energy bolt at the door. Once. Twice. The third blast caused the mahogany to splinter. The fourth shattered the doors, leaving them hanging awkwardly on their hinges.

Shoving the heavy doors out of the way, Ryker led the way up the marble stairs to the turret chamber, his staff at the ready.

"Ky!" he bellowed as they rounded the corner leading to the towers. Kyana soared into view, landing at their feet with a bone-jarring thud. Dodging her fist as she blindly struck out at him, he lifted her off the ground and pinned her tightly to his side.

"This way," Geoff called, leading them into the nearest room.

Ryker locked his arms around Kyana and dragged her backward, his many questions forgotten beneath the frantic need to get her safely away from whatever had caused her panic.

"Seal it," he ordered Silas.

Silas shook his head. "I can't spellcraft. Haven still has my Witch blood."

"Shit." Ryker's gaze quickly took in the blood and bruises on Kyana's face and neck. "How many?"

She shook off his hands and tried to lunge for the door. "Let me go! I have to stop him before he can complete the spell."

It was Geoffrey who snatched her back. "Answer him, lass. How many made it inside the temple?"

Ancient words, in a rhythmic baritone, swelled

until they filled every corner of the small room they'd taken refuge in. They all looked to Silas, but the words weren't coming from him.

"What the hell is that?" he asked.

"It's Cronos!" Kyana bellowed. "He killed Artemis and he claims he can separate my soul from my body. He has something of mine . . . Ryker, we have to stop him!"

Ryker felt his blood drain from his face. He'd never seen such stark terror on Kyana's face before, and the sight of it now shook him to his core. He glanced over her head to Silas. "Can he do that?"

The ghostly pale complexion of the temporary Poseidon was answer enough. Ryker raced to the door, threw it open, and found himself staring at a mesmerizing display of lights. The entire turret chamber was ablaze with golds and greens, blues and reds, and in the center of them all stood a dark figure, hands thrust heavenward.

Determined to wrap his arms around the bastard's head and rip it off his neck, Ryker leaped through the air. But as he prepared to land upon Cronos's back, one of the red lights spiraled upward, then down to coil around Ryker's torso. It threw him up, his head cracking against the rafters before releasing him to fall in a painful heap at the feet of his companions.

"What did he take of yours? It would have to be really personal for him to do what you said," Silas asked as Kyana grabbed Ryker's arm and pulled him safely away from the lights that danced precariously close to his feet.

"I don't know."

The daze was finally wearing off Ryker as he pushed to his feet. Okay, good. Cronos hadn't shown her anything so maybe it was a bluff. Maybe he didn't have anything. Kyana was shaking, her body coated in a fine sheen of sweat.

"Damn it," Silas muttered. "Try your staff, Ryker. It's the most powerful of our conduits. If he really has something, he can do what he threatened. Break through his protection spell, now!"

Ryker seized the staff that had rolled to the other side of the room when he'd hit the ceiling. Kyana's body was in reactive mode, dancing around the lights in an effort to keep them from attacking her as they had him, but her gaze was frozen on Cronos's back. What the hell did he have of hers? Was he lying?

Something inside her told her Cronos wasn't the sort to bluff, but she couldn't think of anything she was missi—

"No. Oh gods, Ryker . . ." She reached for him, her gaze locked on the flicker of silver protruding from Cronos's long velvet coat. Silver that led to black and to silver again. A very familiar design. A very familiar weapon. But it didn't belong to her.

It belonged to Geoffrey.

It was his dagger. The one she'd found at Cronos's camp. The one he'd lost in her room that Cronos must have taken because he'd thought it belonged to *her*.

If Cronos was successful, she wasn't the one in danger.

"No!" She rushed to the lights as Cronos smiled down on her. She didn't need to hear him speak, she could read everything he was thinking in his sadistic smile. He was nearly finished, and she was about to die.

Only she wasn't.

The lights ripped at her skin, searing her like laser beams, but she pressed forward, ignoring Ryker's clawing hands as he tried to drag her back.

But it was too late. The lights began to evaporate. Cronos laughed. He pulled the dagger from his robes and thrust it into the lingering, brightest light.

There came a sickening thump, and a look of confusion washed over Cronos's face as his gaze fell to the floor behind her.

Kyana turned, her legs shaking, her heart splintering as she knew what she was going to find.

Behind her, Geoffrey lay facedown, his body badly broken into distorted angles. His dark eyes blank and unblinking. Kyana had never in her life felt more helpless than she did as she watched his soul tear away from his body and disappear into the night.

He was gone.

Chapter Thirty

Kyana felt herself being lifted. Felt herself being carried from the room in a blur of speed. She was vaguely aware that it was Ryker holding her, vaguely conscious of Cronos's howl of laughter as he realized he'd managed to kill one of his true targets by mistake.

Geoffrey.

Gone.

Violent sobs racked through her until she couldn't see through the tears. He'd been as much her brother as Haven was her sister and he was gone! How was Kyana going to tell Haven? What was she supposed to say? How were any of them ever going to be okay again when there'd never be that annoying Irish accent to taunt and tease them?

How was she ever going to erase the horrible image of his lifeless face and soulless eyes?

She shoved at Ryker's shoulder. "We can't leave him in there with that monster! I won't leave him alone in there!"

"He's gone, Ky," Ryker whispered. "He'd want you to be safe."

She clawed at his face, not caring that she drew blood, only relieved that her actions forced him to let her go. She raced back to the stairs, half blind, near passing out. Silas barreled toward her, grabbed her by her arm, and dragged her back again, this time shoving her inside the throne room before she could register what had just happened.

"Leave him!" he hissed. "Cronos isn't done here, Kyana." He turned away from her, waited till Ryker was inside with them, then yelled to the Witches. "Seal the door!"

They tried but something seemed to be wrong with their spell casting. Kyana shoved Silas away, charged for the door again only to be caught around the waist by Ryker and thrown to the floor. He straddled her, forcing her to stay still.

"Haven!" he bellowed "Seal the door!"

Kyana exhaled, a bit of her madness vanishing as she saw Haven limping toward them. She was alive. She wasn't dead like Geoffrey.

Oh gods, she's going to find out that Geoffrey's dead and it's my fault!

"What about Geoff? We have to wait for him."

"Seal the damned door!" Ryker and Silas ordered.

Cronos had stolen the dagger in an attempt to kill *her*. Geoffrey hadn't even seen it coming.

Oh gods, oh gods, oh gods. No no no no no!

When Haven finished her spell and the door was sealed, the final barrier between Kyana and Geoffrey's lifeless body, she looked at Kyana, a million questions filling Haven's eyes.

Instead of asking them, she looked at Kyana's hand, and as Ryker eased off Kyana and helped her to her feet, Haven narrowed her gaze.

"You got his ring?" Then her eyes opened wider. "Kyana! You have his ring!"

Kyana couldn't speak. She rolled her head so she could stare at the ring lying in her open palm. Somehow, she'd managed to hold on to it throughout her struggle with Cronos. She let it slide from her hand to the floor, watched it roll out of reach.

Who the fuck cared about the damned ring? Geoffrey was dead!

Ryker slid his arms around her shoulder, trying to pull her toward him in a comforting embrace, but she shoved him away, unwilling to be consoled.

Haven's mouth fell open and her gaze searched Ryker in question, but Kyana saw him give a slight shake of his head, effectively shutting her up.

"What about the ring?" he asked, bending to scoop it up.

"If he doesn't have it, it means he's weakened," Haven said. "Since we do . . . it means we have a bit more power."

Zeus appeared over Ryker's shoulder. "She's right. We used the conduits to bind him when we exiled him all those years ago. They're the key to bringing him down."

"That ring is what kept his soul alive. It won't be easy, but with it we have the ability to kill him," Hades added.

What the hell was wrong with all of them? Why weren't any of them falling apart over Geoffrey's death the way she was? She felt as though she were losing all of her limbs, one by one, and there were Ryker and Haven—

Haven didn't know. She still didn't know! How was Kyana supposed to tell her . . .

She gripped Ryker's hand, wishing he could read her mind and speak the words she suddenly couldn't lend voice to.

Cronos's ring lay pressed between their hands and she pulled free, clasping it, shoving it onto her finger. If it really was one of the keys to bringing Cronos down, she wasn't letting go of it. She was going to make him pay for what he'd taken from her today.

Silas and Ryker had Eyes of Power of their own. This one . . . this ring of dark magic . . . it was her Eye of Power now, and it was going to be what she used to send Cronos to his final grave.

Focus. She just had to focus.

"Kyana? Where's Geoffrey?" Haven asked again. "We need his conduit to complete the quartet."

Kyana shook her head, unable to find the words to tell Haven about Geoff.

"I'll go," Ryker whispered. "I'll bring it back."

No way in hell. She couldn't lose him too.

"We both go. I have something Cronos wants. I can make sure you have time to grab the amulet."

"Not if you're not completely in the game, Ky. If you lose it because you're blinded by hurt—"

"I've never been calmer in my life." And to her surprise, it was the truth. The numbness, the pain . . . it all evaporated as she imagined herself killing Cronos. As she imagined them winning.

Geoffrey would be properly mourned. Would be missed more than he could ever have known.

But first, he would be avenged.

Geoffrey and Artemis. They were her primary motivation now.

That and keeping the other pieces of her family from harm.

"Let's go," she said, pushing to her feet and taking Ryker's hand. "Someone unseal the door. It's time to finish this."

Chapter Thirty-one

As she ran up the massive staircase leading to the turrets with Ryker beside her, the ring on her finger pulsed with heat the nearer they came to its master. She was counting on him wanting it back badly enough to focus on her and let Ryker get to the amulet. If he didn't, they could be in for a world of hurt.

Her fears were realized when they turned the final corner and came face to chest with Cronos, casually making his way down each step as though he had all the time in the world to finish off his prey and no worries that he'd fail.

Asshat.

Ryker pulled her back a step with him. She felt him tense as though tempted to run at Cronos, but she held on to him and slowly raised her hand so

Cronos could see the glint of the bloodred sickle in the center of the onyx ring.

"You want it back, Cronos?" she sneered, easing Ryker toward the stone wall of the staircase. "You'll have to come and get it."

She wiggled her fingers at him, praying he'd take the bait.

"What do you want more, Cronos?" Kyana taunted. "The ring or Ryker?"

Cronos tsked. "So very angry for such a beauty. Are you certain I can't persuade you to spread your legs and let me crawl inside you—show you what real power feels like? What a real *man* feels like? A splendid wife you'd make me, Kyana Aslan."

She shuddered, her fist clenched so tightly, tiny pricks of blood trailed down her fingers as her nails pierced her palms.

"I *know* what a real man feels like, Cronos. And for the first time in my life, I can face dying with the knowledge that I have loved one. That makes me stronger than you. That makes me fearless. So come to me, *big boy*, and let me show you what a real *woman* can do to a puppy like you."

Ryker tensed beside her and she knew he understood what her confession meant. She didn't have time for sweet nothings and whispered promises, but if she was going to die, she'd go knowing Ryker had heard her admit that she'd loved him. She wished he'd stop staring at her, though. She was trying to concentrate on not fainting.

She could feel him rethinking their plan. Not breaking eye contact with Cronos, she hissed, "Go!"

He hesitated, then bounded up the stairs, sweeping low beneath Cronos's arms, and barely missed being snatched by clawing fingers.

"I have what you want, not him," she yelled, pulling his attention back to her and away from Ryker, giving him a chance to disappear up the remaining stairs.

Cronos lunged at her, the weight of his body sending her somersaulting down the steps, injuring the few remaining bits of her that weren't already bruised and battered. She held on tight, hoping she'd land on top of him. That he hadn't used magic gave her hope. It meant he was saving his juice and wouldn't toss it around willy-nilly.

She held on to that thought as the last stone step smashed into her spine and her head smacked marble. Stars burst behind her shut eyes. The seconds it took to clear her vision gave Cronos the advantage. He pinned her with one hand, reaching for his ring with the other. She tucked it beneath her body and bucked, nearly successful in throwing him off her.

He grabbed her by the throat and lifted them both to their feet. She hung in the air like a sock puppet, feet dangling and helpless. Then he smashed her against the wall and pinned her arm out, clutching her fist until she was sure every bone in her fingers would snap like twigs.

Then she was falling, once again colliding with the marble floor. Cronos's body flew over her head, followed by Ryker, who landed with a graceful roll back to his feet. He tossed something at her, and she was barely able to make her hands work to catch it.

It was Geoff's amulet.

She clutched it to her chest, stumbling to her feet.

"Get back to the others!" Ryker yelled, sliding his staff from his belt as he tried to pull her behind him.

"Your staff alone isn't powerful enough to kill him, Ryker!" He was like a damned cockroach. The two of them alone didn't stand a chance.

Cronos rose to his feet, his body humming with an energy that terrified her. He was about to release a burst of power that they might not survive.

As Cronos took a step toward her, she took a

step back, forcing Ryker to do the same. If they could just lure him downstairs, there was an entire temple full of gods and goddesses who could help subdue him. One step, two steps. *Come on, bastard, follow me.*

When he was nearly on top of them, she spun, grabbed Ryker's hand, and fled for the throne room, screaming for Haven to unseal the door for them. She could hear Cronos's steady footsteps behind her as she and Ryker skidded into the crowded room.

"Get your trident out!" she screamed, spotting Silas near the door. "We have the amulet—"

"Where's Geoffrey?" Haven demanded, looking truly worried.

Kyana had to look away.

"If all four of the Eyes of Power are discharged at once," Haven continued, "it will destroy him."

Behind them, the door was being locked once again. But it wouldn't keep Cronos out for long. He was definitely powerful enough to break whatever seal the Witches were casting.

"How will we keep him off us long enough to pull this off?" Silas asked, his face suddenly pale as he fumbled with the trident in his hands.

"A shield. It is all we can do." Zeus stepped forward, looking decades older than he had days ago. "All of our powers stem from Cronos and will be virtually ineffective against him. All we can do is try to keep the Eyes contained and try to keep most of us alive in the process."

"Geoffrey isn't here! Does no one realize that? We need him to wield that amulet!"

Kyana shook her head, terrified of the moment this battle was over and she'd be forced to tell Haven the truth. "I can do it. I used Ryker's staff once."

"You'd just received Artemis's powers, Ky," Ryker said. "Unique circumstance. The owner of the conduit is the only one who can bring out its full power."

She felt a firm grip take hold of her biceps and turned to find Haven staring wide-eyed at her. "Find Geoffrey. Let him do it. He's the only one—"

"If we need Geoffrey," Kyana said, her hands suddenly trembling, "then I'll *be* Geoffrey." She spun on heel and pointed to the locked wall on the other side of the room. "Open the siphoning wall."

No one said anything for a moment, then realization seemed to fill the room at once.

"No, Ky," Ryker said, stepping in front of her. "It's not possible."

Kyana turned her gaze to Zeus. "Is it?"

With a regretful look to Ryker, he nodded. "It is possible to wield the power for a short time. But Kyana, it *will* kill you."

Since meeting Geoffrey more than a century ago and Haven and Ryker a decade ago, she'd known in her heart she would have died for any of them. Now it was time to prove it.

"Open the damned wall."

Chapter Thirty-two

Every deity in the room seemed to understand that Kyana's idea was the only one on hand and that, despite the outcome, it needed to be done. Every deity, that was, except Ryker. It took Zeus and Ares taking Ryker's staff and physically restraining him to keep him from stopping Kyana as the sentinels disobeyed their god and opened the wall.

She gave him a look that she prayed conveyed her feelings, but she wouldn't apologize for doing what needed to be done.

"The powers of the Goddess of the Hunt are already fully siphoned," she reasoned aloud. "Another Chosen can take my place if this goes badly."

And judging by the pitying looks everyone was giving her now as she walked toward the wall, it probably would.

A sentinel handed her a rounded bottle that glowed with light blue liquid. "That his?"

He nodded.

"Kyana . . . you can't do this!" Ryker roared from behind her. "I will!"

"You have a power in you already that is far stronger than that of Artemis," Zeus said. "Kyana has a better chance of surviving than you."

"Then let me." Haven lightly touched Kyana's arm, turning her as she opened the bottle and smelled the contents. "I don't have a power in me. I can be a temporary Vessel for Geoffrey like Silas is for Poseidon."

She leaned in closely, her eyes damp and her cheeks ruddy. Kyana could tell she was trying not to break down and was thankful for it. Already, the pain in Ryker's cries of outrage was killing her.

"He's dead, isn't he?" Haven whispered. "That's why you won't answer me. Why you won't look at me. Geoffrey's gone."

Kyana began to shake her head, then gave one soft nod instead. "I'm so sorry, Haven."

Haven lifted her chin, and though her voice was steady, her tears fell freely now. "Then let me do this for him. Please."

Haven needed to avenge Geoffrey as much as Kyana. To have a part of him forever with her.

Who was she to deny her friend this? With a nod, she held out the vial.

"It would take more time than we have for someone without any godly blood to adjust to having the powers of a god in you," Zeus cut in, placing his hand around Kyana's, preventing Haven from taking the bottle. "Consuming all of a god's powers at once instead of letting them gradually infiltrate your system will make you useless."

But Kyana *had* a god's blood within her already. She could do this.

Before anyone else could prevent it, Kyana lifted the bottle and drank. Haven and Ryker begged for her stop, but it was too late. The liquid seared its way through her blood, sending her to her knees. She retched, heaved, nearly fainted as each and every vein in her body expanded to welcome the new cells.

"Open . . . the . . . door!" she roared, terrified that this change would kill her before she could take Cronos with her. "Now!"

She looked up to find Ryker staring down at her in horror. Then he leaped into action, obviously coming to the same fear-based conclusion she had—they had only a couple of minutes to do this right. They'd have to deal with the consequences later.

He and Silas lifted their conduits, aiming them at the door. Kyana slipped the amulet around one wrist and raised her ringed finger, positioning both conduits in front of her face. The ring might not be at full strength without its owner, but with the other three at full capacity, hopefully it would be enough.

The door burst open and Cronos flew through, hovering above them all as flashes of red lights seeped from his body, striking those around them.

Bodies fell beneath tables for protection as Silas was thrown through the entrance, his body colliding with Haven's as they crashed atop the long council table and slid to the other side. A moment later, Ryker backed toward Kyana, his staff raised in his fists.

"Evacuo," Zeus said. "Say it!"

Kyana craned her neck upward to see Cronos hanging from the ceiling by his feet, his arms stretched toward her as he soared downward, his hands groping for hers in his attempt to steal his ring back. She clutched her hands to her stomach and bent over her knees.

"Evacuo!" she shouted, though she knew it would do no good unless she could aim the damned conduits back at him.

But it was hard to concentrate when it felt as

though her body was being ripped apart from the inside out. Like her organs were on fire and her skin was busting open.

Pandemonium exploded all around her as she fought to keep the ring from him.

Hands ripped at her hair but Kyana didn't dare move, didn't dare look up. The shouted orders, the cries of pain, the bodies falling as the deadly red lights bounced around the room.

The weight on top of her doubled and she felt a struggle of bodies on top of her spine. She hunched deeper, pressing her forehead to the cold marble, the ring clenched so tightly, her fingers grew numb.

Something hot seared her cheek, making her eyes burn, but still, she couldn't bring herself to open them.

Then the weight was gone.

"Kyana! Move!"

Kyana didn't hesitate to obey Ryker's command. She fumbled to her feet and made a beeline to the other side of the room, leaping over bodies, too afraid to look down and see who they belonged to. Haven grabbed her arm and pulled her behind the table.

Kyana followed her gaze to the center of the room where Ryker and Cronos were going toe to toe. Ryker's staff burst with light, tossing Cronos off his feet. But Cronos didn't need a conduit to be deadly. He simply raised his arms and spread the bodies around him to give himself moving room as he confronted Ryker again.

"Silas! Ryker! The Eyes! Now!" Kyana shouted, desperate to get help for Ryker before Cronos could unleash the deadly intent that was flickering in his dark eyes. *"Evacuo!"*

Silas spoke the word as well, joined in by Ryker as Zeus maneuvered himself between their fight and took a blow to his gut that granted Ryker enough time to raise his staff and aim again. Kyana cupped the ring and amulet together and aimed as well, the word *evacuo* spilling from her lips over and over in high-pitched desperation.

As Cronos lunged for Ryker, a group of gods around him lifted their arms and a sphere of white light enveloped Ryker. Cronos stumbled, reaching for Ryker and hissing as his hand breached the shield and began to smoke.

Kyana found herself surrounded as well, and watched as Silas was adopted by his own protectors, their spheres coating them all in an aura of defense that angered Cronos as much as it seemed to burn him.

"Evacuo! Say it!" Zeus demanded again, his

own arms lifted as the leader of Ryker's group. "Do not break your focus until it works!"

In her haste to once again aim conduits in Cronos's direction, Kyana fumbled with the ring, catching it before it hit the ground. *"Evacuo!"*

"Evacuo!"

"Evacuo!"

Enraged, Cronos struck out, a blaze of yellow light catching Ares in the stomach and causing him to break his hold on Ryker's shield. If Cronos managed to take down everyone holding Ryker safe, Ryker would be left exposed before the Eyes could do their job.

The blazing red lights were beginning to fade. Cronos was weakening. And as soon as his powers were stripped, they could kill him.

Please, please, please.

Kyana didn't know how much longer she could hang on. She coughed, blood spewing from her mouth as she fought not to double over. Inside, her body was melting with the flames of Geoffrey's powers struggling with Artemis's. One of them was about to win, and in doing so, was going to kill her.

Her chest painfully tight, she held her arm steady, waiting for the power to stream from Cronos. Little slivers of black popped out from his

cloak like slugs, slithering toward the staff, the
ring, the amulet, and the trident. But not many.
Cronos was too strong for that to be all there was
to his power. And so she waited, watching as, one
by one, gods were taken from the fight.

Silas's shield flickered as his protectors went
down, one after another. Helios, Hera's Chosen,
and another Chosen Kyana didn't recognize were
sent to their knees. Athena, thrown through the
massive window behind her, glass shattering
as her body was tossed to the Dark Breeds bat-
tling outside. Her distraught Chosen dropped
her guard and was immediately punished for it.
A green light shot from Cronos's hand to pin her
above the fireplace, where she struggled fruit-
lessly to free herself.

"Coward!" Kyana clenched her fist, shoving it
upward so the ring was clearly visible. "I'm the
one with your ring! Too afraid to come and get
it?"

As he spun to face her, another dozen slug-
gish black oozes crept down his face. He winced,
stumbled again.

"Whore!" His bellow filled the throne room,
causing Kyana's head to pound, but she kept her
hand steady and her gaze taunting him.

Evacuo already!

The process was torturously slow, and as the weight of more black ooze seeped into Cronos's ring, it became almost too heavy to continue clutching with one hand. Her gaze swept to Ryker. He was covered in sweat, his face pale. He looked so mortal at that moment, she wanted to cry.

She coughed again, this time spilling blood from both her mouth and her nose. The world around her was beginning to dim. She had to hold on.

Just a few more minutes . . .

Something struck her hard but the shield kept her on her feet. She craned her neck to find Cronos hovering above her, his hand outstretched toward the old Hades as he ripped his son off his feet. He gave Hades a wicked grin before throwing him outside to join Athena in her fate with the Dark Breeds.

"Who wishes to join him? Zeus? My brave, traitorous firstborn? Or perhaps you, Poseidon? I should have killed you before you took your first breath. A weaker babe I'd never seen. What sort of god have you turned into? Still whiny? Still unworthy? Let's find out."

Cronos's long black hair framed his face like a shroud, leaving Kyana with only the smallest glimpse of his piercing black eyes. But as he moved to glide toward his youngest son, he dropped from the air in the center of the room.

Huddled on his side, he let out a gurgle and pushed himself back to his feet. As he did so, Kyana caught the slightest glimpse of a tremor, and hope lit her on fire as she wobbled on her feet.

It was working. With each step toward Poseidon that Cronos attempted, a hundred black oozes fell from beneath his cloak and slithered across the floor toward the Eyes of Power. His anger renewed, he spit out a string of Latin words that sent the last of Silas and Ryker's protectors flying. Their auras shattered, and panic nearly caused Kyana to lose her focus.

From somewhere deep inside her, beginning with a strange tingling from the amulet perched on her wrist, foreign words tripped through her mind and flitted off her tongue. It was as though Geoffrey was speaking through her, helping her.

By the power within me, I send you to hell.

"Ab intra me, et ego mitto vos as infernum!" She felt the power of those words deep within her soul, giving her the strength and the will to take a step closer, to die on her own two feet rather than on her knees before pure evil.

"No," he hissed. "No!" The hem of Cronos's robe began to smoke and Cronos faltered.

Inch by inch, flames ate up the side of the material and Cronos began to breathe quickly, his fear evident as he struggled to pull the garment from his body.

"Ab intra me, et ego mitto vos as infernum!" she repeated, taking a step toward Cronos. Blood seeped from her mouth and nose, her eyes and ears. Her body was losing the war waging within it. They had to finish this now. Cronos could not win.

She looked at Ryker and Silas. "Say it!"

Ryker stepped forward, placed the tip of his staff in the center of Cronos's chest. *"Ab intra me, et ego mitto vos as infernum!"*

Cronos's chest began to smolder. Pulling himself to his feet, he knocked the staff from Ryker's hand, his eyes so red they looked as though he was being eaten alive by fire.

And the last thing she saw before blackness claimed her was Cronos's face, twisted in pain, as the flames devoured him.

Chapter Thirty-three

Cronos was gone.

Ryker watched the flames lick at the god's head, the stench of burning flesh filling the throne room like a visible fog. Cronos's body fell limp to the floor; the only sound in the room became that of the heavy breathing of the survivors.

Triumphant and so proud of Kyana he could burst, he spun to face her, to lift her into his arms and hold her forever.

She was on the floor.

And she wasn't moving.

He ran to her. In the rush of excitement he'd allowed himself to forget what she'd risked to save them all. Now her cold body lay lifeless. He scooped her into his arms, closed his eyes, and let out a guttural roar of agony that tore at his soul.

His legs wouldn't hold him. He crashed back to

the floor, holding Ky close to his chest to keep her safe as he toppled onto his ass and cradled her in his lap.

He felt Haven beside him, heard her scream, cry, be consoled by Silas.

"Aceso!" His bellow for the Goddess of Healing was answered immediately. She knelt beside him, though Ryker couldn't see her face through the hot, burning tears blinding him. "Save her," he whispered, his voice ragged and breathless.

"I—I can't."

Ryker nearly released Kyana as the need to reach out and throttle the goddess undid him. Everything inside his body was screaming. Kyana had just destroyed pure evil. She should be laughing with pride and relief. She should be kissing him, telling him that she loved him as she'd hinted at before. Finally, he'd gotten what he'd wanted from her and she was leaving him.

"Save her!" he roared, understanding in that moment the agony Kyana must have felt when she'd held Haven this way, when she'd turned her best friend in order to save her life. Anything was better than losing someone who meant so much . . . anything.

Fumbling for the staff that had rolled slightly out of reach in his fall, he seized it and slipped the tip across his wrist, feeling the warm blood ooze from his veins. This had healed her before. It had to work!

He pressed his bleeding wrist to her lips, willing her to drink. Her mouth didn't open. He forced it to. There was no hot breath to warm his arm. No slight suckle to let him know she tasted his blood.

"The blood of a god will not heal another, son." Ares placed his hand on Ryker's shoulder and Ryker couldn't bring himself to shrug it off.

Without looking up, he whispered, "I've never asked you for anything as my father. Please. Save her."

He felt Ares's hand squeeze his shoulder, heard the deep intake of his breath. "I wish I could."

"She's still alive," Haven said, pressing her cheek to Kyana's forehead. "She is still my Sire, and I still have that link to her. She's still alive. It's not too late."

Kyana wasn't breathing. Or was she? He lowered his face until his lips touched hers. There. The faintest trace of warmth coming from her nostrils, caressing the tip of his nose in one last whisper of life.

He looked to Aceso. "Can you perform a siphoning? A switch?"

The goddess shook her head. "You must use a healing Witch or Mystic."

"Then bring me one!" he demanded, his resolve returning as he readjusted her in his arms.

"They've all been taken to Poseidon's realm," Silas said, his eyes damp and red as he helped Haven to her feet.

"What do you need?" Haven jerked away from Silas and crouched beside Ryker again. "Whatever you need a Healer for, I might be able to do." She touched his arm, looking as though she might completely fall apart at any moment. He knew how she felt. "Please. I've already lost part of my family today. I can't lose more. Tell me."

"Siphon Geoffrey's blood from her."

Silas moved to stand in front of them. "That process takes far too long to do any goo—"

"Shut up," Ryker snapped, his gaze focused on Haven. "Can you do it?"

He could tell by the look on her face that she wasn't sure, but she said only, "Give her to me."

She ordered Silas to bring her a vial and commanded the crowd to vacate the hall to give them room. The chaos of footsteps pounding toward the door was drowned out by the sound of Ryker's heartbeat. Unsteady. Off rhythm. But slowly coming back to life as hope filled him.

But he wasn't letting go of Kyana for anything. "I'll hold her. Do what you have to do."

Haven nodded, slipping a dagger from her belt. "It's not sterile but it's all I have."

"She's a goddess," Ryker said. "Infection isn't an issue."

But time was. If Silas didn't hurry the hell up, it would be too late. He glanced up to see Silas picking up the empty bottle that had once held Geoffrey's power. Ryker snatched it from him and handed it to Haven.

She didn't take it. "Hold it to her wrist. Collect every bit of energy you see spill from her. I can't guarantee it will all be . . . G-Geoffrey's." She sobbed, gathered herself, her voice shaky. "Some of Artemis's could—"

"Do it!"

She nodded, chewing on her bottom lip as she took Kyana's hand and laid it carefully in her lap. Then she leaned over Kyana's body and whispered just loud enough that Ryker could hear. "You have to *choose* this, Kyana. Choose to live. For us. Please."

Then she slit a vertical cut over Kyana's wrist, spilling blood onto her jeans. "When I speak the words, the energy should start flowing with the blood. Are you ready?"

He gave a curt nod and clenched his teeth.
She took a deep breath.

Virtutem non pertinent
ad vos, ut vos deserat. Vires intrinsecus fueris tu,
qui te defendere May esvilis futures.

Kyana's body spasmed. Ryker gripped her
arms to keep her steady as Haven dug the dagger
deeper into her arm. She repeated the words three
more times, and Kyana's body bucked a foot off
his lap.

"The energy! Silas, take the bottle from Ryker.
He's going to need his hands to hold her now!"
Haven commanded.

Silas was on the floor beside them in an instant.
He snatched the bottle, sliding it beneath the
wound just as the first crack of blue light shone
through the broken flesh.

The slight rise and fall of Kyana's chest slowed.
The long, low sigh she emitted sounded so close
to a death rattle that it caused them to pause and
glance at one another before returning their gazes
to Kyana.

"She isn't strong enough for this!" Silas moved
the container like a game piece, hurrying to catch
each ray of light as it escaped. "No one can trans-

fer this fast, Haven! It took Poseidon a full day to give me his—"

"Shut the fuck up!" Ryker roared. He glanced at Haven. "Keep going."

Maybe Kyana wasn't strong enough for this, but if anyone was, it was Ky. And without it, there was no chance of her survival. This was the only way.

More blue light flitted out like lightning bugs, only to be snatched by Silas as they drifted upward. Then it was like a dam inside Kyana burst. A flood of energy fled the wound, pouring onto the floor and into the air like water and dust and tiny flames.

Silas moved quickly, catching those in the air, then scooping those on the floor, then repeating. The bottle was half full . . . just a few minutes longer.

Haven repeated the foreign words over and over, and though he no longer had Witch power inside him, Silas spoke them with her. Ryker tried, but his mouth wouldn't work. He was numb to everything—except to the hope that they could save Kyana.

"It's done," Haven whispered.

Ryker turned his gaze to the full bottle of blue liquid in Silas's hands, then to Kyana's lifeless face.

She didn't look any more alive than she had when they'd started.

"How do we know . . ."

His voice trailed off as a soft movement under his forearm stole his breath.

Kyana's chest was expanding. Retracting. Expanding.

She was alive.

Chapter Thirty-four

Cries of pain and anger and sorrow and joy greeted Kyana as the black void slowly released her. She couldn't move, couldn't steady her double vision to take in what was left of Ryker's throne room, couldn't determine who was left standing and who'd given their lives so that they all had a chance to live.

Thoughts of those who'd fallen had her fuzzy gaze settling on the soot and ash that had once been Cronos . . .

It took her a minute to realize she was being held so tightly that the possibility of strangulation wasn't out of the question. It took her a longer moment to remember that she was supposed to be dead.

Pressing away from the imprisoning arms around her as much as her weakened body would allow, she found herself looking into two very blue, very damp eyes.

Ryker.

"Am I dead?" she whispered.

He cupped her face and kissed her so softly, but with such desperation, there was no doubt that she was very much alive. "Haven saved your life."

A half hiccup, half sob sounded from beside them. Kyana turned her head to find Haven blubbering like a fool, her cheeks and nose puffy and red. "It was . . . his idea."

Hiccup.

"Hey, I caught the shit. Wasn't easy either. More like a pinball game from hell." Silas's voice sounded deeper than usual, as though he too was choking on some emotion or another.

"You're all sappy . . . was I that close to death?"

All three nodded. A wave of nausea crept up Kyana's stomach. Whether it was the aftermath of her ordeal or sickness at the thought of how close she'd come to death, she wasn't sure.

"Thank you," she whispered, desperate not to turn as teary as the trio around her. "We won . . . right?"

For all she knew, Cronos had escaped and that pile of ashes belonged to someone else.

"Yeah," Ryker said, smiling down at her. "We won."

"Some of us anyway," Haven whispered.

Kyana's heart gave a painful tug and her fight not to get teary was lost. "I'm sorry, Haven."

The loss of Artemis and Geoffrey was going to stay with her for a long time, but Kyana couldn't imagine being in Haven's shoes, losing someone who held so much of her heart and yet had never had a chance to see where it could have gone.

She wasn't going to make that mistake with Ryker.

Haven gave Kyana's hand a squeeze and she pulled herself to her feet. "Where is he? I . . . I need to say good-bye."

Ryker told her, and as she stepped away, he looked at Silas. "Go with her. She shouldn't be alone."

Kyana stopped him. "She needs to be. Let her go."

Haven glanced back at her with a thankful smile, then cast her gaze toward Ryker. "You should prepare her in case . . ."

"In case what? Prepare me for what?" Kyana's head was aching like a bitch and her wrist was on fire, but the concerned expression on Haven's face was like a psychic painkiller. "Oh gods . . .

did someone turn me to save me? What the hell am I now?"

Ryker smiled and Haven vanished up the stairs to mourn in private. He glanced at Silas and ordered him from the room.

When he was gone, Ryker kissed her, holding her close enough to smother her again. "Really Ryker," she insisted. "I'm fine. Or I will be, anyway."

There were people now gone from her life that she'd miss forever, but she was definitely going to be fine. She couldn't believe their struggle with Cronos was finally over. That they'd finally won.

He released her slightly, letting her breathe freely again. "So what are you supposed to tell me?"

He sighed and buried his head in her hair. "There's a slight chance that Artemis's powers left you when we drained Geoff's from your blood."

An ugly pit filled her stomach. "So I could have no powers at all?"

He leaned back, scrutinizing her.

"You might. You might not. Not sure this has ever been done before."

"What?" she asked, realizing he was waiting for her to throw a fit, and on top of that, realizing she didn't want to. A few weeks ago, power had meant everything to her. Now the thought of losing everything she'd gained meant little to nothing. She'd lost people she'd loved, but she'd taken on the biggest, baddest evil to come along in ages. The people in her life didn't care about her because of what she was—they'd care regardless of whether she was the most powerful or the least.

Even Ryker.

All the work she'd done to convince herself that his feelings for her were growing because she was no longer a Dark Breed vanished. He knew there was the possibility that she could revert to what she'd been . . . and yet he was still looking at her with love in his eyes.

She touched his cheek. "Whatever happens, happens. What I am has nothing to do with *who* I am."

He smiled, kissed her cheek. "And who are you, then, Kyana?"

"A woman who might not be afraid to admit she's in love with a man."

"Might not?"

"Definitely not. I love you. And if you break my heart, I'll kill you."

His smile widened. "Deal."

When he kissed her, she used the last of her energy to show him how much she truly did love him, willing him to grasp that she was letting go of the notions she'd lived with forever—that she wasn't meant to be with one man and find happiness like everyone else.

The realization that she did deserve those things made her feel more powerful than she'd ever felt in her life.

Kyana slept until sunrise, her body aching even in sleep. She woke to the feel of a soft hand on her cheek and opened her eyes to find herself in her own bed, Haven staring sadly down at her.

"Hi," Haven whispered.

She looked like hell.

"You all right?"

Haven nodded, then shook her head. "I should have told him what he meant to me."

"He knew."

"Did he?" She raked her hair away from her blotchy face and shook her head. "Tell them I'm ready for my sentencing. Right now. So much . . ." She sobbed. ". . . has happened to me. I don't like this world anymore, Kyana."

"Bullshit." Kyana had spent every minute of every damned day for the last few months trying to keep Haven alive. She wasn't going to let her friend give up now.

She sat up, feeling as though she'd been run over by a freight train. "The Haven I know loves this world more than anyone. If you give up now . . . if you let them sentence you without even fighting, Geoff will have died for nothing. He wasn't fighting for the world today, Haven. For him, saving the world just meant saving *you*."

Haven had been through the worst time of her life. It could only get better from here. But Kyana knew well the agony of grief, and it would take more than a few meaningless words to make her better.

"He loved you," Kyana whispered, hoping those words weren't so meaningless.

Haven nodded. "I know."

Haven fiddled with the whistle dangling from Kyana's neck and took a deep breath. "So . . . ready to see how much of you I took out?"

Kyana smiled. "You didn't take out any of me. You took out bits that were on loan."

Haven gave the whistle a tug. "Yeah, well, let's just see who's still in there."

Willing to play along, even though a part of her was terrified to see how empty of powers she might really be now, Kyana nodded. "How?"

"The dogs will only answer to their goddess. If she's still in you, they'll obey and come out. If she's not, then . . . nothing."

Since she was too weak to try any of the other daunting powers, Kyana pulled the chain from around her neck and gave the whistle a blow. Would she truly be as okay with reverting back to her old self as she'd bragged to Ryker?

The smile in Haven's eyes held the answer.

Yes. She would be. Life wouldn't change so long as the people in it remained. And now that she knew the heartbreak of losing loved ones again, she wasn't going to lose any more.

She would be fine, no matter what . . .

The whistle glowed, breaking through her thoughts and calming her erratic pulse. Then she was buried under the weight of three enormous puppies, covering her in puppy drool and dog hair.

"I knew it," Haven whispered. "The Goddess of the Hunt is still in there."

Relief swelled within Kyana and she laughed. "Oh? How did you know?"

"The spell I used to siphon the blood from you . . . it roughly translates to 'The power that does not belong to you, may it leave you now. May the strength within you protect you as you become who you were meant to be.' You were meant to be Artemis, Kyana. It was never supposed to be me."

Kyana lay back on her pillow, her body lightened as the burden of guilt lifted from her soul. The gaze staring down at her held no anger over the fact that Kyana had become what Haven had been meant to be. Kyana could finally embrace all that being the Goddess of the Hunt entailed. Every last bit of it.

Even the nasty fertility bits.

"Will we ever be as we were before all this?" she asked.

Haven's smile didn't quite reach her eyes. "I don't know. One way or another, we won't be together anymore. Either I'm going to be sent to Tartarus after my trial, or I'll return Above. You'll be here."

"I could have a portal put into the house and one put here, in my room," Kyana said, only half joking. "I could go back and forth whenever . . ."

Haven chuckled. "You have a life here, Kyana. And I . . . well, I have to figure out if I have one anywhere." Her eyes closed, and she let out her breath in a long string of whoosh. "Have my sentencing hurried along, will you? I . . . Kyana, I desperately need to move on."

And with that, Haven strode from the room and closed the door quietly behind her.

Chapter Thirty-five

"I thought I'd have to wait until evening to find you. Thought for certain you'd be at Kyana's side."

Ryker turned to find Ares standing in the doorway of the dining hall where many of the injured were being tended by Healers. "I would be, but she was having a fitful sleep. I was afraid lying next to her would be too painful."

Ares moved slowly through the crowd and sat beside him. He seemed to have aged twenty years in the last two hours. Dark circles rimmed his eyes. Lines creased his forehead that hadn't been there the day before. Blood splatter painted his tunic, and his red cape was dirty and torn.

"How many dead and wounded?"

A Healer appeared beside them and spread her hands out inches from Ares's skull, where a massive lump was taking form and turning green.

As the Healer worked, Ares closed his eyes and shook his head. "Too many bodies from both sides to determine that. Sentinels are searching for wounded. My Elite Guard is dealing with securing the prisoners. Henry insisted on collecting our dead and preparing them for burial."

Ares cleared his throat. "Artemis would have been proud of her today. You chose your mate well."

"Yes," Ryker agreed. "I did."

He studied Ares, saw pride in his eyes. When Ryker had been ten years old, Ares had come to claim him, and since then, he'd wanted only one thing from Ryker. It was time to let bygones be bygones and finally give the old man the only thing Ryker had of value.

"Ares, please pass word along that I'd like all gods and goddesses of Olympus to gather in my council room this evening for a feast."

The Healer stepped away from Ares, brushing her hands on her tunic. Ares rotated his shoulders, obviously feeling much better after the tending, the lump already pea-sized.

Ares stood and started for the door. "What is the reason I am to give?"

Smiling, Ryker said, "I think the time has come to formally recognize you as my father."

Ares opened his mouth. Closed it again. And before he turned to leave and do as Ryker asked, Ryker saw the faint trace of a grin on his father's face. "As you wish."

"That was kind of you." Kyana's voice turned Ryker in his seat.

She was standing just a few feet away, wrapped in a thick blanket, her face pale, but her mouth smiling.

He pulled her onto his lap as gently as he could. "He's wanted it for years. Seems foolish to me since the entire Order already knows I'm his son, but . . . it means something to him to have me say the words."

Because for so long, Ryker didn't want to *be* Ares's son. Times had changed, however, and loyalties had been proven. Ares deserved no less than Ryker's now.

She pressed her lips to his. Tenderly, softly, she caressed his face before pulling away to stare him in the eyes.

"As a human, my father treated me like property, sold me like cattle, took his payment, and I never saw him or my mother again. My husband, Mehmet, was a beautiful man. When he visited our home, he was kind, attentive, and smiled at me all the time. I fell so deeply in love with the idea of someone being nice to me that I confused it with love. I discovered on my wedding night how wrong I was."

He wanted to find her father and ex-husband and kill them both again. Very slowly and with an eternity of pain.

"No man had ever told me he loved me. Desired me, hated me, terrified of me, yes, but never that he loved me. And when you said those words, I thought it was just like when Mehmet smiled at me."

"I'm nothing like that bastard," he said. "I don't want anything from you but who you are and what you have to give."

She opened her mouth, nodded, but didn't say anything. Ryker smiled and squeezed her hand. "You said the words once. Are they so hard to find again?"

"No, I just—"

"I'll take whatever you can give, and if you'll stick around long enough and give me the chance, I'll do everything in my power not to disappoint you, Ky. I'll make mistakes. I can't promise you perfection. But I *won't* disappoint you."

Despite his words, he wanted her to say she loved him again so badly his stomach ached. Until recently, he'd never heard anyone tell him he loved him. That gift had been delivered by his father. Now he wanted more of it. From the woman he saw at his side for the rest of his life, her hair fanned out on his pillows and her venomous tongue lashing out at him when he screwed up.

"I love the way you make me laugh and the way you make me want to hit you. I love the way you smile when you're pleased and scowl when I've pissed you off again. I love the way you smell, and the way you kiss me, and the way you show me every time we're together how much you care about me."

He smiled against her mouth, but she pulled away.

"But mostly," she continued, "I love *you*, Ryker. Believe me, I tried not to and I don't like failing at anything I try to do. But I failed at this. Despite all my efforts, I love you."

Warmth spread through Ryker's body like wildfire. Finally, she was his and he was hers and *something* about this fucked-up world made sense. This time when her lips covered his, Ryker tasted her surrender.

They stayed like that for a long while. When Kyana finally pulled away, the lines of grief were still etched on her face, but a renewed spark of life had filled her brown and amber eyes.

"If you think I'm living here, you're wrong," she muttered, standing.

Ryker grabbed her hand, smiling. "I didn't ask you to."

She shrugged. "You would have. Pack your stuff, Surfer Boy. I want you in my bed tonight . . ." She walked away, pausing when she reached the door. "Every night."

As Ryker watched her go, he couldn't stop the shit-eating grin spreading across his face.

"She shouldn't speak to the God of Gods in such a disrespectful manner," a nearby Healer said. "You're not to be ordered about like a slave."

Ryker chuckled, knowing the woman could never understand why Kyana's demanding nature turned him on. Taming Ky would be fun. Difficult as hell, but fun. And he had an eternity to do it.

Tonight would be explosive. Especially when she found out he'd had her things moved to his temple that morning.

Epilogue

Kyana sat as regally as possible at the table in Ryker's council room, the smell of the prepared feast gnawing at her until she was woozy. She wished he'd get on with it already so they could eat, drink, be merry and then . . . go to bed. Even if it *was* his bed and not hers. She was still miffed about that, but her promise to withhold sex from him as punishment wasn't going to happen.

She'd have to think of something else to make him pay for his trickery of moving her to his temple without her permission. But that could wait. Right now, she was weary from the sadness that had come from burying their dead today. As Artemis's broken body had been grieved over, Kyana had been unable to watch. The goddess had been the closest thing to a mother Kyana had ever had. Watching her final descent into the Underworld had been too much to bear.

Even Geoffrey, who'd had no body to bury, had been eulogized. For that, Kyana had left her place among the gods to stand beside Haven and hold her. She had hope for Haven, however. The old Haven would have crumbled and dissolved with such a loss. But this one . . . whatever Haven was to become, she would be strong. She would survive it.

Now, as the sun made way for the moon and the feast had been prepared, all the gods and goddesses and Oracles and every member of the Order who'd fought for them today sat packed at the tables, ready to eat and be praised for their victory.

Her gaze lingered on Silas and his girlfriend, Sixx, involved in a heated discussion by the window. Poor Silas. Haven had had to confess to him that the Dark Mage who'd struck her in the battlefield had stripped her of Silas's powers—which had been the only thing that had saved her life.

When Poseidon found his permanent Chosen, Silas would be left with nothing. He'd pretty much be human with a slightly longer longevity. He looked absolutely pitiful as he sat with that knowledge now.

Sixx caught Kyana staring and threw her a glare. Kyana turned her attention to her empty plate, wishing she could make food appear on it. But she couldn't. Not until a few matters had been settled. The first of which, Ryker was now standing to address.

"It is no surprise to any of you," he said when the room quieted, "that I was brought into the Order nearly four hundred years ago when I was ten."

Kyana choked on her cider. Four hundred years ago? Gods, was he really that old?

"It is also no surprise that, while Ares claimed me as his son, I have never claimed *him* as my father." All eyes were on Ryker, but Kyana held hers steady on Ares, who was looking rather uncomfortable yet proud in the back of the room. "I wish to remedy that today. A father protects his child. Stands beside him and offers him words of counsel. Ares is my father, by rights and by blood. I give that acknowledgment to the Order of Ancients and wish it to be set in the annals of our history."

A loud cheer erupted and smiles beamed their way at the old God of War, who nodded his acknowledgment with a stoic face.

Ryker cleared his throat. "That said, we have

one more matter to attend before we can enjoy the
fine meal Kyana's Nymphs have prepared for us
tonight."

Kyana's Nymphs. Not Artie's. The well of sadness would never be completely filled again with
small thoughts like that. That Ryker had brought
Artemis's Nymphs and dogs to live with them at
his temple reassured her that he knew how great
Kyana's loss had been. She loved him even more
for that.

But the topic he was broaching now had her
shifting uncomfortably in her chair. The crowd
parted and Haven was led down its center by
Henry. When she reached the dais, Haven knelt
but kept her head lifted, her gaze on Kyana.

"Haven Monroe's trial was to take place when she
finished her purging," Ryker said. "A purging that
was interrupted by the events that have plagued us
these last few days. It is the wish of Goddess Kyana
that the trial be held here tonight. By consent of the
Ancients, her wish has been granted."

As his gaze drifted to Haven, Ryker's voice softened. "Is there anything you wish to say, Haven?"

Haven shook her head, her gaze never wavering from Kyana's.

If she needs my strength, it is hers.

"Then on behalf of the Ancients, I proclaim your

freedom. Your actions in this war have proven your loyalty. You will be monitored until we are certain you've not embraced the Dark Breed blood you now possess. If you desire to continue your work with the Order, you are welcome here, Haven. But regardless, you will check in with us each week until your monitoring is finished. Are you agreeable to these terms?"

"I—what?"

Ryker cleared his throat. "I asked if you were agreeable to the terms I have laid out."

"I—yeah." She gave a slight nod, swaying on her feet. "I'm . . . free to go?"

Kyana made her way around the table to take Haven's hand. "You're free, Haven," she whispered. "It's what Geoffrey would have wanted. It's what you *deserve*. Take the opportunity to return to your work and prove to all the doubters that we didn't make a mistake."

"Then I wish to leave now." Haven glanced around the room. "I don't belong here. If I'm truly free, let me go."

"Tonight we celebrate. You're as much of the reason for that as any of us."

"I don't *want* to celebrate!" Realizing she'd shouted, Haven leaned in closer to Kyana. "I want to be alone."

The pain in Haven's eyes was too much for Kyana. She looked to Henry. "Escort her to our home Above. Make certain the house is protected." Then to Haven she said, "You must check in with me in a week, Haven, but if you need me before that . . . any time . . . I'll be there."

Haven nodded and turned away, allowing Henry to take her arm and lead her out of the temple. With a heavy heart, Kyana returned to her seat, grateful when Ryker gave her thigh a supportive squeeze.

"She'll be all right," he whispered, and Kyana nodded, glancing out the window to watch the chariot take her best friend to another world. "She's almost as strong as you are."

"Yeah," she whispered. "She is."

The humans would never have any idea what was sacrificed for them here today. But that didn't matter. As Kyana's gaze swept across the grinning faces of the Order members accepting their plates of food and goblets of wine, she felt the lump in her throat dissolve.

Humans might never know, but the Order of Ancients would never forget.

K.I.S.S. and Teal: Avon Books and the Ovarian Cancer National Alliance Urge Women to Know the Important Signs and Symptoms

September is National Ovarian Cancer Awareness month, and Avon Books is joining forces with the Ovarian Cancer National Alliance to urge women to start talking, and help us spread the **K.I.S.S. and Teal** message: Know the Important Signs and Symptoms.

Ovarian cancer was long thought to be a silent killer, but now we know it isn't silent at all. The Ovarian Cancer National Alliance works to spread a life-affirming message that this disease doesn't have to be fatal if we all take the time to learn the symptoms.

The **K.I.S.S. and Teal** program urges women to help promote awareness among friends and family members. Avon authors are actively taking part in this mission, creating public service announcements and speaking with readers and media across the country to break the silence. Please log on to *www.kissandteal.com* to hear what they have to share, and to learn how you can further help the cause and donate.

You can lend your support to the Ovarian Cancer National Alliance by making a donation at:
www.ovariancancer.org/donate.
Your donation benefits all the women in our lives.

KT1 0912

This September, the Ovarian Cancer National Alliance and Avon Books urge you to K.I.S.S. and Teal:

Know the Important Signs and Symptoms

Ovarian cancer is the deadliest gynecologic cancer and a leading cause of cancer deaths for women.

There is no early detection test, but women with the disease have the following symptoms:

- **Bloating**
- **Pelvic and abdominal pain**
- **Difficulty eating or feeling full quickly**
- **Urinary symptoms (urgency or frequency)**

Learn the symptoms and tell other women about them!

Teal is the color of ovarian cancer awareness—help us K.I.S.S. and Teal today!

Log on to **www.kissandteal.com** to learn more about the symptoms and risk factors associated with ovarian cancer, and donate to support women with the disease.

The Ovarian Cancer National Alliance is the foremost advocate for women with ovarian cancer in the United States.

Learn more at www.ovariancancer.org

KT3 0912

*At Avon Books, we know your passion
for romance—once you finish one of our
novels, you find yourself wanting more.*

May we tempt you with . . .

- **Excerpts** from our upcoming releases.

- Entertaining **extras**, including authors'
  personal photo albums and book lists.

- Behind-the-scenes **scoop** on your favorite
  characters and series.

- **Sweepstakes** for the chance to win free books,
  romantic getaways, and other fun prizes.

- Writing **tips** from our authors and editors.

- **Blog** with our authors and find out why they
  love to write romance.

- **Exclusive content** that's not contained
  within the pages of our novels.

Join us at
www.avonbooks.com

Next month, don't miss these exciting
love stories only from
Avon Books

Lord of Temptation by Lorraine Heath
When Lady Anne Hayworth hires the protection of buccaneer Crimson Jack, she never expects he'll demand a kiss as payment. What happens when Lady Anne finds herself in the unchartered waters of desire? Enjoy the last book in the Lost Lords of Pembrook series!

How a Lady Weds a Rogue by Katharine Ashe
Diantha knows society expects her to wed and settle down, but she's got other plans—plans that include danger at every turn. But when Diantha is rescued by the handsome secret agent Wyn Yale she's suddenly sure he's the man for her. Focused on a mission certain to land him in a noose, Wyn doesn't have time for her dimples and lips . . . so why can't he keep his hands off her?

Sacrifice the Wicked by Karina Cooper
Parker Adams knows better than to like the manipulative, spying, conniving Mission Agent Simon Wells. But this famed ice queen melts at the sight of him. Simon is everything Parker has been trained to avoid, but that doesn't stop her from sleeping with the enemy . . .

Head Over Heels by Susan Andersen
Back home in Fossil, Washington, Veronica Davis wants nothing more than a one way ticket to anywhere else: and that's what she'll get once the family saloon is finally sold. Cooper Blackstock—bartender and former marine—has his own agenda and dangerous secrets. But as Veronica's family faces growing trouble in the town, Cooper lends a helping hand and these two misfits find themselves growing closer by the day . . .

REL 0912

*G*ive in to your Impulses!

These unforgettable stories only take a second to buy and give you hours of reading pleasure!

Go to *www.AvonImpulse.com* and see what we have to offer.

Available wherever e-books are sold.

AVONIMPULSE

IMP 0811